A Beautiful Glittering Lie

A Novel of the Civil War

J.D.R. Hawkins

Printed in the United States of America.

Library of Congress Control Number: 2012902220

ISBN	Paperback	978-1-64361-994-1
	eBook	978-1-64361-995-8

Westwood Books Publishing LLC
11416 SW Aventino Drive
Port Saint Lucie, FL 34987

www.westwoodbookspublishing.com

Emotionally Charged and Beautifully Written!

This was such a beautifully written novel, with intense imagery and narrative that made me feel as though I was right there alongside the characters. Knowing the outcome of the Civil War made me even more emotionally invested, as I knew what was in store for them. Despite being armed with that knowledge, my hope for Hiram's safe return only grew as I dove deeper and deeper into the story. Hawkins writing made everything seem new, and it was almost a surprise when the outcome was revealed.

I would highly recommend this emotionally-charged novel to anyone who reads, not just those who are fans of historical fiction. I would also love to see this being assigned in school. I know I would have greatly enjoyed reading it in AP US History!

I have absolutely no qualms about this novel, and can definitely see why it was awarded 2013 John Esten Cooke Fiction Award, the B.R.A.G. Medallion Honoree, and honorable mention at the Los Angeles Book Festival. As for the last one, I am highly surprised it was not in first place. There is no question about it, this book definitely earned its 5 out of 5 stars.

By Alexia Bullard
E-Book Review Gal

A Really Worthwhile/Entertaining Book

This is a prequel to "A Beckoning Hellfire" That also is a great book. This covers the time leading up to the events in the first book. It is a must read for Civil War buffs, but also carries a great message about the strength of the families left behind by their warriors. Again, the history is correct and the story line is very believable. I'm sure hoping for a sequel.

By Raymond H. Mullen
Vine Voice

2012 B.R.A.G. Medallion Honoree

We are so proud to announce that A Beautiful Glittering Lie: A Novel of the Civil War by J. D. R. Hawkins is a 2012 B.R.A.G. Medallion Honoree. This assures readers that this is a book well worth their time and money!

By indieBRAG

This book is the recipient of the 2013 **John Esten Cooke Fiction Award**, given by the Military Order of the Stars and Bars.

ACKNOWLEDGMENTS

I would like to express my deepest heartfelt gratitude to the following people (listed in alphabetical order) for all of their insight, support, criticism, and guidance. Without them, this novel could not have been written.

Decatur Public Library, Decatur, Alabama
Someone on staff sent pertinent information regarding one of my main characters without receiving a specific request from me. Everyone is very accommodating and supportive.

Fredericksburg and Spotsylvania National Military Park, Virginia
The park rangers are amazing in their knowledge of the battles, as well as the park. When I visited, they went so far as to dig out old maps that provided fascinating information.

Horn Lake Public Library, Horn Lake, Mississippi
The librarians and staff are friendly, knowledgeable, courteous, and helpful. If they grew tired of my interlibrary loan requests, they certainly didn't express it. On the contrary, they went out of their way to offer assistance.

My Son, Jeremy
He has been more of a help to me than he will ever know. Regardless of his overwhelming responsibilities at work, school, etc., he has unconditionally assisted me with finding ideas, words, and phrases, and has served as my first editor. Thank you so much, Boomer.

Museum of the Confederacy, Richmond, Virginia
I would like to specifically thank Mr. John M. Coski, Historian and Director of Library & Research. Mr. Coski, you are so humble, and yet so very helpful.

R. T. Cole (posthumously)

Mr. Cole served as an adjutant in the 4th Regiment, Alabama Volunteer Infantry. Because he had the foresight and fortitude to record his thoughts and actions in his diary, the events in this novel are very accurate. Without this documentation, many of the specifics detailing what the 4th Alabama went through would be lost to history.

The Smithsonian Institution, Washington, D.C.

I would like to especially thank Mr. David Miller, Associate Curator, Military and Diplomatic History, National Museum of American History, and Ms. Jennifer L. Jones, Chair, Military and Diplomatic History, National Museum of American History. Thank you both for your insight and unending assistance, regardless of how ignorant my questions seemed.

FOR DAD

Table of Contents

"Any people, anywhere, being inclined and having the power, have the right to rise up, and shake off the existing government, and form a new one that suits them better. This is a most valuable - a most sacred right - a right, which we hope and believe, is to liberate the world. Nor is this right confined to cases in which the whole people of an existing government may choose to exercise it. Any portion of such people, that can, may revolutionize, and make their own of so much of the territory as they inhabit."

—*Abraham Lincoln, January 12, 1848*

Chapter One

"Oh, look! Here he comes!" Jenny exclaimed.

The crowd exploded with cheers.

David looked over to where she was pointing, his hazel eyes squinting in the bright sunshine. An elegant black lacquered carriage drawn by six white horses pulled up to the steps of the regal Greek revival-style state capitol building. Eight musicians burst into "Dixie's Land." A slender, stately, middle-aged gentleman stepped out of the carriage and was escorted by military personnel to a waiting platform, where he took his seat.

"He looks a mite sickly to me," remarked David's father, Hiram.

Mr. Kimball concurred.

"Well, I'll be glad when this here circus act is over," grumbled Hiram's longtime friend, Bud Samuels.

He was an amusing man with a scraggly beard and a constant twinkle in his eye. David thought of him as an uncle. But the distressed tone in Bud's voice alarmed him, for it was unusually out of character.

"I thought you wanted to bear witness to this," Hiram fired back.

He looked at his son and winked. David saw a glimmer of devilishness in his father's blue eyes.

"I did, till I had that vision last night," Bud replied.

"Vision?" asked Mr. Kimball.

Bud frowned. "I'll tell y'all about it later."

A pastor stood, walked up onto the platform, and requested that the people bow their heads before he started a short prayer. The crowd chanted, "Amen," in unison, and the middle-aged man who had arrived with his entourage approached the podium. Withdrawing his notes from his inner coat pocket, he began to speak.

"Gentlemen of the Congress of the Confederate States of America, friends, and fellow citizens. Called to the difficult and responsible station of chief executive of the provisional government which you have instituted, I approach the discharge of the duties assigned to me with a humble distrust of my abilities…"

1

David glanced over at the spectators standing beside him, who were listening intently. He noticed several soldiers on horseback, patrolling the area. The stately man's voice brought him back, recapturing his attention.

"I enter upon the duties of the office to which I have been chosen with the hope that the beginnin' of our career as a confederacy may not be obstructed by hostile opposition to our enjoyment of the separate existence and independence which we have asserted, and, with the blessin' of Providence, intend to maintain."

Looking at his friend, David nudged him with his elbow. "Hey, Jake, what do you think of ole Jeff Davis?" he asked in a hushed voice.

"Ain't sure yet," came the reply. Jake grinned at him, his young face beaming and a gleam in his brown eyes. "I jist hope he keeps it short."

"Our present political position, achieved in a manner unprecedented in the history of nations," continued Jefferson Davis, "illustrates the American idea that governments rest upon the consent of the governed, and that it is the right of the people to alter or abolish governments whenever they become destructive of the ends for which they were established..."

David found himself swaying slightly and shifting from side to side. His feet grew tired from standing. He had been in the same spot for over an hour, waiting for the president's arrival. His tall, lanky frame slumped as he shoved his cold hands deep into his coat pockets. Unintentionally, his mind drifted, and he began daydreaming out of boredom, thinking about the changes that had taken place. In his opinion, it had all started two years ago and had escalated from there. First was John Brown's raid, followed by his hanging. After that came Lincoln's election, and now, one by one, Southern states were seceding. His own beloved Alabama had been the fourth to leave the Union only a month ago. Since then, three more states had disaffiliated. The country was splitting in two. A slight breeze blew by, causing him to shiver from the cold February chill. He forced himself to listen once again.

"If we may not hope to avoid war," Jefferson Davis read, "we may at least expect that posterity will acquit us of havin' needlessly engaged in it. Doubly justified by the absence of wrong on our part, and by wanton aggression on the part of others, there can be no cause to doubt that the courage and patriotism of the people of the Confederate States will be found equal to any measures of defense which their honor and security may require..."

"It's mighty cold out here," Jake complained. His vaporized breath floated away like a small, wispy cloud.

"Sure is," David responded with a sniffle.

"Will you two please hush up?" Jenny quietly growled, her dark brown pipe curls swirling out from under her amber bonnet, encircling her porcelain-like face.

"Sorry, sis," Jake said with a smile.

She rolled her brown eyes at him before looking back up at the platform.

"There can be but little rivalry between ours and any manufacturin' or navigatin' community, such as the Northeastern States of the American Union," said the president-elect. "It must follow, therefore, that mutual interest would invite goodwill and kind offices. If, however, passion or the lust of dominion should cloud the judgment or inflame the ambition of those states, we must prepare to meet the emergency and maintain, by the final arbitrament of the sword, the position which we have assumed among the nations of the earth ..."

"Is he sayin' that we're fixin' to go to war?" Jake asked his father.

"Don't rightly know what it means," Mr. Kimball replied. He gave his son a sidelong glance before returning his gaze to the platform.

"I reckon he's referrin' to the fact that Northern tyranny has suppressed us here in the South," Jenny's husband, Nate, said softly, giving an affirmative nod. "And if the Yankees don't allow us to leave peaceably, we'll take up arms if need be."

A horse nickered from the street, distracting David. His gaze meandered over the crowd of a few hundred. Although it was a Monday, most were dressed in their Sunday finery, complete with hats, shawls, topcoats, and hooped skirts. Some had their children in tow. People, both black and white, stood in awe of the newly elected official, and David wondered if they had the same thing on their minds as he did. *Where is this man leading us?*

"There should be a well-instructed and disciplined army," Davis continued, "more numerous than would usually be required on a peace establishment ..."

Jake and David threw awestruck glances at each other from under their slouch hats.

"It's jist as I thought," Bud whispered ominously.

Hiram gave him a doubtful look.

"I also suggest that, for the protection of our harbors and commerce on the high seas, a navy adapted to those objects will be required," said Davis.

"Well, I'm jinin' the navy, then," Jake proclaimed.

"I'm fixin' to jine the army," added David.

They both snickered at each other and were unable to stop. Afraid their laughter would spark an outrage, David covered his mouth with his hand, trying to suppress the urge.

"Shhh!" Jenny's stare bore into them, making their snickers cease.

Hiram leaned in close to his son. "You two young'uns need to keep it down," he growled.

Biting his lower lip to regain his composure, David glanced at him, noticing his father's lofty stature, and the concerned expression on his clean-shaven face as he listened to the president's words. Looking back at the dignitaries, he could pay attention only momentarily before his mind drifted again. Instead of the army, he envisioned himself enlisting as a Pony Express rider, even though he knew they only allowed orphans. For a few moments, he imagined riding through the wilderness, alone on horseback across the dusty desert, pursued by marauding Indians. It was a dangerous adventure, just like those in dime novels he had read, about his hero, Kit Carson. In order to do it, he would have to run away from home, and steal his father's horse as well. Even though he was only fifteen, enlisting in the army would probably be easier for his kinfolk to accept.

Jefferson Davis rambled on. "Should reason guide the action of the government from which we have separated, a policy so detrimental to the civilized world, the Northern states included, could not be dictated by even the strongest desire to inflict injury upon us; but otherwise a terrible responsibility will rest upon it, and the sufferin' of millions will bear testimony to the folly and wickedness of our aggressors. In the meantime, there will remain to us, besides the ordinary means before suggested, the well-known resources for retaliation upon the commerce of an enemy..."

"Those are fightin' words if I ever did hear them," remarked Mr. Kimball.

"It's jist as I feared," Bud muttered, dismally shaking his slouch hat-covered head. "It's the end of all things as we know them."

"Your generosity has bestowed upon me an undeserved distinction, one which I neither sought nor desired," said the president-elect. "Upon the continuance of that sentiment, and upon your wisdom and patriotism, I rely to direct and support me in the performance of the duties required at my hands."

"At least he's humble about it," observed Jake.

David glanced at his friend's sister, who scowled at him. He felt himself recoil, for although he had known Jenny nearly all his life, he was still painfully shy, especially in front of girls. Even his own sisters made him self-conscious at times. But he reasoned it was because he was the only boy left in their family, and the oldest sibling at that. Deciding to keep quiet, he merely nodded in agreement.

"We have changed the constituent parts, but not the system of government," Jefferson Davis went on to say. "The Constitution formed by our fathers is that of these Confederate States..."

Expelling a sigh, David felt his stomach rumble. The president's lengthy speech was becoming nothing more than a long-winded drone. Turning his gaze toward the soldiers, he wondered what it must be like to be one, and what adventures were in store for them. He couldn't imagine a war igniting, and yet, there was much talk of it. Noticing Bud, who was also staring at the military men, he inexplicably felt a twinge of apprehension. The soldiers stood clustered together, waiting for an uprising. He suddenly realized that it wouldn't take much provocation for them to dispense their ammunition into an unruly crowd.

"It is joyous, in the midst of perilous times, to look around upon a people united in heart, where one purpose of high resolve animates and actuates the whole, where the sacrifices to be made are not weighed in the balance against honor and right and liberty and equality." The president's voice rang out like a church bell, his words becoming more fervent. "Obstacles may retard, but they cannot long prevent the progress of a movement sanctified by its justice and sustained by a virtuous people. Reverently let us invoke the God of our fathers to guide and protect us in our efforts to perpetuate the principles which, by his blessin', they were able to vindicate, establish, and transmit to their posterity, and with a continuance of His favor, ever gratefully acknowledged, we may hopefully look forward to success, to peace, and to prosperity."

With that, Jefferson Davis folded his speech and stuffed it into the breast pocket of his long coat. The crowd erupted with applause. Another man stood, joined Davis on the platform, withdrew a Bible as the audience grew silent, and requested that Davis place his right hand upon it. Everyone present stood in silent admiration while he took his oath of office. The president echoed the man's sporadic phrases, and ended by lifting his eyes and his hand toward the sky, saying, "So help me God!"

For a moment, all were stunned, stirred by the impressive scene, but then several started applauding enthusiastically, and the rest followed. The band broke into a jaunty rendition of the "Bonnie Blue Flag," and a few men tossed their hats into the air. Upon completion of the ceremony, swarming admirers and the media quickly surrounded the president, while the militia stood by.

"Well, that monkey show's over," remarked Bud.

He followed David, Hiram, and Jake's family across the frosty lawn to their waiting carriage. Mr. Kimball, who limped along behind them, was the last to climb aboard.

While they rode back to Jenny and Nate's small two-story house, their conversation centered on the inauguration they had just witnessed.

"What did you think of his speech, Pa?" asked Jake.

Mr. Kimball smiled. "I reckon he'll make a fine president. Don't you, Hiram?"

Jake looked across at his best friend's father, who was seated between David and Nate. "Do tell, Mr. Summers."

Hiram nodded thoughtfully. "I'd have to agree with your pa," he said.

"What if everything he says is true?" asked David. "And he asks for volunteers to jine the army?"

His father shrugged. "We'll cross that bridge when we git to it."

"I don't reckon they'll take me, due to my bum leg," stated Mr. Kimball forlornly.

"You already paid your dues in Mexico," Bud remarked.

Jake and David glanced at each other from across the carriage.

"Can I enlist?" David asked.

"Oh, here we go," Bud muttered under his breath.

Hiram chortled, causing his son to frown. He said, "Now, David, you're mighty young..." but seeing his disappointment, he added, "We'll discuss it later with your ma."

David smirked. His mother would give in, he was certain. Removing his hat, he ran his long fingers through his thick shoulder-length hair, dark brown in color like that of a pecan shell.

Taking notice, Jake followed suit and did the same, although his hair wasn't nearly as long and was much darker. "If Zeke's jinin', then I should, too," he said, referring to his friend by using the nickname he had given him years ago.

"Jist as Mr. Summers said, we'll discuss it later." With that, Mr. Kimball extinguished the fire.

Changing the subject, Hiram said, "We're much obliged to you, Nate, and to you, too, Miss Jenny. It was right kind allowin' us to stay here in Montgomery with y'all. Reckon the hotels are all filled up due to the inauguration."

"You're quite welcome, dear sir," replied Jenny with a sunny smile, accepting his graciousness.

David looked over at Jake again, who winked at him. Each knew what the other was thinking. If there was adventure afoot, they'd pursue it.

For the rest of the afternoon and into the evening, the family enjoyed each other's company. Mr. Kimball apologized that his wife couldn't be there, for she was required to stay home due to a sprained ankle. His faithful slaves, Percy and Isabelle, were looking after her. They were newlyweds, and seemed happy to oblige. Therefore, Mr. Kimball brought his son down to see Jake's sister and her husband, who had moved to Montgomery two years ago. Jake insisted that his best friend come along, and when asked, David requested the presence of his own father, too. Hiram then invited Bud, knowing that if war broke out, he would want to be one of the first to know.

They enjoyed a delectable meal Jenny had prepared and laid out on her banquet table, complete with fine china, crystal, and linens. She prided herself on her domestic abilities, and Nate raved about her cooking. Following an evening of quiet discussion in front of the quaint marble fireplace, they retired to their designated bedchambers upstairs: David with Hiram, Jake with his father, and Bud in his own small room. Early the following morning, they arose to enjoy breakfast with Nate and Jenny before catching the nine o'clock train. Their ride to Huntsville took most of the day. Once they arrived, they checked into a nearby hotel, sharing one room. After dining in the hotel, they returned upstairs and promptly fell asleep.

Loud voices outside awoke them in the morning. David and Jake immediately sprang to the window to find out what was causing the commotion, and saw groups of people rushing toward the train depot. Quickly dressing, the travelers went downstairs, where the hotel clerk informed them that President Davis had just arrived via the Memphis and Charleston Railroad, so they rushed out into the street, and hurried to the depot to investigate.

As they walked, Bud commented under his breath, "This is it, Hiram. This is how it all starts."

Overhearing the comment, David frowned. Bud wasn't acting like himself at all, which deeply concerned him. Remembering the vision Bud had mentioned before, he promised himself to riddle the man about it later.

A crowd had gathered. Seeing the president emerge from a passenger car, they broke into cheers. The president raised his hand to say a few words, and all fell quiet. After greeting everyone, he alluded to the causes that had imposed the formation of what he called the "Southern Republic." According to him, the South had no desire to aggravate hostilities with other sections of "this great continent."

"The North," he continued, "will find that while we are their best customers in peace, we will become their worst enemies in war."

The congregation reveled in his proclamation. Someone near the rear shot off a pistol, startling the horses. David saw Bud jump at the noise. Mr. Davis waved to the crowd before disappearing into his passenger car.

Jake and David looked at each other and shrugged. Now it seemed obvious that war was imminent. They followed their fathers to the city livery to retrieve their horses.

While they rode home, Hiram, Bud, and Mr. Kimball immersed themselves in discussion, most of which went over the boys' heads. Talk about the Constitution and the right to secede, the Founding Fathers, and how Lincoln had won with only 40 percent of the popular vote, beating out their favorite, John C. Breckinridge, dominated their conversation.

"By electin' ole Abe, the Yankees made a declaration of war," said Bud.

"He wasn't even on the ballot in ten states, all Southern, of course," stated Hiram. "They burned him in effigy, right here in Huntsville."

"The stock market plummeted because they elected that black Republican," said Mr. Kimball, referring to the fact that Lincoln's ticket supported abolition.

"Well, before all this occurred," said Hiram, "there was talk of incorporatin' us North Alabamians with Tennessee, and makin' it a whole new country in and of itself."

"I heard about that," responded Mr. Kimball. "They were fixin' to call it the Free State of Nickajack, so's it would be a neutral state between the North and South."

David grinned at the name. He wouldn't have minded living in a state named "Nickajack," for it had a nice ring to it.

"I don't suppose that'll happen now," Hiram said. "The troops have already seized Fort Morgan and Fort Gaines down in Mobile Bay."

"And they've elected our new president," stated Bud, "along with his cabinet, and a revised Constitution."

Hiram nodded. "He's been elected for six years, instead of the usual four. Talk is they wanted Huntsville to be the capital for the C.S.A.," he informed the others.

"I'm glad it's in Montgomery," Jake interjected, "because it gives us a chance to see Jenny."

His father chuckled, amused by his fifteen-year-old's naiveté about the events taking place around him.

Recalling Bud's earlier comments, David decided to probe him. "Mr. Samuels, if you please, tell us about the vision you had."

Bud's demeanor suddenly turned dark. He sighed. "There ain't much to tell," he finally said.

David and Jake looked at each other, both raising an eyebrow.

"Now you've got us all scared!" remarked Hiram with a chuckle.

Bud glared at him. "We should be scared. If my vision is any indication, there's a mighty dim future in store for us all. I reckon we'll be seein' a heap of bloodshed."

"Oh, Bud," said Hiram. "Now you're soundin' like one of those radicals, or ole John Brown himself."

"Mark my words, Hiram," Bud said seriously. "There's only sadness in store for us. For you, for me, and for the young'uns here. It ain't good. Tain't good at all."

The smile faded from Hiram's face. He looked away.

David couldn't help feeling an ominous presence, like a storm cloud was gathering over him. He shuddered, impulsively attempting to shake it off.

As dusk approached the following day, Bud, Mr. Kimball, and Jake bid their farewells and went their separate ways, splitting off down a frozen dirt road. Hiram and his son continued on until they finally arrived home. Relieved that he was back with his family, David volunteered to unsaddle their mounts, while Hiram went inside their wood-slat dogtrot house. As David led the two horses into the tin-roofed barn, his yearling colt whinnied a greeting to him.

"Hey, Renegade," he called out to the colt, who snorted in response, stomping a forefoot.

The yearling was his pride and joy, the offspring of Hiram's stallion. Renegade was piebald, a dark chestnut highlighted with white patches spanning under his belly, and white socks reaching up to his knobby knees. His mane and tail were light flaxen, and his uniquely colored eyes were hazel, the same color as David's.

Whistling the "Bonnie Blue Flag" while he removed the horses' saddles, David curried his father's grand stallion, Cotaco, named after a famous Indian chief who had lived in their parts long before the Trail of Tears took place. It was also the name of a creek that ran through the back end of their property. The stallion had been gifted to Hiram by an Indian acquaintance in Texas, and was a magnificent mustang, covered with brown and white splotches that transformed, if David used his imagination, into faces of people and animals. To him, Cotaco was all-knowing, and a sly devil at that. It was he who had bred with the neighbor's prize thoroughbred mare, thus creating Renegade. The owner, Mr. Collier, insisted that David's father purchase the foal, or "mistake" as he called him, so Hiram was obliged. He gave Renegade to David, let him choose a name, and was teaching him how to gently break the colt.

Because Renegade was still too young to ride, David's current mount was a Standardbred mare named Sally, and she was a fine animal as well. Not as special as Cotaco, but pretty, just the same. She actually belonged to his mother, who allowed him to borrow the mare when the need arose. Sally's shiny brownish-black coat glistened with sweat from where the saddle on her back had been positioned, so he gently rubbed her down. He gave the horses their oats, stroked Renegade's muzzle, and went inside, where he found his family gathered around the rough-hewn pine table his father had constructed.

"And ole Jeff Davis said somethin' about bein' ready by recruitin' an army," Hiram was saying. His mother and sisters looked over at David as he entered.

"Come sit down and eat your vittles before they git cold," his mother instructed, motioning him toward her with a swoop of one hand while she brushed a stray strand of dark brown hair away from her face with the other.

David took his seat. He folded his hands, quickly gave thanks in silence, clutched the fork in his left hand, and started shoveling in grits.

His mother shook her head. "Worked up an appetite, did you?" she remarked.

Josie, his youngest sister, laughed. "There's a whole potful out in the kitchen Ma made jist for you!"

David grinned, exposing grit-covered teeth.

"Ew!" Josie squealed.

"David, you mind your manners," his mother scolded.

"Beggin' your pardon, Ma," he mumbled through his grits.

"As I was sayin', Caroline," his father continued, "the president sounds like he means business. He ain't takin' no muck off the Yankees."

"Hiram!" she exclaimed. "I'll not have you talkin' like that at the dinner table."

He chuckled, but suddenly became somber. "We're in for a fight, all right," he declared, "so we'd best hold on tight."

"I'm all for the fight!" David hollered.

His sister Rena glared at him. "You're fixin' to go fight the Yankees? Did Pa say you could?"

"No, I did not," Hiram responded. "I said I'd discuss it with your ma."

"I'll have none of it," Caroline announced, rising as she took up empty plates. "You're much too young to go gallivantin' off to chase Yankees."

"But Ma!" David protested.

"That's all I'm sayin' on the subject," Caroline said firmly, and walked out of the room.

David glared at the doorway through which she had just exited. "It ain't fair," he muttered, shoveling a piece of ham into his mouth.

"You don't know that there will be a fight, anyhow," said Josie.

With a frown, Hiram solemnly remarked, "For the good Lord's sake, I hope there won't be."

Several weeks went by. The air grew more static with anticipation. David and his father traveled to the nearby mercantile one afternoon in mid-March. As soon as they entered, they were absorbed into a debate.

"Governor Moore has authorized establishin' an army in Alabama," said Mr. Skidmore, a local resident who was standing near the wood-burning stove in the center of the store with several others. "He's called for two thousand troops to garrison the coasts."

"Well, now that Lincoln has been sworn in," said Mr. Banes, a finely dressed man about the same age as David's father, "it'll really git the ball rollin'."

"I hear tell that the Spotsworth Apothecary up in Huntsville is flyin' the Stars and Bars now. The first merchant to do it, so they say," Joseph Ryan informed the group.

Ben Johnson, the shopkeeper, put his two cents-worth in by informing the crowd, while he dusted, that during the Secession Convention in February, the Republic of Alabama flag was severely damaged by a storm, so it was moved to the governor's office, and he hoped it wasn't a bad omen. Because the flag had flown just once, he had only seen a drawing of it in a local publication; the Goddess of Liberty was on one side, holding an unsheathed sword in her right hand and a flag with one star in the other. The words "Independent Now and Forever" were arched above her head. On the other side was a cotton plant with a coiled rattlesnake. Beneath the plant, in Latin words, it read, *"Noli Me Tangere,"* or, "Touch Me Not."

Kit Lawrence, a childhood friend of David's father, protested. "We should support the Union by not takin' up arms," he growled.

"Why in God's name would we support the Yankees," said Mr. Skidmore, "when all they want is to take away our livelihoods and privileges?"

"I'm supportin' the state, and the majority has voted for secession, so it's our duty to protect her!" ranted Mr. Copeland. David had been friends with his daughter, Callie, ever since they started school together nine years ago.

"Now that there's a call out for troops, we'd best be thinkin' about signin' up," said Mr. Powell, a lanky, fine-boned gentleman.

"This war won't go on for long, anyway," remarked Mr. Garrison, another neighbor, who lived in nearby Arab. "Why, I'll be amazed if it lasts more than ninety days."

"We should all sign up now, put those Yankees in their place, and git on back home before harvest," said Bud.

Mr. Foreman looked up from the newspaper he had draped over the countertop. "It says here that on the twenty-seventh of last month, Russian troops in Warsaw shot five people who were protestin' Poland's rule." He shook his head slowly. "It's as though the whole world is ablaze with violence."

"Well, I'm fixin' to enlist, so I can put this fire out before it gits any worse!" exclaimed Billy Ryan, who was Joseph's cousin.

"Those damn Yankee nigger lovers will pay dearly!" proclaimed Mr. Copeland.

The gentlemen agreed boisterously by hollering, "Here! Here!"

David glanced around at the gathering, taking it all in, and wished Jake was there to witness it.

"I'm fixin' to enlist, too," announced Bud.

Hiram glared at him. "This is the first I've heard of it," he said concernedly.

Bud nodded. "It's what's required of us, and I, for one, am a patriot's son." He grinned. "Well, grandson, anyhow. This is *our* war for independence."

Frowning, Hiram patted David's shoulder. "We'd best be headed home." He placed his slouch hat on his head. "See y'all later."

David followed his father outside, and they climbed up onto the buckboard. Taking the reins, Hiram slapped them against the withers of their big white Percheron.

"Git up, there, Joe Boy," he commanded. He clucked to the gelding, who lurched, pulling the wagon behind him.

During the ride home, Hiram said very little, which was fine with David, who preferred not to discuss what he knew his father was thinking. One thing was for certain, though. If his father enlisted, so would he.

On March 27, the *Huntsville Democrat* reported that a company known as the Madison Rifles was being called into service, and a few days later, so were the Huntsville Guards under Captain Egbert Jones. Alabama was preparing for war, and things were heating up. The entire Southern nation was up in arms, waiting for a reason to fight.

The weather grew milder, and soon it was April 2. David went about his farm chores as usual, anticipating with excitement what might be in store for him later in the day. He saw the family's hogs, all five of them, wandering around on a nearby hillside, and noticed his father busy at work building a pen.

Curious, he walked over and asked, "Whatcha doin', Pa?"

"I'm buildin' a pen for the hogs," he replied.

"Why?"

"Because I decided they'd be safer penned up." Hiram pounded several nails as his son watched. Stopping momentarily, he said, "I want you to make sure they stay in this pen, you hear?"

"Yessir."

"Now go fetch me some more nails and help me finish it."

David did as he was told, even though a strange knot formed in the pit of his stomach. His father had never been concerned with confining the livestock before. Instead of prying to find out more information, he dutifully went about his tasks, and when the pen was finished later that afternoon, he rounded up the hogs with the assistance of his two black-and-tan coonhounds, Si and Caleb. Renegade whinnied from behind the pasture fence the entire time, wanting to come out and frolic with the pigs, but David knew that would only mean trouble. When he was finished, he dragged himself to the well to wash up. Exhausted, he decided to find time for a nap before supper, so he went in through the breezeway of the saddlebag house and entered one of the two doors on the right side of the dwelling to his room. Throwing himself onto his bed, he quickly dozed off.

"Wake up!"

Startled awake, he looked around the room frantically and saw Josie standing in the doorway, a huge grin on her face. Her long auburn locks hung down past her shoulders, and her hazel eyes glistened.

Sitting up, he asked, "What's wrong, Josie?"

"Nothin', silly! Come on out to the kitchen for your surprise!" She giggled before bounding off.

He rubbed the sleep from his eyes, rose to his feet, and sauntered outside to the summer kitchen. As he entered, his family greeted him by yelling in unison, "Happy Birthday!"

David's grin grew to be so huge that it spread across the faces of his family members. "Why, I thought y'all forgot!" he said bashfully.

"Oh, darlin', we could never forget you!" his mother said before smothering him with a kiss and a hug. "Now sit down!"

Rena came toward him with a small vanilla pound cake in her hands. She set it in front of him. "Cut the cake, and make sure all the pieces are the same size this time."

"Yeah. Last year you got the biggest one," remarked Josie, plopping down beside him at the long table.

They took their seats, said a quick blessing, and enjoyed their cake.

Hiram stood. "You know we don't have much money, son," he said, "but we all chipped in and bought you this." He pulled a white cotton sheet away from what had been hidden beneath it to expose a saddle.

"Oh," David uttered, his eyes widening in delighted surprise.

"When the time comes for Renegade to wear this, you'll be ridin' in style," said Caroline. "In the meantime, you can break it in on ole Sally."

"I… I don't know what to say," he stammered.

"Thank you would be right appropriate," remarked Rena with a radiant smile.

"Yes, thank y'all very much." David stood and walked over to the saddle, which was balanced on a slat-back chair. Running his hands over the tanned leather, he admired his gift with awe.

"It really ain't new," admitted ten-year-old Josie. "Pa got it off a feller in Marshall County whose brother kicked the bucket—"

"That's enough, Josie!" Caroline intervened. She smiled at David. "Your pa has another surprise for you."

Looking over at his father, David saw that he was hiding something behind his back.

"It ain't really what you wanted," Hiram said, smiling, his blue eyes dancing, "but I made you this." He withdrew the instrument from behind his back, and held it out to his son. "I know how musically inclined you are, so I thought you could learn to play this, and think of me when you do."

David took the stringed instrument, sat down, and balanced it on his knee. Strumming the strings, he asked, "What is it, Pa?"

"It's a guitar. They're mighty popular up North. I started makin' it for you before all this talk of war broke out." He withdrew a small hand-drawn booklet from his vest pocket. "This shows how to play chords on it, kinda like a pianee." Giving it to his son, who began studying it intently, he added, "I know you wanted a banjo, but I'm hopin' this will suffice."

"Pa, it's beautiful," he said, turning the instrument over to look at the remarkable craftsmanship. Different colored woods, consisting of maple, rosewood, and mahogany, were combined over the hollow body and neck of the instrument, and sanded down to form a rich, lustrous finish. He had never seen anything like it. "I'll cherish it always," he said. Smiling, he strummed an off chord, causing everyone to wince.

That evening, before the family went to bed, Rena entered David's room and handed him a small package wrapped in brown paper. Her long amber hair hung down haphazardly around her shoulders, so she brushed it back while grinning at him.

"How's come you didn't give this to me earlier?" he asked, eagerly tearing into it. "It's *Ivanhoe*!"

With a snicker, she said, "I knew how much you wanted this book, and I finally secured a copy from Miss Callie."

"Miss Callie? She had a copy?"

Rena nodded, her violet-blue eyes sparkling. "I didn't give it to you sooner because it's a hand-me-down."

"Pshaw," David said. He gave his sister a hug. "I'll read it and give it back to you when your birthday comes next month."

She laughed, aware that he was joking. "No. That's quite all right. I have certain things I would prefer to receive instead. After all, I am nearly fourteen, and I must prepare for ladyhood."

Amused, he chuckled and blushed at the same time. "All right, then. Thank you, sis."

He gave her a swift kiss on the cheek before she shuffled off. Reclining on his bed, he opened the pages to discover fantastic wood-carved illustrations depicting characters in cathedral-like settings. Soon, a tap came at the door. His mother entered.

"Darlin', I brought you an extra blanket," she said, setting the quilt at the foot of his bed. "The *Farmers' Almanac* says it's fixin' to git cold as a witch's... heart tonight."

David chuckled at her hesitation, but then shuddered, for the thought of witches terrified him. "Thanks, Ma." He sat up and closed his book.

"Oh, I see Rena gave you that book she got from Callie."

"Yes'm."

"She wasn't sure if she should or not, but I told her you'd treasure it."

"That I do."

Caroline sat beside him and smiled, her hazel eyes misting. She slowly shook her head. "I can't believe my boy is already sixteen years old!" She took his hand and kissed his cheek. "I'm so very proud of you."

"Thanks, Ma." He hesitated, wondering what had brought this on. "Is everything all right?" he prompted.

She nodded. "It's jist that we've had so much loss the past few years, what with your brother, Elijah, passin' on to our Lord after bein' sick with the cholera, and then your granny last year. I only hope this war we're headed into..." Her voice trailed off.

"Ma, there ain't gonna be a war. We'll whip the Yankees good, and it'll all be over before harvest. Least that's what Jake's pa says."

"Well, I hope he's right." She patted him on the knee, and stood. "I'll see you in the mornin'." With that, she left the room.

David turned down the kerosene lamp, and lay back on his bed in the dark. Closing his eyes, he pondered the situation. Mr. Kimball had to be right, didn't he? The war would probably end before it even began. Smiling to himself as he thought of the gifts he'd been given, he fell into a blissful slumber.

Two quiet weeks passed. He helped his father plant rows of peas, and tilled the soil, preparing it for corn and sorghum. Their peacefulness didn't last long, for news came that Fort Sumter, off the coast of South Carolina in Charleston Harbor, had been bombarded by Confederate forces and captured. Two days later, President Lincoln called for 75,000 volunteers, evidence that a war was now truly imminent. On April 17, Virginia seceded, and two days later, a mob of Southern sympathizers in Baltimore attacked the 6th Massachusetts Regiment while it marched through on its way to Washington. Newspapers reported that four soldiers and twenty rioters were killed.

By April 20, every state in the Confederacy was bracing for war. When David rode to the town of Arab for supplies, he couldn't believe his eyes. Excitement filled the streets. People hustled about, and small groups of men and boys, firearms in hand, practiced drills. Two would-be soldiers attempted to play a fife and drum. A newspaper boy hollered out the latest news from an intersection. David's heart pounded with exhilaration. His moment was close at hand. When he returned home to report the news, to his amazement, his father seemed disinterested, said very little about the event, and told him to tend to his duties.

On the following morning, Hiram addressed his family at the dining room table. "I have some news for y'all," he said, his voice strained with seriousness. "Your ma and I have discussed it, and I'm enlistin' in the army." He looked around at his children, who gaped at him. "In fact, I've already signed up." At a loss for elaboration, he fell silent.

"Pa," Rena said with apprehension, "when are you leavin'?"

"I ain't quite sure yet," he replied somberly. "Bud's enlisted with me."

David scowled, his mouth dropping open. "Pa, you know I want to go, too."

Hiram shook his head authoritatively. "No, son. We've discussed this. You're too young, and your ma needs you here."

Clenching his teeth, he glared at his father momentarily before he jumped to his feet and stomped outside, his face burning with anger and resentment. How could his father leave him with the womenfolk when there was excitement commencing elsewhere? He had always longed to escape his mundane life, and did so by burrowing his nose in books. His paternal grandfather, a Baptist minister, had taught them all how to read at a very young age, and David prided himself on his ability. But now, the likelihood of seeing anything besides the crops growing seemed like a pipe dream.

He stood at the split-rail fence with his arms folded over the top rail and stared out at the empty fields, noticing dark clouds gather on the horizon. Thunder rumbled far off in the distance. Renegade nickered to him from across the barnyard, alerting him to the impending storm. Across the field, a mourning dove began its melancholy song, so David responded by calling back. Using a method his father had taught him, he

18

cupped his hands, blew into them to produce a low, whispery whistle that rose to a high note, and followed it with three short notes. Presently, Hiram came out of the house and walked over to him.

"David, you and I need to have a talk." He was well aware that his son was fuming. "Now, don't be gittin' yourself all worked up. I won't be gone long." He hesitated, waiting for David to look at him. "I need you to stay here and look after the place for me. I'm dependin' on you."

Unable to resist his father's stare, David relented. "I was hopin' I could go," he stated softly.

"I know. With everyone leavin' to go fight, someone has to stay here and protect the womenfolk. You're the man of the house now."

"I don't have a gun."

"I'm leavin' you with the shotgun."

"What are you fixin' to take?"

"My ole flintlock. It shoots straight enough to hit a few Yankees."

The grin on his face made David smile back. "All right, Pa. I won't let you down."

"And I have your word you won't run off once I'm gone?"

"No, Pa." He chuckled. "I mean, yessir, you have my word. I promise I'll stay here and tend to the farm."

"That's my boy," he said, giving his son a pat on the back. "Best tend to your chores, and then go on in and apologize to your ma and sisters. It looks like there's a storm over yonder." He gestured toward the darkening horizon. "And it's fixin' to come this way."

"Yessir," David responded. Obediently, he walked off toward the house.

Hiram watched him, watched the slow, gangly gait he knew so well. A storm was brewing, all right, in more ways than one. That much he knew. Hopefully, it would all blow over soon.

"War! An arm'd race is advancing!—the welcome for battle—no turning away;

War! Be it weeks, months, or years—an arm'd race is advancing to welcome it."

—*Walt Whitman*

Chapter Two

Later that afternoon, Kit Lawrence arrived. David watched the lanky man ride up the lane to the house, dismount, and saunter to the porch on long, spindly legs. Unsurprisingly, he was scowling, but at a loss for words.

"Cat got your tongue, Kit?" he asked, holding back a snicker while he slowly swayed back and forth in one of the rockers.

Kit shook his head. "No, it ain't that." He tapped his booted foot nervously. "Where's that pa of yours?"

"Reckon he's out yonder at the fence line," David responded, pointing in the direction indicated. "Why do you want to see him?"

"Well, it ain't none of your business," Kit barked.

David's large hazel eyes widened at the unexpected escalation of Kit's voice, and he abruptly stopped rocking.

"But I'm here to ask him somethin'."

"Oh. What would that be?"

"I want to know why he's runnin' off to jine the army." With that, Kit stomped back to his haggard horse, mounted, and rode off.

Deciding to follow, David went to the barn to retrieve Sally. He knew he'd be eavesdropping, but curiosity compelled him. Once he arrived at the corner of their property, he stopped Sally far enough away so that they were hidden behind a small coppice of white oaks, but he could still overhear.

"What's got into that thick head of yours that you'd want to run off and leave your kinfolk to go fight the United States government?" Kit asked gruffly.

Hiram grunted. "Because it's my duty to defend my home, Kit," he responded slowly, as if contemplating every word. "I'm jist surprised you didn't enlist."

Kit grumbled, "I ain't jinin', because I don't believe in it."

"What do you mean? You don't believe in fightin' for your country?"

"I ain't sayin' that. But I live in Tennessee now, which has not seceded. Least, not yet. I'm supportin' whatever she decides."

"Suit yourself," Hiram snapped.

David could tell by the tone in his father's voice he was becoming agitated with Kit's narrow-mindedness.

"I'm choosin' to fight for Dixie," Hiram went on, "so my son can grow up free from oppression."

Biting his lower lip, David felt somewhat guilty. He didn't want to be the reason for his father's enlistment. Controlling himself, he refrained from protesting aloud.

"There ain't no need, Hiram." Kit seemed to be pleading. "This war nonsense will all be over in a few months. Besides, we're too old to go. Hell, we're both thirty-eight, for God's sake. And I'd hate to see you blacklisted because you fought against your homeland."

"But this *is* my homeland, Kit," Hiram said, exasperated. "That's what I've been tryin' to tell you." He was quiet for a moment. "Are you afraid I'll be labeled a traitor?"

"It ain't that," replied Kit. "For all I know, I could be the traitor."

Hiram snorted. "For all you know, you could be." He climbed aboard the wagon. "I've made up my mind, Kit," he said. "If you want to go up to Huntsville and see me off, I'll be obliged. But if you don't, then so be it."

He slapped the reins while commanding Joe Boy to get up. As he drove onto the road, he saw David, and faintly smiled from under his slouch hat.

Soon, Kit appeared on his scruffy steed. "I suppose you heard the whole thing," he growled.

"Why don't you want Pa to go fight?" David asked.

Kit spat and rode past him down the road without responding.

Sitting atop Sally for a moment, David pondered, until the realization hit him. He knew why Kit didn't want his father to go. It would make him look bad for not going himself. Kit was nothing but a low-down coward. Disgusted, he turned his mare and returned home.

Five days later, Hiram was requested to attend a flag presentation with the rest of the newly enlisted North Alabamians, Company I. The *Southern Advocate* described the festivities that had transpired the evening before, when the Huntsville Guards were presented with their flag, which rivaled that of another new company, the Madison Rifles.

According to the newspaper article, Miss Sallie McKie presented the silk flag to Lieutenant Gus Mastin, who in return gave a "strong, manly, and striking address, which was in good taste and well received."

Arriving at the Huntsville Female College with Bud and his wife, Hiram and his family entered. College students escorted them to a gala dinner being held in their honor. David sat quietly watching the guests and their soldiers, men of the recently created Company I. He was already acquainted with some. He knew William Caldwell, because he had gone to school with his son, Tom. He had also met Matthew Curry, a farmer from neighboring Lawrence County, and two other young enlistees who were barely older than he was, cousins by the names of James Alexander and William Rivers. Taking note of their excitement and anticipation, he wished to be a part of it, but he had made his father a promise, which he fully intended to honor, so he ate without speaking, and swallowed his disappointment.

After the banquet, a ceremony commenced, beginning with a patriotic oration given by one of the officers. A banner sewn by the Ladies Aid Society in Huntsville was presented to the new company by Miss Carrie Gordon, who was appropriately dressed in Southern homespun. It was accepted by Private E. S. McClung, the color sergeant, who advanced with his corporals and gave a stirring speech.

"Ladies, with high-beatin' hearts, and pulses throbbin' with emotion, we receive from your hands this beautiful flag, the proud emblem of our young republic. To those who may return from the field of battle bearin' this flag in triumph, though perhaps tattered and torn, this incident will always prove a cheerin' recollection, and to him whose fate it may be to die a soldier's death, this moment brought before his fadin' view will recall your kind and sympathetic words, he will bless you as his spirit takes its aerial flight. May the God of battles look down upon us as we register a soldier's vow that no stain shall ever be found upon thy sacred folds, save the blood of those who attack thee and those who fall in thy defense. Comrades, you have heard the pledge; may it ever guide and guard you on the tented field, or in the smoke, glare, and din of battle, amidst carnage and death, there let its bright folds inspire you with new strength, nerve your arms, and steel your hearts to deeds of strength and valor."

Binford, Slaughter & Co., the Huntsville druggists, bestowed a fully stocked medical chest to the company, and the citizens of Huntsville donated one thousand dollars. Professor Hermann Saroni sang "To Arms Ye Braves." Afterward, the pastor from the First Presbyterian Church offered up a short, reverent prayer.

"Dear Lord," he began, "please do all you can to preserve these young men in their pursuit of securin' our freedom from the tyranny that threatens to disempower us, and keep them from harm's way. Let them walk in the path of righteousness, and never waver from your truth and light. Theirs is the banner of glory, given to them this day that they might virtuously protect us in their quest. May you bring health, safety, and well bein' to each and every one of these fine soldiers. It is in your name we pray."

"Amen," the group chanted in unison.

Following the ceremony, each officer was given a bouquet of flowers, and to each enlistee, a newly constructed Confederate uniform was distributed. The jackets were gray homespun wool with a row of nine shiny brass buttons down the front. Kepis were allotted as headwear, and brogans for footwear. Every man was instructed to bring his own firearm and ammunition if possible, as well as knives and hygienic items. The pastor dispersed small Testaments, blessing each soldier while he went down the line, and telling them that they were expected to learn not only duty to their country, but also how to fight the great moral battle of life. The recruits were then ordered to return the following Monday to the Huntsville Depot for departure. Before the evening's festivities ended, members of the new company exchanged vows with each other, stating that they would protect one another like brethren "to the death."

On the way home, David and his sisters sat in the back of the wagon, listening to their mother and Mrs. Samuels converse beside them. Hiram and Bud rode up on the driver's seat.

"I'm jist so proud of my Bud for wantin' to go off and fight those Yankees," Mrs. Samuels gushed.

David turned his focus toward what the men were saying.

"That was a mighty nice ceremony," Bud commented, to which his father agreed. "Two days ago, I heard that the Marion Light Infantry received a banner made of blue silk, which came from a young lady's weddin' dress."

"Ours is jist as fine," said Hiram with a smile.

Bud went on with his news. "I heard tell Colonel Lee resigned from the U.S. Army so's he could fight for Virginee," he informed Hiram. "He's married to Mary Custis, you know. She's the great grand-daughter of Martha Washin'ton."

"Is that a fact?" responded Hiram.

"Yessiree."

"Reckon there's a lot of fellers who don't know which side of the fence to roost on," commented Hiram.

"Most of the commanders are West Pointers, too," added Bud. "They all went to school together."

"That's right sad indeed. Them havin' to take up arms against each other."

David sighed. The all-too-familiar ache in his heart returned. He wanted more than anything to go with them, to be a part of what he knew would be history in the making. As he glanced at Josie, she winked at him, so reluctantly, he smiled back.

Once they arrived home, Hiram tended to last-minute chores he needed to complete before he departed with his company. David joined him in the barnyard and helped feed the livestock. They spent the remainder of the day repairing fences and finishing up with the planting. When they were done, they went to the summer kitchen, where Caroline had supper waiting for them.

Afterward, David excused himself to his room. He sprawled out on his bed, and began reading *Ivanhoe* for the third time. After a few minutes, his eyelids grew heavy. He yawned, rolled over, and unintentionally fell asleep. Above him, he saw wispy clouds gradually morph into the shape of a soldier. The cloud-soldier slowly raised a gun and pointed it at him. With a start, he awoke to find his room dark. Quickly shaking off the alarming dream, he went outside to feed the animals, but Rena informed him his chores had already been done. He ambled back to his room, lit the kerosene lamp, and picked up his guitar. Perched on the edge of his bed, he gently strummed it. Already, he had managed to figure out five different chords, and could play his favorite, which was the "Bonnie Blue Flag." For some reason, that song made him proud, not only of being a Southerner, but also for believing in the cause his father was about to defend, even though the concept was rather vague to him. He knew a few other melodies, too: "Old Zip Coon," "Aura Lea," "Old Dan Tucker," and another favorite, "Cindy." When he had gone through his repertoire a few times, long enough for his fingertips to start hurting, he put the instrument back in the corner.

Deciding to go outside, he stepped onto the breezeway. He heard voices coming from just beyond the corner, so he moved up close enough to see around it. His mother and father were sitting side by side, their silhouettes illuminated by the pale moonlight as they conversed on the front porch. Caroline's voice sounded strained, while his father's was consoling.

"I reckon the workload is caught up enough," Hiram was saying, "and I won't be leavin' David with too much of a burden." She didn't reply, so he went on. "I don't want to overwhelm the boy, because his studies are important, too, but I know certain things will have to be dealt with in my absence. He'll be accountable for balin' hay, weedin' crops, and tendin' to the livestock, as well as keepin' up with his schoolwork before this ninety-day war is over."

"I know," she finally responded, so quietly David could barely hear her.

"Still," Hiram said, "I have confidence in him. He's mature and responsible enough to handle it."

David grinned. The drone of their voices ceased momentarily, replaced with the high-pitched chirps of crickets.

"Don't forget to write to me every chance you git," Caroline said.

He snickered. "I won't forget, honey."

"And I expect you to attend services every Sunday."

"I will."

"I'll send you packages every week."

"That'll be jist fine."

They sat in the dark momentarily, the faint hoot of an owl punctuating the silence.

"I don't want you to go," she finally said, "even though I know it's your duty to uphold."

"Now, Caroline, darlin', you know I'll be fine."

"Yes, I do. But I'll still fret about you."

He softly chuckled. "There ain't no need for you to worry your purty li'l' head."

She took his hand. "I'll miss you, my dear," she tenderly whispered.

There was another extended silence, and then Hiram responded in a low, passionate voice, "I'll miss you, too. You know that, Caroline. My heart belongs to you, and it always will."

David stepped back into the shadows to the sanctuary of his room. He quietly closed the door behind him. For some reason, he felt consumed with gloom, but pushed the feeling aside. His father was leaving for duty, honor, excitement, and glory. He forced his heartache to turn into anticipation.

The next morning was a Saturday. Because Caroline wanted to make Hiram's last day at home special, she prepared a hearty breakfast, so they all sat down together to indulge in biscuits, sausage gravy, eggs, cornbread with sweet cream butter, and coffee. Afterward, Josie, Rena, and David agreed to ride over to their friends' homes, thus giving their parents some time to be alone together. The girls rode off on Joe Boy, and David bid his folks good-day before he set off down the road on Sally. Although sprightly, the mare didn't obey his commands to gallop, but instead bounced him along at an uncomfortable buck trot. Deciding the ride was too bumpy, he pulled her back to a walk, thankful the day was clear and mild. Sunbeams filtered down through blossoming trees, casting pastel, flickering reflections on the puddle-riddled ditches. The scent of fragrant wild azaleas floated on the whispering breeze. David crossed over Cotaco Creek, passed Apple Grove, and continued for a few miles before turning onto a lane. At the bottom of a sloping hill stood the familiar white farmhouse he had known since childhood. He rode up to the veranda of the Greek revival-style house and stepped down off his horse. As he ascended the steps, a familiar voice called out.

"Dat you, Massa David?"

He withdrew his slouch hat and looked around. "Percy?" he asked. "Where are you?"

"I'ze up here!"

His eyes lifted upward to see a black man grinning at him from over the edge of the roof.

"What're you doin' up there?"

"Fixin' a hole. It been leakin' since las' winter." He raised an index finger and then disappeared.

Deciding their conversation was over, David rapped on the screened door. Momentarily, a lithe Negro woman answered. She wore a black dress with a white apron over it, tied at her waist, and had a white scarf wrapped around her head.

"Come on in here," she said with a shy smile. "I'll tell Massa Jake you's here."

"Thank you, Miss Isabelle."

He knew her as Percy's new bride, for they had been married only a few months. As he started to enter, Percy ran around the side of the house.

"I'll tend to your horse, Massa," he said jovially.

He wore homespun brown pants held up by suspenders, a tattered slouch hat, and a tan shirt with the sleeves rolled up to his elbows. As Percy reached over to take Sally's halter, David stopped him.

"That's quite all right, Percy," he responded. "It looks like you're busy. Sally will be fine out here on the lawn."

He smiled assuredly at the slave before entering the house. While he stood waiting, he heard Isabelle speaking upstairs, announcing his arrival. Another recognizable voice answered.

Isabelle came downstairs, and said, "He'll be right here, Massa David," before vanishing through a doorway.

Moments later, Jake thumped down the steps, rubbing his eyes. "Zeke," he croaked. "Why are you here so early?"

"I came to roust you out, you ole lazy possum," he replied with a grin.

"Well, you succeeded in doin' that." Jake licked the palm of his hand and smoothed back his collar-length, dark brown hair. "Come on, then. Let's go fetch us some vittles."

The two walked through the parlor, down a hallway, and into the kitchen, where Isabelle was busy stirring a cast iron pot on the wood-burning stove. "You two boys sit on down now," she instructed.

They did as they were told while she carried the pot over and poured the creamy contents into two bowls already waiting for them on the table.

"What else you want?" she asked.

"This is fine, Isabelle," mumbled Jake, his mouth full of grits.

She grimaced before turning away.

"Thank you," David added.

Flashing a faint smile at him from over her shoulder, she set the pot down and exited the room. The two boys shoveled in their breakfast, barely speaking until they finished simultaneously.

"Where are your folks?" David asked.

28

"They went into town for the day," replied Jake, who then suggested, "Let's head out back. I'll saddle up ole Stella, and we can go for a ride."

David agreed. He followed his friend outside, feeling the cool breeze blow through his shoulder-length, dark brown hair before flopping his slouch hat on his head.

"I'll go fetch Sally," he said.

By the time he returned, Jake was sitting atop a large black Morgan mare, similar in appearance to David's mount, but more swaybacked.

"Let's head on up to that cave we found last week," said Jake.

They rode down a trail back into the woods for a few miles, until they came to a crevice in the side of a hill. Dismounting, they tethered their mares, cautiously walked toward the cavern, and entered.

"It's mighty dark in here," remarked David.

Suddenly, three small bats fluttered past them, escaping out the mouth of the cave, which caused them to duck and holler in surprise. Once they had settled down, they decided to carve their names into the walls.

"My pa's leavin' on Monday," David remarked.

Jake said nothing.

"You want to go up to Huntsville with us when we see him off? We're leavin' tomorrow afternoon."

Pausing for a moment, Jake finally replied, "Naw. It should only be your kin."

David grunted. He was hoping his friend would accompany him for moral support, but perhaps Jake had a point. "Yeah, reckon you're right," he concurred. "Besides, Kit Lawrence might be there, and I know you don't like him."

Jake simpered. "It ain't that I don't like him, it's jist that I don't care for him much."

"Ain't that the same thing?"

"No. He ain't done nothin' to me personally, but he made snide remarks to the help, and I don't take too kindly to that."

"What kind of remarks?"

"Oh, you know. That Percy's too old for Miss Isabelle, and they should be kept chained up like all slaves."

"What does he know about it? He don't have any slaves."

"I know. He don't even have a wife or young'uns either, because no one will take him!" Jake chuckled, but seeing his friend's sober expression, stifled himself. "Are you all right?"

David raised an eyebrow at him. "Why do you ask?"

"Because you've been dreadful quiet, that's why. More than usual."

With a sigh, he admitted, "I jist feel bad that I don't git to go fight, and I miss Pa already."

Jake laughed. "He ain't even gone yet!"

"I know. But he's fixin' to go off for such a far piece, and I don't know when I'll see him again."

"I wouldn't fret," Jake reassured him. He folded his pocket knife and shoved it into his trouser pocket. Seeing the forlorn look on David's face, he decided to change the subject. "Let's go over to the ole McGovern place!"

That ole place? It's haunted."

"I'll race you over there!"

Jake ran outside with David at his heels. They jumped onto their horses and kicked them to go. To David's surprise, Sally broke into a canter, easily passing Jake's aged mare. He reached the decrepit, run-down farm first. While he waited for Jake to catch up, he looked around at the deteriorating outbuildings, the neglected, overgrown fields, and the dark, empty house. The thought occurred to him that the Yankees could attack and take away everything they owned. His farm might someday look just as derelict. A shiver ran down his spine. He shook it off, thinking his imagination was running away with him.

The Yankees come down here? he thought. *That'll never happen. Our army will whip them before they ever git the chance.*

Jake neared the farmhouse, so David dismounted, all the while teasing his best friend.

After exploring the empty dwelling, and finding only a few spider webs and some mouse droppings, the two returned outside to mount their steeds. They rode to one of the pastures on the Kimballs' property, and sat beneath a stately old live oak dripping with Spanish moss while they allowed their horses to graze. It was their secret meeting place, where they often sat to converse and share confidences, and where they were both growing up, rapidly approaching manhood.

"So when are you fixin' to bring that guitar over and play me a tune?" Jake asked. Plucking a long blade of grass from the soil, he stuck the root end into his mouth.

"As soon as I can play well enough to not mess up," he replied, and followed suit by pulling a blade out, too, but instead of chewing on it, he rolled it around in his long fingers.

"How's your ma takin' to your pa's leavin'?"

"I don't rightly know," he casually stated. "She don't talk about it."

Jake slowly munched on the root. "Sure must be hard sometimes, bein' married."

David glanced at him and grinned. "Speakin' of which, have you decided when to propose to Miss Callie?"

Glaring at him with a strange sneer on his face, he exclaimed, "I ain't proposin' to Miss Callie!"

"No? Seems that's all you've been talkin' about for the last four months."

With a shake of his head, Jake attempted to disguise his feelings. "Miss Callie says she's fixin' to marry me, not the other way around!"

David smiled. "I've heard tell of it both ways."

"Why, I'm too young to git hitched, anyhow," Jake proclaimed. "I want to sow my wild oats for a spell first."

"Me too," David agreed. "There ain't no one in this county I want to marry, anyways."

"Not even Alice Walker? I've seen you two google-eyein' each other. Or at least, she's been google-eyein' you. You're jist too bashful to return the gesture."

David snorted. "She's too plain for me." He leaned back against the rough bark of the oak's corrugated trunk. "I'm fixin' to marry someone exotic, like a foreigner."

Jake exploded with laughter. "You ain't gonna find a foreigner in these parts! Best be settin' your sights a little lower, and settle for someone around here." He stood and walked over to Stella.

As David rose to his feet, he thought to himself, *I will too find someone exotic*. Suppressing a grin, he stepped up onto Sally, and teased his friend about his upcoming nuptials.

They returned to Jake's house, and finding nothing to do, the boys decided to spend the afternoon fishing at a nearby pond, where they discussed everything from the worms they were using for bait, to the

31

Choctaw Indian mounds down by the creek, to the new crop of spring lambs. They wondered what it must be like to march off to war, the mystique of fighting an unknown foe, and discovering places they had never seen before. And then they commenced into listing off places they wished to see.

After a few lazy hours drifted by, and still they had been unable to catch any fish, they returned to the house. Isabelle had a snack already prepared, so they devoured their sandwiches while lounging outside on the front porch. When they had finished, David decided it was time to go. As he stood, one of Mrs. Kimball's calico cats promenaded up onto the porch and began to preen.

"Sure you don't want to come with us tomorrow?" he asked in a last-ditch effort of persuasion.

Jake shook his head. "No, thanks, but come on by when y'all git back," he requested. Glancing at the cat, he pointed to her and said, "Lookee there."

"What?" David asked.

"You know what that means, don't you?"

He shook his head in perplexity.

"When a cat washes behind its ears, it means it'll rain tomorrow. Best bring along your rain gear!"

Giving his friend a wry grin, David said, "See you later," and rode off toward home.

Once he arrived, he became immersed in his usual chores. He ate supper while his sisters chattered excitedly about their father's departure, after which he excused himself and went to bed. His head throbbed from the day's activities, and he wished with all his heart his father wasn't leaving after all, that somehow, the far-away war would be called off, but he knew his wish wouldn't likely come true.

Before sunup, he tended to the hogs and chickens, and hitched Joe Boy to the wagon. He readied himself for church, and joined his family for a quick breakfast of biscuits and honey before it was time to leave. They rode to a small, white, steepled chapel nestled in a valley, the same Baptist church David had been baptized in, had grown up in, and had known all his life. Family members were buried in the church's graveyard, including grandparents from both his mother's and father's sides, as well as aunts, uncles, cousins, and his own little brother, Elijah. The service was similar to that performed every Sunday, except this time, Pastor Tidwell made a point of including Bud and Hiram in his prayer so that they might be sheltered by the Almighty on their journey "to protect the Southland," as he put it. Once the service was over, his family stood outside greeting well-wishers. David waited patiently at the wagon until the last members of the congregation had gone, and as his family approached, he climbed up onto the driver's seat.

On the ride home, he glanced over his shoulder to see his parents holding hands, something he rarely witnessed. Josie jabbered excitedly about her morning in Sunday school class, and Rena added that hers was also interesting. When they arrived home, the girls helped their mother prepare dinner. David assisted his father with the midday chores, and afterward, they went into the house. Seating themselves at the pine dining room table, the family was treated to fried chicken with cornbread, spring greens, smashed Irish potatoes, and candied carrots Caroline had canned from the previous year. For dessert, they relished sweet potato pie. When the meal was over, the family readied for their journey. David went outside to the wagon, and watched as his sisters solemnly filed out of the house. With Caroline on his arm, Hiram followed, dressed in his new uniform. Seeing David gape at him, he grinned back.

"Don't your father look handsome?" Caroline asked with glee, sounding like a schoolgirl.

"Yes'm, he surely does." He tried to hide his apprehension while assisting his mother and sisters into the wagon before he climbed up onto the driver's seat.

Hiram placed his satchel and musket into the bed, and took his seat beside him. "All right, then, let's go!" he exclaimed with a smile.

David slapped the reins, and the family set off for Huntsville. After riding for several hours, they stayed overnight at a tavern in Lacey's Spring. In the morning, they traveled through intermittent sprinkles, across the great Tennessee River, and over mud-pocked roads, until they finally reached their destination.

Other members of the North Alabamians, as well as the Huntsville Guards, had already arrived, along with a throng of spectators. All were standing before the courthouse, a white, three-story Greek revival structure with a large copper-clad dome, and seven wide steps leading up to the entryway. The building and its manicured lawn took up an entire city block.

David parked the wagon, jumped out, and assisted his sisters, while Hiram helped Caroline down. He led his wife by the hand, and the children followed. Ladies dressed in their finest dresses, complete with lavish hats and parasols, stood beside their men, who were attired in fine gray woolen uniforms.

Following his parents through the crowd, David noticed his schoolmate, Tom Caldwell, who was standing with his family. Tom saw him at the same time, and the two boys waved at each other, both caught up in the excitement of the momentous occasion.

Hiram found Bud and his wife near the center of the crowd. The men shook hands, and Bud offered his to David, who happily took it.

"Have you seen Kit?" asked Hiram.

"Not a sign of him," was Bud's response.

The men stood in line to have their likenesses reproduced onto tintypes. Once Hiram's photograph was finished, he gave it to Caroline, who smiled lovingly at the portrait before sliding it into her vestibule.

After several minutes had passed, the mayor captured everyone's attention. He proceeded into a heartrending, lofty farewell address, in which he complimented the soldiers for their bravery, patriotism, and chivalry. Following his eloquent speech, the young women from Judson College performed, a cappella, a song with a melancholy melody but uplifting lyrics, which produced high hopes for the new enlistees.

The soldiers were ordered to form lines eight souls across and march to the train station. Their families followed, and when they walked around the three-story brick depot, they saw a train waiting to take the new recruits to their destination. Steam vaporized up around the mighty driving wheels of the locomotive. The Stars and Bars flew from a flagstaff above the engine, and every passenger car lined behind was decked out in patriotic bunting. The soldiers stood milling about, waiting for their orders while conversing with loved ones. Through the throng, an officer emerged, and raised his voice above the din.

"Attention!" he commanded. "May I have your attention, please!"

Bud said to Hiram, "That's Captain Egbert Jones. He fought in the Mexican War." Looking over at David, he said to him, "Same as your friend, Jake's, pa."

"Ladies and gentlemen." Jones said, his voice as clear as a church bell. "We will be departin' directly. The good Reverend Barnes has a few words he'd like to share."

An elderly gentleman with spectacles, a balding head, and gray hair stepped forward. "Let us pray," he requested, and he delved into a prayer, similar to the one Pastor Tidwell had given the day before.

"Amen!" Everyone exclaimed together.

The crowd grew louder, and a five-piece brass band commenced into "Dixie's Land."

David couldn't help but tap his foot to the music. He watched ladies approach the men in gray, giving them kisses and flowers, along with personal mementos of their affection. Men in finely tailored dress suits and top hats intermingled with the new soldiers. Some handed them money. A shrill whistle came from the locomotive, piercing the air. Steam spewed out onto the sidewalk.

"All aboard!" a uniformed officer hollered.

"Well, reckon this is it," Bud said. He grabbed his wife around the waist and gave her a fervent kiss.

"I'll see you soon, darlin'," Hiram said to Caroline, who struggled to hold back tears.

She smiled as he gently took her in his arms and kissed her tenderly. Releasing her, he grinned, picked up his satchel, and followed his friend to the line of soldiers already waiting to board.

The men began stepping up into the cars, all bubbling with enthusiasm, ready to embark on the adventure of their lives. Bud waved with a silly grin on his face, and climbed aboard. Hiram turned to look at his beautiful bride one last time, gave her a reassuring smile, and boarded. He took a window seat beside his comrade, and gazed down at his brood. Caroline brushed a tear from her cheek, but still retained her smile.

With his hands in his coat pockets, David stood absorbing the scene. His sisters jumped up and down beside him, waving frantically. Several of the young men inside took turns waving back, all with enormous smiles on their faces. He glanced over at his mother, wondering if she was weeping from joy or sorrow, or perhaps a combination of both. Strangely, a twinge of pity pulled at his heartstrings, so he stepped over and took hold of her hand to steady her in case she swooned.

The brass band broke into a melodic, upbeat melody that sounded like a march, which was no doubt meant to inspire the men. Once again, the locomotive whistled. It suddenly lurched forward with a terrible clank. The giant wheels began rotating, grinding on the iron rails until they took hold, and pulled the cars behind. It reminded David of some terrific beast, churning and belching as it picked up speed. The men inside waved exuberantly until the last passenger car had passed the platform. Again, the train whistled before it chugged off into the distance, trailing smoke, and was gone.

The joyous fanfare now over, Caroline and her daughters wandered off to converse with others in the crowd, but all David could do was look out at the distant horizon where the train had disappeared. He couldn't take his eyes from it, and kept staring while he imagined what adventures lay in wait for his father.

Inexplicably, his heart began racing. Hiram was going off to protect his rights, his property, and his family. He was among Alabama's finest patriotic sons, the cream of the crop, and the best the South had to offer. For this, David was immensely grateful, awestruck by the nobility of it all. He could almost feel the exhilaration his father must be experiencing.

He came to the realization that he was now responsible for protecting his family, tending to the farm, and taking his father's place as head of the household. Silently, he made a solemn vow, convincing himself he would do everything in his power to keep the promise he had made. He would faithfully uphold his duty, and make his father proud. When Hiram returned, he would see the man David had become. And if the war was still going on, he would convince his father to allow him to enlist. With that idea in mind, he smiled to himself.

"For it was the first Field of Glory I had seen in my May of life, and the first time that Glory sickened me with its repulsive aspect, and made me suspect it was all a glittering lie."

—*Henry Morton Stanley, C.S.A.*

Chapter Three

The train rumbled on, into dusk and throughout the night, slowing occasionally before accelerating again. Hiram found it difficult to sleep, even though he knew he should, and noticed Bud didn't seem to be having a problem. Every time the train changed velocity or went through a town, Hiram startled awake. Just before dawn, he finally fell asleep, only to be awakened once more by the shrill whistle of the locomotive. The train slowed, coming to a stop.

A sergeant near the front of the passenger car stood, and turned to face them. "Gentlemen, you are to exit after me. Once you are outside, line up in single file."

He went out the door, and slowly, the human contents of the car spilled out after him into the bright morning sunlight.

"Where are we?" a sleepy soldier asked.

The sergeant glared at him with bulging, steely blue eyes. His leathery face was testimony he had spent too much time in the sun. "We're in Chattanooga, boy," he replied before sneering at the young man, who slinked off to find his place in line.

Once the car was empty, the sergeant started down the line, calling roll while he moved amongst the new recruits. Hiram glanced down the row, noticing how one sergeant was assigned to each passenger car, and they were all walking up and down their lines, too.

"Soldiers of the Confederate States of America!" the nearest pacing sergeant hollered, staring each enlistee in the eye. "I am your superior officer, Sergeant Meadows!"

Bud choked a chuckle as he stood beside Hiram, who knew what he was thinking. For such an ugly fellow, the name didn't fit.

"For the next few days, y'all will be accountable to me! I am here to make y'all into the finest soldiers our country has to offer! By the time I'm done, y'all will be the best damn fightin' army there is!"

A few of the men clapped, but seeing the sergeant stare them down, quickly suppressed their response.

"Each man is responsible for his own belongin's, and if somethin' gits lost, I don't want to hear y'all whinin' about it! Understood?"

Some hesitant souls mumbled in acknowledgment, while the others stood in silent awe.

"*Well?*"

"Yessir!" a third of them chanted.

"Men, you are to report back to me at that location over yonder..."

He pointed to a grand, century-old sycamore. Underneath, several staff officers stood, some smoking fat cigars, all staring at the new recruits, and summing them up, Hiram was certain. He and Bud gave sidelong glances to each other. Bud suppressed a smirk.

"...at seven o'clock. Dismissed!"

The men let out sighs and started for the baggage cars.

Hiram withdrew his pocket watch to check the time. "We have half an hour," he observed.

The North Alabamians gathered their belongings, mingled about, and then scavenged for something to eat, bartering off one another. The passenger train that had delivered them departed, leaving the soldiers standing haphazardly around the depot. They learned their destination was Dalton, Georgia, where an Alabama regiment was being formed. At the designated time, they congregated near the enormous sycamore tree, and waited in the warm sunshine. Nearly an hour passed before a freight train arrived. Ordered to line up, the men were loaded into boxcars. Several complained about being treated no better than cattle, but the circumstances didn't improve. Soon, the train pulled out.

Bud and Hiram sat down in the musty straw beside their comrades, listening to the rhythmic clunk of the rails beneath them, and the low hum of men's voices. Light filtered in, streaming through the wooden slats. Hiram glanced over at a young man who was busy scribbling in his journal with a nib.

"Whatcha writin'?" he asked.

The recruit looked up at him. "I'm jist takin' notation of our travels," he said with a grin. He protruded his hand, and Hiram courteously took it. "Name's Anderson," the young man stated. "George Anderson."

"Hiram Summers. Glad to meet you."

"And you, sir." George reached his hand across to Bud as the two exchanged introductions.

"Well, I noticed ole Kit never did show up yesterday to see us off," Bud observed.

Hiram glanced at him. "Reckon he was too busy."

"Or too chicken. I have a new nickname for him."

"What's that?"

"Kit, Kit, chicken... crap!"

Hiram snorted. "Couldn't you think of somethin' that rhymes better than that?"

A few of the boys around them chuckled.

The train embarked on a long ride through pine-covered countryside. After two days of rugged riding, the North Alabamians reached Dalton on May 2. They were the last company from Alabama to arrive. Once the recruits were out of the cars, their respective sergeants began calling roll, and the men responded to their names, after which they were assigned tent partners. Each soldier was given half a small white tent, and taught how to combine the two pieces in order to provide shelter. After they had built their temporary homes, they stood in line again to receive rations, and were served breakfast on tin plates that they were instructed to keep, as well as tin cups. They indulged in cornbread, steak, fried potatoes, eggs, and coffee, all provided by the local townsfolk. Upon finishing their meal, they lined up to receive additional provisions, including haversacks, gum cloths, canteens, blankets, and roll straps. Smooth-bored muskets were distributed to those without their own guns, to which the men grunted, knowing the weapons were relics. Some of the soldiers who had brought along extra money purchased additional accoutrements from the commissary, but they soon found out the items were significantly overpriced, so most did without.

Almost immediately, voting began to determine who would lead what was now known as the 4th Alabama Infantry Regiment, consisting of fourteen hundred men and ten companies: the Governor's Guards and the Magnolia Cadets from Dallas County, the Tuskegee Zouaves from Macon County, the Canebrake Rifles of Perry and Marengo Counties, the Conecuh Guards from Conecuh County, the Marion Light Infantry of Perry County, the Lauderdale Guards of Lauderdale County, the Huntsville Guards and North Alabamians from Madison County, and the Larkinsville

Guards of Jackson County. The regiment included men from all walks of life, from planters and clergymen to lawyers and physicians.

By 3:00 p.m., the votes had been cast. Huntsville's Egbert Jones, whom Bud had drawn Hiram's attention to upon their departure, was elected colonel. Jones instantaneously commanded respect, not only because of his demeanor, but also because of his stature. At nearly six and a half feet tall, he towered over most of the other men, who averaged in height at around five foot seven. He was wide-shouldered and clean-shaven, with kind, yet penetrating eyes, and a direct way of speech.

Evander McIvor Law of Florence was unanimously chosen as lieutenant colonel on the first ballot. Law was considered an accomplished officer, despite his lack of combat experience and field command. He was of slight build, with a goatee covering his twenty-six-year-old face, thus concealing his youthful appearance. On the second ballot, Charles Lewis Scott was elected major. He had been a two-term congressman from California at the onset of the war, at which time he returned to Alabama to defend his native state. Edward Dorr Tracy, a Georgia-born lawyer, was elected as captain for the North Alabamians, the company he had created. Tracy's law partner, David C. Humphreys, was considered to be a Douglas Democrat who had staunchly opposed secession, but once the war became certain, he enlisted in his colleague's company as a private. He was an experienced military man, having previously served as a militia colonel.

The men were fed supper before settling in for the night. Early the following day, they boarded another train, and traveled in old boxcars, with forty-one packed into each car. At sunset, the train stopped to pick up hay that was spread across the floors for bedding. The next morning, the soldiers reached Jonesborough, Tennessee, and were allowed to exit the cars. Ladies from the town turned out to welcome them, questioned them about their home state, and exchanged opinions about the war. After a six-hour delay, the train finally continued on, destined for Virginia.

Two days later, at 10:00 p.m., the men arrived in Lynchburg amidst pouring rain. Through the drenching downpour, they managed to erect their tents, light measly fires, and cook meager meals consisting of stale cornbread and bacon. Some of the new recruits complained incessantly, but Hiram only snickered at their whining, chalking it up to inexperience and youthfulness. Many enlistees were fresh off the farm, he could tell, and had never endured inclement weather. For their sake, he hoped they would toughen up quickly.

On May 6, Arkansas seceded from the Union, and on the following day, the 4th Alabama was inducted into Confederate service, mustered in for the duration of one year. Following several days of idleness, the recruits embarked yet again via train to Strasburg, Virginia, arriving on May 11. The weather had become partly cloudy, to the men's delight. They rested in the afternoon, and prepared rations for the next day's march that evening.

While Hiram reclined on his back with his head resting on the satchel he had converted into a pillow, he listened contently to his comrades, their voices low and calming in the cool evening breeze. The smell of spring hung in the air, and thoughts of home seized his mind. He glanced over at Bud, who was struggling with his boiler.

"Dag nab it!" Bud finally cursed in frustration.

Hiram chuckled in response. "Didn't your wife ever teach you how to cook?" he asked sarcastically.

"Now, why would she do such a dang fool thing as that?" He touched the handle, singed his fingertips, and cussed some more before shoving them into his mouth.

Struggling to contain himself, Hiram suppressed a snicker. "Here, let me help." He pulled himself up from his comfortable position to assist his friend with supper.

They managed to put together an interesting concoction of cornbread, wild onions, carrots, and the army's allotted pork, heated it through, and poured it into their tin cups, making stew. To their gratification, it tasted quite delicious, so much so that Bud bragged to the tent mates next to them. Before they knew it, their comrades were putting their own rations in, and a few others contributed as well, combining their efforts into a spectacular feast. By the time they were finished, they complained of being too full, and lounged by the cozy campfire, listening to a fiddler squeakily draw his bow across the strings in an attempt to play "Nelly Bly." One of the young men who had been drawn in to the banquet was George T. Anderson, the soldier Hiram had met on the train ride to Dalton. George sat scribbling in his journal while the other men relaxed, exchanging stories of their home lives.

Hiram noticed. "What's that you're writin', George?" he asked.

The young man looked up at him with a twinkle in his eye, and smiled. "Would you like for me to read it to y'all?"

"Yes!" the men coaxed.

George cleared his throat. "Old Abe is the greatest fool that I have ever heard of."

The men chortled.

"If he had good sense, he could see that the South could not be coerced. We are all united as one man, and can whip any lot of Yankees on equal terms. It is useless for them to wage war on us, for we can defy the world if they invade us."

One of the men, George Washington Jones, who was an assistant quartermaster of the regiment, guffawed. "All the South wants is her independence!" he declared.

"I'll drink to that!" another man, Enoch Campbell, exclaimed. He raised his tin cup, which contained questionable contents.

"This war will be over as soon as we git there!" hollered Matthew Curry, the farmer Hiram and Bud had previously been acquainted with from Lawrence County.

"Each one of us can whip ten Yankees!" laughed James Alexander.

"With one hand tied behind our backs!" added his cousin, William Rivers.

Hiram smiled at the young men's zeal. He glanced at Bud, who rolled his blue eyes while grinning with amusement. Their excitement was catching: Hiram felt their fervor as well. He hoped the Yankees would see they meant business, turn tail, and run. Perhaps the war would be just a farce, and fizzle out after all.

The following morning, Hiram and his band of brothers set out on a twenty-mile march, learning the reason why they were ordered to prepare rations in advance, for those who had failed to follow orders suffered by having empty stomachs. With four drummer boys keeping rhythm, they arrived in Winchester late in the day to a welcoming reception. The town's residents greeted them enthusiastically by waving Confederate flags and handkerchiefs that resembled fluttering butterflies, and cheered the soldiers, who tiredly marched through town.

One young lady called out to the men in Hiram's company as they marched by. "Where are y'all from?"

William Rivers responded, "Alabama's sons come to fight for Virginia's daughters!"

The young woman joyfully squealed to her friends. Some of the soldiers around Hiram sniggered at her reaction while keeping step with their marching comrades.

Once they had passed through town, the soldiers were ordered to set up camp, where they wearily retired. To their relief, they were allowed to rest the following day, but were required to break camp the next morning and move some thirty miles upstate to Harpers Ferry.

The regiment joined with General Joseph E. Johnston's Army of the Shenandoah, and was attached to Brigadier General Barnard E. Bee's Third Brigade. For the remainder of the week, the recruits enjoyed their leisurely life, faithfully attended Sunday services, read their prayer books, and learned how to fend for themselves by performing duties traditionally left for the womenfolk, such as cooking and darning. The soldiers received sewing kits called housewives, and variations of religious literature from the Army Christian Association, pamphlets that were referred to as tracts, and titled, "Prepare for Battle," "A Mother's Parting Words to Her Soldier Boy," and "Sufferings of the Lost." The Alabamians filled their time with scripture, or sang hymns, such as "Nearer My God to Thee" and "How Sweet the Sound."

The camp chaplain, William D. Chaddick, preached fervently, quoting scripture, although he distorted the content to justify their cause by inferring the enemy was evil, and the Confederates were right and noble: "And if thy right eye offend thee, pluck it out, and cast it from thee: for it is profitable for thee that one of thy members should perish, and not that thy whole body should be cast into hell. And if thy right hand offend thee, cut it off, and cast it from thee: for it is profitable for thee that one of thy members should perish, and not that thy whole body should be cast into hell."

"You ought to be the one up there inspirin' us with scripture," Bud quipped. "After all, you're the son of a preacher."

Hiram merely grinned and shook his head. "I'll leave it to the good chaplain," he humbly replied.

Soon, their situation drastically changed, as more drills and fatigue details were continually expected of them. The men were driven through a gauntlet of routines. Following reveille at 4:00 a.m., they were drilled as an entire regiment from 4:30 until 7:00 a.m., when they broke for breakfast. General inspection was at 8:00 a.m., and the company drill lasted from 9:00 until noon. After midday break, another drill session commenced, lasting from 2:30 until 5:30. A dress parade immediately followed. Supper was served at 6:30, roll call was at 9:00, and tattoo was at 9:30, when all lights were extinguished. Most drill sessions were led by Colonel Jones' protégé, Private Humphreys.

Within a few weeks, the infantrymen became disenchanted with their new colonel, for he rigorously sent them through routine drills, and relentlessly imposed discipline, which the North Alabamians found repetitious and boring. Anxious to fight the Yankees, they grew resentful of the monotony forced upon them, and they were concerned about the colonel's lack of fighting experience while he had served in the Mexican War. The soldiers' disgruntlement led to their passing a petition around camp that called for Jones to resign.

During the month of May, the Confederacy's capital moved from Montgomery to Richmond, and another southern state, North Carolina, seceded. Hiram learned the reason for his regiment's relocation was because Union forces had moved into Virginia and seized Alexandria, which was nearly seventy miles away. Although the situation seemed to be worsening, strangely enough, visitors from Huntsville steadily arrived to see their boys, bringing gifts and letters. Citizens from home temporarily took their own places in the ranks as privates, readying for the fight, but the Yankees failed to appear, and rumors of the Federals' impending advances proved to be false.

On Sunday, May 19, the soldiers behaved as if it was a weekday, which was how many Sundays had become. They fired off their guns, played cards, cooked, and held a dress parade. Afterward, they attended an Episcopal service performed by their camp chaplain. Another dress parade followed, and then the men were ordered to bed as rain set in, lasting all night.

Word reached the troops that on May 24, a New York infantry regiment led by Colonel Elmer Ellsworth arrived in Alexandria. A large Southern flag had been displayed from the Marshall House Hotel, which was visible from Washington. The colonel attempted to remove it himself, but was shot in the chest with a double-barrel shotgun by the proprietor of the hotel, James W. Jackson, who in return was shot and bayoneted to death. Few members of the 4th Alabama expressed remorse for the loss of Ellsworth, especially since he had been a close friend of President Lincoln. In their opinion, it was only a shame Jackson had been murdered for defending his rights.

The Alabamians rotated between standing guard and preparing for battle, all the while becoming more frustrated with their situation. Jones was presented with the petition demanding his resignation on May 27. He immediately brought it to the attention of General Johnston, who warned the men they should either draft a formal complaint or drop the subject altogether.

Jones confronted his fellow soldiers by assembling them. He rode up on his big bay horse, which the men had named "Old Battalion," dismounted, and expressed his regret for not living up to their expectations.

"I am certain that a battle will occur very soon," he proclaimed. "But if you men are still dissatisfied with my performance, I will dutifully resign afterward."

This declaration seemed to quell the 4th Alabama's discontentment, at least for the time being.

May gave way to June, and a week later, Tennessee seceded from the Union.

Bud didn't hesitate to bring it to Hiram's attention. "I wonder if Kit, Kit, chicken crap will jine up now that Tennessee is with us," he quipped. "Don't you suppose we would've seen his sorry hide by now?"

Glancing up from the letter he was writing, Hiram shrugged. "I received a letter from Caroline this mornin', but she didn't mention Kit's enlistment."

"I ain't surprised," retorted Bud. "He's jist another Tory."

Expelling a sigh, Hiram nodded. "He calls himself a cooperationist instead of a secessionist, but I reckon you're right. He ain't jinin' up to defend us."

Deeply saddened his childhood friend had betrayed him, Hiram knew he had no control over Kit's decision, so he resigned himself into accepting it. Redirecting his attention, he continued composing.

Dearest Caroline

I write to inform you of my current condition. We have been camped here at Harpers Ferry for several weeks as you well know. It is strange to think of this as the place of John Brown's uprising only two years ago and that our own Colonel Lee captured him. We have seen the arsenal where he staged his raid and it looks so calm and peaceful that you would have a hard time telling something terrible happened there.

My dearest wife your letters have served as a great comfort to me during this time of unease. I am being well fed and our mutual friend Bud Samuels is learning to cook. We have befriended many others. All are prepared for the fight.

Sweet heart please keep us in your upmost prayers. Give our daughters a kiss for me and tell David not to fret about the heat. Know that my love for you is endless. If the Union keeps procrastinating this war should be over in a matter of days.

All my love
Hiram

News came that Union General George B. McClellan had driven the Confederates out of the Allegheny Mountains, thus bringing the western portion of Virginia under U.S. control. By doing so, he secured himself the nickname, "Little Napoleon." A short time later, it was reported the U.S. Sanitary Commission had been founded by a group of New York women who intended to promote healthful practices within the ranks. Although Rebel forces had no such committee, they followed suit with similar designs.

The Fourth of July was observed with a speech by President Lincoln, whose plea to Congress led to the authorized call for five hundred thousand Federal volunteers. By making such a request, Lincoln apparently had made a total declaration of war, and the Confederates took it as such. Two days later, Private Humphreys was discharged. He returned to Alabama to raise a brigade, and elected himself as colonel.

By mid-July, the Union Army finally began to move, and on Thursday, July 18, the Alabamians received orders to strike tents and cook two days' rations in preparation for a march. The sick, who were principally suffering from the measles, were left behind in Winchester.

While the men marched through town, women, old men, and children came out to see them, calling, "Please don't leave us to the Yankees!"

The foot soldiers set off, marching throughout the day and all night, until they were finally allowed to sleep, but only for two hours. At daylight, they resumed their march, continuing on through the day, from the Shenandoah through Ashby's Gap across the Blue Ridge Mountains. Their uniforms were beginning to show signs of wear, in that shoes and wool coats had sprouted holes; kepis, forage caps, and Egyptian-style havelocks were beginning to fray, and rations were becoming sparse.

Storm clouds mushroomed, thickening to a dark gray by dusk, and obscured the setting sun. Around 10:30 p.m., the Confederate soldiers arrived at Piedmont Station in a miserable, torrential downpour. They sloshed through mud while trying to keep their gunpowder dry. Completely exhausted, the men struggled to obtain what little rest they could under their temporary shelters, which failed to provide much remedy from the rain. At midnight, they took a train to Manassas Junction, arriving at approximately 9:00 a.m. on the morning of July 20.

The men marched about two miles north of the junction before being allowed to bivouac near what they learned was referred to as Ball's Ford. They rested in their temporary camp for a few hours prior to assuming their position, defending a stone bridge that spanned a creek known as the Bull Run River. It was along this road that the enemy was expected to come. Shortly after sunrise on July 21, a Sunday, the distant boom of cannons announced their foe's arrival.

It wasn't long before the Yankees came into view: their appearance seemed surreal. The men of the 4th Alabama were confronted with the entire advancing Union Army. As they neared, the regiments on either side of the North Alabamians fell away. Colonel Jones ordered his men to hold fast their line of defense while he had them march up a hill to a low fence surrounding a cornfield.

General Bee galloped over to the regiment and commanded them by calling out, "Up, Alabamians!"

The men rushed over the fence and advanced at a double quick to the top of the hill. Colonel Jones ordered them to lie down just below the crest, to fire, load, and fire again. The Federals became entrenched only about one hundred yards from where Hiram and his comrades were positioned.

Struggling with their obsolete weapons, the soldiers bit off cartridges and loaded their muskets as rapidly as they could. All the while, Colonel Jones sat calmly atop Old Battalion with one leg draped across the pommel of his saddle, observing the enemy's movements. Upon his command, the North Alabamians rose to deliver a volley, and after waiting for his signal, fell back upon the cool, damp earth. They were spread from the cornfield on their right to a pine woodlot on their left. The men fought on for over an hour, with only artillery to support them.

Glancing at his comrades, Hiram took a moment to catch his breath. The situation at hand was dangerous, yet dreamlike. He had envisioned this moment for months, and had discussed it with his comrades. Still, the realization that it was actually taking place was difficult to comprehend. His heart was beating so hard it felt like it was in his throat. He glanced at Bud, whose face was blackened from powder. Obviously concentrating with all his might, Bud continued to jump to his feet, fire and fall down again while grimacing. Men around them fell with thuds like acorns from oak trees. Bullets whizzed all around them, sounding like angry wasps. Some whistled and ricocheted, haphazardly hitting and missing men as they screamed, moaned, and cursed the wretched Yankees.

One man who thought he could fire better if he remained standing, bragged to the men close to Bud, "Watch how nicely I can take that officer off his horse."

Just as he took aim with his rifle, a Yankee bullet penetrated his skull. He fell in a heap, his brains splattered onto the field. Bud glanced at Hiram, shook his head in dismay, and kept firing like nothing had happened. Stunned, Hiram forced himself to shake it off, continuing to fight as well.

For some reason, the Union Army ceased firing at noon. Bracing themselves for another attack, the Rebels utilized the time to check their firearms. Word came that artillery was running low, which caused a slight panic, but Jones assured his men they could win the battle before their ammunition ran out.

After two hours of quiet, the Yankees resumed their assault, and the Confederates fought off several Union advances. Men in colorful garb fashioned after French Algerian Zouaves attacked first, but were driven back. Then came, one at a time, three other regiments, but all eventually broke and ran. Their uniforms caused confusion, for men on either side were dressed in both blue and gray, including Colonel Jones, who wore the blue uniform he had donned while previously serving in the U.S. Army.

The men spied two unknown regiments clad in gray, approaching in a line on their right. Assuming they were Confederates, the Alabamians signaled by raising their hands to their caps while giving the password, "our homes," and the unknown regiment signaled back by mirroring the action. Law ordered his soldiers to form a line behind the new arrivals. As soon as the 4th unfurled their flags, they were quickly surprised when the culprits turned and opened fire on them. Several men were shot, screaming in agony while the deceivers perpetrated their lines. Others reacted by bursting into hysterical laughter, contrary to what the situation demanded.

The 4th Alabama was finally flanked. As the regiment was commanded to retire, Old Battalion was hit in the leg, forcing Colonel Jones to dismount. In a hail of bullets, he too was hit in both thighs, and crumbled to the ground with a broken left leg. Law immediately took command, managing to retire his troops, but was compelled to leave Jones on the field because Union soldiers had forded Bull Run River. Major Scott went down, shot through the leg. Law fell next, his arm broken by a Yankee's bullet, and was quickly taken from the field. The remaining Alabamians now had no one to guide them. They stood in mass confusion while men writhed around them on the ground, bloody and dying. Smoke and thunder filled the air.

Hiram and his comrades fell back through a skirt of woods, descended a hill, and formed a line, trying to regroup, regardless of the humid, withering heat, their parched thirst, and the horror that engulfed them.

Captain Tracy delivered a patriotic speech, saying, "Strike for the green graves of your sires. Strike for your altars and fires, God and your native land."

He then asked for volunteers to retrieve Jones, but was convinced by another captain that the effort was futile. At a loss, the regiment awaited orders, watching survivors from other divisions scatter or huddle together in a nearby ravine.

Generals Johnston and Beauregard arrived on their right.

Johnston asked, "Where are your field officers?"

"They've been left on the battlefield," came a response.

Another man asked the general to place the regiment in position, to which Johnston replied he would once he analyzed the situation, and the generals rode off.

It was now two o'clock. Suddenly, General Bee rode up on his steed, excitedly waving his sword.

"What body of troops is this?" he hollered at them.

"Why, General, don't you know your own troops? We're what remains of the Fourth Alabama!" Enoch Campbell exclaimed.

The general appeared calm but perturbed. "This is all of my brigade I can find," he stated to the soldiers. "Will you follow me back to where the firin' is goin' on?"

"Aye, sir!" hollered one of the men.

"We will, sir!" yelled Hiram, barely recognizing his own voice.

"To the death!" added George Anderson.

Bee immediately set the men into action, leading them forward into the fray. On the other side of the ravine awaited a brigade of Virginians commanded by General Thomas Jackson, who sat stoically upon his steed.

General Bee brought him to the men's attention, and said, "Let us go and support Jackson! See, he stands like a stone wall! Rally behind the Virginians!"

As the regiment moved left, an artillery battery cut through their ranks. Bee and his army veered right, while the rest of the regiment moved forward into the woods.

Mayhem prevailed. The men were unable to distinguish friend from foe. Forced to fall back, they retired in a hurricane of bullets to await further orders. Suddenly, James Alexander fell, a bullet piercing his abdomen, and sending his entrails splattering. Bud witnessed the young man's terrible injury, but was unable to assist. Although in shock, he retreated with his regiment in a tornado of chaos. He and Hiram trailed behind, and as they retreated, Hiram overheard Bee address Jackson.

"General, they're pushin' us back!"

Jackson replied calmly, his blue eyes barely visible from beneath his forage cap, "Well, sir, we shall give them the bayonet."

General Bee ordered his men to retreat to a nearby hill. The Rebels fell behind it, and fortified the hill. Surprisingly, the field began to grow quiet, except for the frantic wails of injured soldiers. To the Alabamians' relief, the Federals were retreating. With one hand, Hiram withdrew his pocket watch, and wiped sweat from his brow with the other. Clicking the timepiece open, he saw it was nearly five o'clock. The battle had gone on for seven hours.

Bud glanced over at him, sweat trickling down his darkened face, leaving streaked rivulets, but he said nothing.

The Yankees fled northeast toward Washington, and in their chaos, became more panic-stricken, until their escape became a rout. The 4th Alabama, however, could only observe from a distance, since their exhaustion immobilized them.

"Has anyone seen my cousin?" asked William Rivers in a daze.

Bud wiped the sweat from his face with his shirtsleeve. "I seen him over yonder," he said to the young man, his voice hoarse from breathing smoke. He stopped William by clasping onto his arm. "I don't recommend you go over there," he said quietly. "He's in a bad way."

William glared at him for a moment, contemplating his words, but then hurried off.

The men were requested to return to the field and gather the fallen. It wasn't long before Hiram wished he had been assigned to a less gruesome task. All across the field, swarming flies swirled about strewn body parts, broken soldiers cried out in pain, and the wounded, both men and horses alike, writhed in agony as gathering buzzards slowly circled overhead. A white clapboard house that had been at the center of the commotion was now splattered with bullet holes, the wooden sideboards shattered from gunfire. Hiram passed his canteen from one thirsty casualty to the next until it was drained, and still they cried out for more. Finally, an ambulance arrived. Litter-bearers carried off the wounded. Colonel Jones was discovered where he had fallen, and was transported to a nearby hospital at Orange Court House.

Hiram came upon James Alexander. His cousin, William Rivers, was kneeling beside him, holding a white cloth to his cousin's wounded stomach, which was soaked with bright red blood.

"Can you help me?" William pleaded, his voice quivering as he neared tears.

Unsure of what to do, Hiram could only stare in piteous distress. James reached up, took hold of his cousin's arm, and smiled.

"It's all right, Will," he said. "I don't feel a thing." Suddenly, he gasped, spurting blood from his mouth. A final sigh escaped him. He grew silent, and his eyes glazed over.

William began to cry. Hiram could see he was overwhelmed, so he offered to help him up, but William refused. Finally, Bud came along, and insisted. Slowly, William rose to his feet, dropped the bloody rag, and allowed Bud to escort him away. Hiram remorsefully followed, glancing back over his shoulder at James' lifeless body while he stumbled off. It was too easy for him to picture his own son lying there, lifeless on the darkening earth. Biting his lower lip, he expelled the ghastly thought from his mind as sunset approached.

Noticing another young casualty, he drew closer, and recognized him to be George Anderson, the young diarist. All the horror of what had happened started sinking in. Unable to contain his emotions, sobs escaped him. He turned away, and ambled off to join his surviving comrades.

Later in the day, President Davis rode at a gallop past the regiment on his way to the front. At sundown, the men found their way back, and rested in their bivouac, reflecting on the day's events. They felt miserable about their performance, because they had turned their backs to the Yankees and retreated. The camp died down, with only the sounds of chirping crickets in the distance.

"I never expected to see anything like that," Bud quietly said.

"Neither did I," agreed Hiram in solemn realization.

"But it was jist like the vision I dreamt," elaborated Bud. "As if it was foretold."

Hiram was still so shaken that he had difficulty finding appropriate words. "I saw that young feller, George, lyin' there dead," he finally muttered.

Bud only nodded. The firelight flickered across his face.

"It was right strange," Hiram finally said, breaking the foreboding silence. "Last summer, I read about a meteor shower that happened over the Hudson River. They were sayin' it was a sign of what was to come."

He glanced at his comrade, who lay motionless beside him. "I laughed it off at the time."

Bud turned his head and glared at him. Both agreed without saying as much. It had been their first introduction into hell, their baptism of fire.

In the morning, the men assisted with gathering their wounded, and delivered them to the tent of Dr. Slaughter, who promptly amputated limb after limb with the assistance of chloroform to help prevent gangrene from setting in. Others sadly helped to bury the dead.

Later in the day, it was learned that General Bee had died from wounds he received. The white clapboard house at the center of the battle belonged to an invalid old woman by the name of Judith Carter Henry. Unable to leave her bed, she had been riddled with bullets. The Federals were commanded by Brigadier General Irvin McDowell. Generals Johnston and Beauregard of the Confederacy had proven themselves as worthy foe, and apparently had defeated the Union soldiers. Hiram and his comrades hoped that, by showing their mettle, they would bring a rapid end to the conflict, thus winning their right to secede.

Soldiers from other regiments wandered into camp, describing the turmoil that had swirled around them. Brigadier General J. E. B. Stuart, Confederate cavalry commander, had hurled his cavaliers into the New York Zouaves, and as the Yankees retreated, all hell broke loose. Civilians from Washington City had driven over to witness the battle, bringing along their ladies, complete with picnic lunches, parasols, and fine carriages. However, when the Federals "skedaddled," they almost killed the Washington elite. An artillery shell worsened the situation when it hit a wagon, clogging the road that had been their escape route. Congressman Healy was captured by the Confederates and taken prisoner. The Rebels were calling it the "Bull Run Races."

As other reports came in, it was estimated the 4th Alabama lost nearly two hundred men. Those who survived could feel nothing but animosity toward their foe, for the northerners were indeed their enemies, out to kill them all … but not if the Rebels killed them first.

"Our brave men fell in great numbers, but they died as the brave love to die—with faces to the foe, fighting in the holy cause of liberty."

—*Captain Thomas Goldsby,*
4th Alabama Infantry Regiment

Chapter Four

Word of the battle quickly spread to Huntsville, and within days, filtered down to Morgan County. Caroline had mentally prepared herself for what she anticipated would happen, but when the first battle finally did take place, she found herself ill-equipped. Doing her best to shelter her brood, she realized it was just a matter of time before they heard of the event.

A week later, she learned that a list of fatalities had been posted, and knew she had to drive to Ben Johnson's mercantile to have a look, but all the while, her heart felt as though it was breaking. She dreaded the list, dreaded the result of the terrible fighting, dreaded what the war might be doing to her home, and especially, dreaded seeing Hiram's name listed. Traveling alone, she reached her destination, climbed down from the wagon, hitched her draft horse, and approached the two-story wooden structure. Her ankle boots clunked up the wooden steps and across the porch's pine slat floorboards with every step she took. She pulled the front door open, and a tiny bell above it announced her arrival. Upon entering, she saw several others gathered around a notice tacked to a wall. Ben Johnson nodded her way. He threw a glance toward the posted list. She knew what it meant.

Slowly, feeling like she was floating, she approached the others, passing by the dry goods, the glass cases displaying pottery, clothing, and sewing notions, and under farm equipment hanging from the ceiling rafters. Some of the women were sobbing, covering their faces with handkerchiefs, while others turned away, or stared at her with vacant eyes. As they drifted off, she stepped toward the ominous poster, held her breath, and forced herself to gaze upon the names. When she had reached the bottom, she breathed a sigh of relief. Hiram's name wasn't on the list, although she recognized one that was. Turning toward the counter, she wiped a trickling tear from her cheek, walked over, and requested a copy of the *Southern Advocate*.

Initially at a loss for words, Ben cleared his throat. "I reckon Hiram's name ain't on there," he finally said.

The revelation started sinking in. Caroline smiled. "No, thankfully not."

Ben returned the smile. "Right glad to hear it." He handed her a newspaper. "The editor of this paper, Mr. William Figures, has a son who's with your husband's regiment."

"Oh?" she replied cordially. "He's all right, ain't he? I mean, I didn't see..."

"Yes, ma'am, far as I can tell."

"That's mighty fine. Well, I'll be on my way. Good-day, Mr. Johnson." Turning to leave, she opened the paned-glass door.

Ben called out, "When you write to that man of yours, tell him I said hello."

"I surely will," she replied.

Returning to the wagon, she untied Joe Boy, climbed aboard, slapped the reins, and drove out of view from the mercantile before pulling the vehicle to a stop. Uncontrollably, she burst into tears, sobbing convulsively until the ache in her heart finally subsided. She couldn't show her weakness to her children. For them, she had to be strong. Wiping her eyes with her handkerchief, she drove on toward home.

After she arrived, she went into the summer kitchen to prepare supper. Her son would return from the fields soon, and he was always famished. She smiled at the thought. He had grown so tall in the last year that he now towered over his father at six feet. She wondered if he would ever stop growing. Counting her blessings, she said a silent prayer to her maker for preserving her family, her Hiram. The war couldn't end too soon.

Josie and Rena rode into the barnyard on Sally.

"Where have you two been off to?" she hollered through the screen.

They slid off the mare and came into the kitchen. "We went over to Miss Lizzie's," Rena replied, referring to her friend Elizabeth Ryan, who was the same age as her. "And you'll never guess what we learned today!"

"Do tell," Caroline responded, smiling at her lovely daughters.

"Miss Lizzie's pa and two of her brothers were talkin' about the battle up in Virginee," said Josie excitedly, her childish voice squeaking. "And they said we won!"

"That's grand news, Josie." Caroline hugged her. "Is your brother still out yonder in the bean field?"

"No, ma'am," answered Josie.

"We didn't see him out there on our way home," Rena added. "I'll be in my room if you need me."

She gave her mother a peck on the cheek, and shuffled off in her long blue calico day dress.

"Me, too," said Josie, who was dressed in a shorter, greener version of her sister's dress. She kissed her mother's cheek as well, and trotted after Rena.

Caroline watched them walk away. It was difficult to believe her girls were already twelve and fourteen years old. It wouldn't be long before they were grown and married to local boys. She thought back to her courtship with Hiram. They had met during a church function, at the same little Baptist fieldstone church where his father had preached. That was seventeen years ago. Within months of their marriage, she discovered she was expecting, and not long after, along came David. Where was that oldest child of hers, anyway? She proceeded to knead a loaf, wondering where her son could be. Finally, she heard the faint thunder of horse's hooves. He rode up the lane on his father's stallion, pulled the mustang to a halt, jumped off, and came into the screened kitchen.

"Where in tarnation have you been?" she inquired. "You weren't off chasin' trouble with Jake, were you?"

"No, ma'am. I went down to the creek." He held up two large catfish strung on a line. "Lookee what I caught for supper!"

"Darlin', that's splendid!" she exclaimed. "And here I thought you were out gallivantin' around."

"No, Ma. I quit doin' that." He handed her the fish. Noticing the newspaper lying on the table, he gazed at the front page. "Governor Moore gave a speech about Pa's regiment!" he exclaimed, and read on. "It says here that he praises the accomplishments of the 4th Alabama for chasin' off four regiments of Yankees. And in return, the state legislature has given its official thanks and distinction for their remarkable display of cohesion and fightin' ability. They're heroes!" He grinned, and with a laugh, added, "They're callin' it the Great Skedaddle, because the Yankees ran away!"

"That's enough, David," she growled. Suddenly overcome, she wiped her hand across her forehead.

"Ma? Are you all right?"

She sank down onto a cane-back chair, struggling to contain her emotions. "I'm fine."

"You don't look it. What's wrong?"

Caroline shook her head. "Did your father say you could ride his horse?"

He grimaced. "Well, no. But I couldn't let Cotaco jist waste away out there in the pasture. I'm fixin' to race him, and make us some extra money."

"David Ezekiel Summers! You know you ain't supposed to be ridin' that wily beast. He's a heap of trouble, because he's too unpredictable."

"No, he ain't, Ma. He jist needs some discipline. I'm fixin' to break Renegade, too."

"I'm fearsome you'll git hurt on that stallion," she admitted. "And I don't want you bettin' on him. That's the devil's way."

"I won't," he assured her, all the while grinning from ear to ear, amused by her mother hen attitude.

"Wipe that smirk off your face, young man," she said. "You heed what I tell you, and mind your mother."

He frowned. "Ma, I'll be fine. You needn't fret. Besides, you know I'll jist ride him anyways."

Caroline scowled, but seeing her son's large eyes gazing earnestly into hers, she softened. "All right," she relented. "Go tend to your chores."

He smiled at her, went outside, and sauntered off toward the barn.

Aware he was growing too fast for her liking, she also knew keeping the truth from him was futile. He would find out soon enough, one way or another, so later that evening, she decided to confess what she had discovered. Finding him in his room, she sat beside him on the bed.

"David, I learned some terrible news today."

He glared at her. "What, Ma?"

"James Alexander was killed," she said. "You remember him, don't you? Him and his cousin jined up together with your pa's company."

"Yes'm, I remember." He sat contemplating momentarily. "That's right sad, indeed. How did you find out?"

"They posted a list at Ben Johnson's place. Praise God, your pa's name wasn't on it."

He took her hand. "Don't fret, Ma. You won't be seein' Pa's name on any death list."

She smiled, squeezing his hand as he gave her a reassuring kiss on the cheek. *I certainly hope not*, she thought to herself.

Although he knew he was going against his mother's wishes, David went out of his way to learn what was happening in Virginia, and he read every detail he could find about the battle. He found out that on July 27, General McClellan was appointed to Commander of the Department of the Potomac, replacing General McDowell, who had failed at the battle, which the Northerners were calling Bull Run and the Rebels were referring to as Manassas. A few days later, on August 6, the Confiscation Act was passed, which permitted the seizure of all property that was being used for insurrection, including slaves. It stripped the slave owners of their property rights, but didn't actually free the slaves, so they were considered property of the U.S. government.

On a sultry afternoon two weeks later, he and Jake decided to go swimming in a pond near Jake's. Returning to the house, they treaded barefoot along a dirt path, passing by the slaves' shanty, and overheard Percy speaking to Isabelle in a hushed tone. Deciding to eavesdrop, they crept to the open window as close as they dared to without being detected.

"Dat Confiscation Act is our freedom ticket, Izzie," he was saying.

Isabelle replied, "Hush yo' mouth! I ain't goin' nowhere and leavin' dese nice folks. Who'll take care ob us if we go?"

"Why, we'll take care ob ourselves," stated Percy, a sincere twinge in his voice. There was an extended moment of silence, until he said, "All right, den. We'll do it yo' way. Least, fo' now."

Isabelle insisted he put it out of his mind, and walked out of the cabin toward the main house as David and Jake ducked behind a cluster of shrubs. Momentarily, Percy followed her.

"Do you reckon they'll run off to Yankee land?" David asked in amazement.

Jake shook his head and grinned. "Naw. At least, I hope not. No tellin' what might happen to them if they try to go up there."

David gaped at him. He hoped, for their sake, Percy and Isabelle didn't decide to flee. It could be their ticket all right: their ticket to death.

That evening, the boys sat out on Jake's veranda counting fireflies, and making up tunes to fit the rhythm of the cricket chirps. Cicadas and tree roaches added to the chorus. Every once in a while, a whippoorwill chimed in, it's haunting call echoing out in the darkness.

"Ain't you boys comin' in soon?" asked Mrs. Kimball as she stepped out of the house and into the cool evening air.

She was a beautiful woman, an older, feminine version of her son, with dark hair and eyes that glistened with contented peace. David thought she looked like a regal Indian maiden, for rumor had it that Jake was a descendant of Cherokee heritage.

"In a while, Ma," responded Jake. "David is takin' Mrs. Summers up to Huntsville tomorrow. Is it all right if I go along?"

"I reckon so," she replied with a slight smile.

As she turned to leave, David asked, "Would you like to go, too, Mrs. Kimball? My ma's helpin' some other ladies sew clothes for the soldiers."

"I'd be happy to," she said. With that, she went into the house, closing the door behind her.

Lying back upon the hard, varnished pine boards of the veranda, the boys gazed up at the spectacle of silent stars shooting across the sky. They oohed and aahed at the sight, talking well into the night, until they finally fell asleep.

Early the following morning, they awoke at the sound of a rooster's crow. The sun was just beginning to peek over the horizon. David bid farewell to his friend, rode Cotaco home, and quickly tended to his chores, finding time to coddle his colt. Renegade returned the gesture by nuzzling up to him, and David promised to spend extra time with him, but it would have to wait until later. He went into the kitchen, ate a quick breakfast, returned to the barn, and hitched up Joe Boy. Once Caroline was ready, they set off for Huntsville, stopping first at the Kimball's.

The foursome traveled to Lacey's Spring, where they spent the night in a local tavern that also served as a room and board. Early the following morning, they continued on their journey. The day was already hot, and by the time they reached Huntsville, it was midday. David delivered the women to the First Presbyterian Church, escorted them inside, and returned to the wagon, where Jake was waiting. They stood out in the sun for a while, but inevitably grew restless.

"Let's see what's goin' on around town," suggested Jake.

They unhitched Joe Boy, and rode the large white Percheron bareback down the thoroughfare. Traveling along Adams Street, they took in the beautiful Italianate homes, headed back up Franklin Street while observing the enormous Classical revival-style mansions, and wondered what life inside them was like, living in the lap of luxury within their walls. Although Jake's family had slaves, they were treated more like family than servants, and the thought of having someone obey their every command like genies was an inconceivable concept. Riding in a square, they noticed how very few people were outdoors because of the heat.

"It's plum hot out here!" Jake exclaimed.

"Let's go find us a shady spot," suggested David.

Digging his heels into Joe Boy's flanks, they rode toward the edge of the city. They turned a corner, and noticing a small division of soldiers marching ahead, they decided to follow, staying back far enough so as not to be detected. The soldiers kept marching to a wooded area along Big Spring Branch, where hundreds of others were drilling. Behind the soldiers, rows of horse stables lined the edge of the woods. David and Jake slid off Joe Boy, tied him to a shrub, and stealthily stole to the top of an incline. They looked down upon the regiment, watching as the group they had followed fell in, took their place among the others, and obeyed their commander's orders to "About face." The men moved in unison, responding to each call the officer made. He hollered, "Attention," and they stood erect in anticipation of his next command. The officer barked other orders. The men lifted their fire irons simultaneously, raised them as though they were taking aim, and placed them back down when the officer yelled, "At ease."

"What are you two doin' here?"

They wheeled around to see a young soldier eyeing them from under his forage cap, and aiming his musket at them like he was ready to shoot them.

"Nothin'," replied Jake. "We were jist observin'."

"Is that a fact?" The young man looked them over. He relaxed his weapon

"That's right," said Jake. "We ain't never seen anything like this. It's spectacular!"

"That it is," the young soldier agreed with a grin. "Welcome to Camp Jones, named after Colonel Jones. Y'all ever heard of him?"

"I have," David volunteered. "He's the commander of my pa's regiment."

"Oh! So your pa is off fightin' the Yankees!"

"Yessir."

"Y'all considerin' jinin' up?"

David flit a glance at his friend. "Not at present," he said, "but it's always a possibility."

"How old are y'all, anyway?"

"I'm fifteen, and he's sixteen," said Jake. "But my birthday's next week."

The soldier chuckled. "Y'all are too young to be soldiers. Want to be drummer boys?"

Jake shrugged. "I reckon we could learn."

"We're here with our mothers," David informed him, "and we're jist curious about what y'all are doin'."

Jake nudged him hard with his elbow. David flinched in pain.

The young soldier smiled. "See that feller down yonder?" he asked, pointing to an officer who was decked out in full uniform, despite the heat.

Jake and David looked over to where the soldier directed.

"Yeah?" asked Jake.

"That's First Lieutenant Joseph Wheeler. He's formin' this here regiment, the nineteenth Alabama."

"Oh," David replied in awe.

They stood watching for a moment. The men below marched in unison, their feet stomping in rhythm, and dust billowing up to their knees.

"Are y'all goin' to Virginia?" David asked.

"Don't rightly know where we're headed," came the response. "We might stay close by. I hear tell there's Yankees lurkin' 'round every corner, and it won't be long before they come here, scrappin' for a fight."

"How long have y'all been trainin' here?" asked Jake.

"Not long. Fightin' Joe—that is, Lieutenant Wheeler—wants to move our trainin' ground. He says the city offers too much temptation for us."

The young soldier simpered. "Reckon you boys don't know what I mean by that." He chuckled again. "By the way, I'm Private Samuel Shepherd. Pleased to make your acquaintance."

"Likewise," said Jake. He reached out his hand to the young private, who refused to take it.

"If y'all plan on becomin' soldiers, you'll have to learn to salute your superiors." He put his hand to his forehead in a military gesture, obviously enjoying his self-appointed promotion.

The boys grinned and followed suit. Jake raised his right hand, David his left, so that their elbows collided.

Private Shepherd chortled. "Well, y'all can learn that when y'all enlist." He glanced at his comrades. "Reckon I'd best mosey on down there, and let y'all git back to your mothers!"

He walked off, snickering to himself.

"Why did you go and do that?" Jake growled, exasperated.

"Do what?"

"Tell him we were here with our mothers?"

"Because it's the truth."

"Well, he didn't need to know it. Now he thinks we're sissies." Jake glared at his friend, whose hazel eyes were swirling to dark brown.

"Sorry if I embarrassed you."

Jake grimaced. "Never mind, Zeke," he said, seeing his friend's discomfort. "It don't really matter." He knew David was far too sensitive for his own good, so he quickly changed the subject. "Let's ride back into town. Maybe we'll see some purty girls."

He started down the knoll to where Joe Boy waited, and David followed.

"I don't know, Jake," he said as they rode back into town. "I promised Pa I'd look after the farm while he's away, so I can't rightly jine up. Besides, as soon as this war is over, I'm fixin' to be a Pony Express rider and go out West."

"Yeah, me too," Jake agreed.

As though his previous wish had willed itself, Jake saw two young women walking down the street with parasols in hand.

"Good afternoon, ladies!" he called out, withdrawing his slouch hat and waving it in their direction.

The two girls giggled in response.

Jake slid off the draft horse. He commenced conversing with them while David remained on Joe Boy's back, looking out at them from under the brim of his slouch hat, too awkwardly bashful to mimic his friend's bold actions.

Once they returned to the church, they discovered that the women were ready to leave, so David hitched Joe Boy up to the wagon. On the ride home, their mothers talked about the soldiers they had heard about, and how some were faring better than others. They took pity on the poor boys who were suffering from homesickness, missing their mothers. David glanced over to see Jake leering at him, and felt his wrath.

The following day, Alabama's new governor, John Gill Shorter, was elected. Kit stopped by the farm the next morning to notify Caroline, as well as to express his thoughts on the matter, while she hung clothes on a line with her older daughter. Hearing the sound of his voice, David stopped mucking stalls in the barn and sauntered over to listen.

"I hope he can do more for this great state of ours than the last one did," Kit grumbled while chewing on a plug of tobacco. He turned to spit the juice out into the yard, causing Rena to wince.

"This ain't your great state any longer," Caroline fired back. "You went off to live in Tennessee, remember?"

"Course I know that! I'm jist sayin' he should be required to find a way to git us out of this mess, same as Jeff Davis should. Before any more fellers git killed."

Caroline glared at him.

"Well, now, Caroline…" His voice softened. "You know it's true. If this war don't end soon, we'll be sendin' off more of our menfolk."

"I don't see how that affects you, Mr. Lawrence," she snarled. "You don't have any kin, 'cept your brother, and he's jist as likely to jine up as you are."

Kit squinted. "My brother's got an impediment, and I told you why I ain't fixin' to go."

David raised a skeptical eyebrow at his sister.

"There must be a more peaceful way to resolve this," Rena reasoned.

"Reckon they've already tried talkin' it out," remarked David, "but it didn't do any good."

"That much is true," Kit agreed. "Congress wasn't willin' to listen to us Southrons."

"Let's hope you're right, then, Mr. Lawrence," said Caroline. "We should all pray that the new governor will change things around for us."

David frowned. He didn't foresee a change taking place merely because one man was being replaced. It would take something far more remarkable.

Two weeks later, on August 29, Caroline received a letter from her beloved, the first since the great battle in July. A courier arrived at the farm to deliver it, and before he had ridden away, she eagerly tore open the envelope. Extracting the letter, she pulled it out, unfolded it, and began reading.

> *My dearest wife*
>
> *Words cannot express how sorry I am that I have not been able to return to you yet. As you might now know we were successful in whipping our opponents at Manassas Junction and have been in camp ever since preparing for the next advance. Our commander Jones was seriously wounded and it seems doubtful he will recover. We have elected a new colonel Ivander Law from Huntsville to take his place.*
>
> *Please send more socks when you get the chance my darling. I am eating well so far but rations become sparse at times. Bud says to tell you hello. Keep us in your prayers and tell the children I said hello.*
> *Your devoted husband*
> *Hiram*

Caroline clutched the letter to her chest while tears trickled down her cheeks. Great relief swept over her. She had finally received word from him, although she had known by intuition he was safe. Regaining her composure, she put on the same masquerade, pretending everything was all right, but the truth was that the situation scared her to death. Hiram might not return alive, and the war could turn even uglier. She vowed to keep her children safe no matter what, but the amplification of more troops terrified her.

Colonel Jones died four days later, not from his wounds directly, but from blood poisoning he acquired as a result. His body was returned to Huntsville, and on September 6, the city turned out for the largest procession it had ever witnessed. Caroline thought it only proper to attend, so taking her children along, she traveled with Bud's wife, meeting up with a few other women whose husbands were serving for the North Alabamians as well.

The spectators stood along the curbside, watching as a detachment of forty soldiers from each of the eleven companies training at Camp Jones marched by in full uniform, complete with glistening bayonets and polished boots. Next came the glass hearse, decorated with white plumes and crepe, drawn by four white horses draped in black. The coffin lay inside, swathed with black cloth. On top of it was displayed a Confederate flag, the deceased's sword, and wreaths of fresh flowers and evergreens. Pallbearers, including both citizens and soldiers, walked on either side of the hearse while it made its way down the street. Behind it, an infantryman rode Old Battalion, who had come home with his master. Members of the 4th Alabama marched behind to a requiem the band played in accompaniment, followed by the mayor and Huntsville aldermen. Next were the colonel's relatives, who rode in a black carriage, and various citizens in vehicles and on foot, trailing behind in a long succession.

The mourners made their way through town to the Court House Green, where a funeral ceremony commenced. The coffin was carried across the lawn and set before a platform that had been erected for the clergy, who spoke to the audience of nearly twenty-five thousand. Once the service ended, the procession continued on to the city cemetery, where the celebrated colonel was laid to rest beside his deceased wife, fulfilling a request he had expressed as a premonition of his death. A wailing dirge played, three shots were fired by a newly formed company, the Huntsville Greys, the grave was filled up, and the congregation dispersed.

As the Summers family drove back home with Mrs. Samuels in tow, they discussed the particulars of the event they had just witnessed, including the fact that Jones' men had sent him messages of regret and sympathy before his death. It was apparent the glamour of being a soldier was starting to wear off, while realism was taking its place. Their celebrated hero and patriot had fallen, the first of his kind, and they all knew in their solemn observance of his funeral there would be more to follow. Bud's wife and Caroline grew quiet at the revelation. Both had the same thought in mind, wondering if their spouses would be next. The uncomfortable silence proclaimed their apprehension.

On October 7, state leaders announced that Alabama had supplied twenty-seven thousand troops to the Confederacy thus far. This included sixty infantry regiments, thirteen cavalry regiments, six battalions, and twenty batteries. The war was ramping up, that much was certain.

Caroline spent her evenings sitting out on the porch in the cool evening air after saturating her soul in scripture, smoking from her corncob pipe, and rocking while she listened to her son strum his guitar, or her older daughter sing like a meadowlark. The land she had known since her childhood took on a calming characteristic in autumn, when the leaves transformed into various degrees of amber and scarlet. She could look out across the valley and see grazing livestock, hear the distant cry of hovering hawks, and occasionally, the shrill yelp of a coyote. She wondered if soldiers would encroach on her farm, and whether she could supply them if need be. Already, her family had managed to store enough honey, elderberry jam, and canned garden vegetables to last them through the winter. The only thing left was to harvest what remained in the fields: fodder for the animals, black-eyed peas, squash, beans, and corn. She let out a sigh of contentment. All was well ... for now.

Three weeks of quiet calm drifted by. David had graduated from school the previous session, for which he was thankful. It wasn't that he disliked school. On the contrary, he enjoyed learning. It was one particular schoolmate he disliked immensely. Owen Ridgeway was a thorn in his side, and he was glad to be rid of him.

Every morning, David worked in the fields, and when his sisters returned home from school in the afternoons, they helped harvest the crops. The three siblings assisted their neighbors, taking turns in each other's fields, until the last plant had been procured.

David learned that on October 24, the first transcontinental telegraph message was sent to President Lincoln in Washington from California by Chief Justice Stephen J. Field, and his heart sank when he read the news. He knew it was just a matter of time before the Pony Express would become obsolete. Therefore, his hopes of ridding himself of his mundane existence by riding off into the Western sunset atop Cotaco were dashed. He rode over to Jake's immediately to report the news.

"Well, I reckon we'll jist be stagecoach drivers instead," Jake said as he sat contemplating while chewing on a grass blade.

"There's likely to be an age limit for that," said David, "and I'll wager we're too young."

Jake simpered. "Want to go to Decatur with Pa and me tomorrow? We're fixin' to be gone for a few days."

"What is there to do in Decatur?"

"There's an auction on Thursday. Pa's been hired to put in a bid for Mr. Primrose," Jake explained.

"I'll ask Ma. If it's all right, I'll be back by sunset."

The boys agreed, and he set off for home. Once David arrived, he was obligated to carry out his chores, but then his mother released him, so he rode Sally back to the Kimball's.

Early the next morning, the boys and Jake's father set out. Traveling in the Kimball's buckboard wagon, with three days' rations between them, they arrived in Decatur the following afternoon. It was All Hallows Eve. David's family didn't observe the pagan ritual, since they were strict Baptists, but he knew of several families who did, and the occasion enthralled him. Although Jake was the superstitious one, David found himself believing in ghosts and goblins, despite his upbringing. Sometimes, he swore he could hear strange voices whisper to him on the wind. When he was younger, he thought they were the voices of his grandparents, or Indians who had lived on his family's land long ago. He knew he had heard them, but convincing anyone else was simply out of the question, so he kept his premonitions to himself. On this particular afternoon, however, a strange chill ran through him, and he knew something uncanny was about to transpire.

Mr. Kimball parked in front of an old warehouse, where a large gathering of men had congregated. Some milled about, while others went in and out of the wooden building. The boys jumped off the wagon and followed Jake's father, who walked with a slight limp, due to the fact that he wore a leg brace to support an injury he had acquired in the Mexican War. They entered to see a large, dark, dank, dingy room with filthy wooden floors. Rafters above sported dangling cobwebs. The air hung heavily, filled with the pungent aroma of cigars. Enough sunlight filtered in through the half-opened windows to provide ample light, even though the air was hazy from billowing smoke.

David glanced around at the strange men in the room, who were looking through printed lists and talking boisterously. Suddenly, they cheered. At the front of the room, a man in a vest and topcoat with a top hat on his head stepped up onto a platform. He motioned for the audience to quiet down.

"Gentlemen, we are about to begin!" he announced. "Please bring up the first specimen!"

An ogre of a man led up a frail-looking Negro. The black man's hands and feet were shackled. He wore only a loincloth, and looked to be about forty, although deep wrinkles in his face made him seem twice that age.

David glanced at his best friend in wonder. Jake winked at him.

"What can I git for this fine fellow here?" asked the auctioneer. "He comes from sturdy stock, is a hard worker, and has been a loyal servant to his current master for the past twelve years!"

"I wonder why his master's gittin' rid of him?" David asked Jake softly.

His friend merely shrugged in response.

The bidding was lively, until a final price was declared.

"Goin' once, goin' twice, sold!" the auctioneer exclaimed, cracking his gavel upon the podium before him.

The thin black man was led away, and another, younger Negro was brought up. This time the bids came fast and furious. The young man was told to turn around, open his mouth to show his teeth, and stand obediently while the throng hollered out cash amounts in a frantic attempt to outbid one another. David realized that the young men were the most sought after for their virility. Inexplicably, he felt a twinge of pity for the poor soul, and wondered if the black man understood the humiliation he was undergoing by being treated no better than livestock. He equated it to horse trading, and imagined the young "buckra" being branded like a calf. To his astonishment, he discovered his imagination was accurate, when another man was exhibited on the stand, complete with whipping scars across his back. The auctioneer boasted that the man was reliable, but the bids dwindled, no doubt because the spectators realized he was untrustworthy, and therefore, had obviously been disciplined many times.

A young woman was brought up for display, naked from the waist up.

Mr. Kimball glanced over to see Jake and his companion gawking in disbelief. "You two go on outside now," he ordered.

The boys did as he commanded, but stopped just outside the doorway and peeked back in around the corner. The bidding was again brisk. Husky voices rose up around the shivering, slender woman, who kept her eyes downturned. She was also forced to turn around, bend over, and open her mouth like a horse. Tears streamed down her ebony face as she was led off the stand in shackles. While she was escorted off, she sadly gazed over her shoulder at two young children who were waiting in line to be auctioned.

David realized they must be her offspring. The sight made him suddenly nauseous. He had to turn his head away, alarmed by his own benevolence. The feeling persisted, so he walked over to the wagon to catch his breath.

"You all right?" Jake stood beside him, patting him gently on the back.

"Yeah. It's jist ... I ain't never seen anything like that before."

"Me neither. They don't call it our 'peculiar institution' for nothin."

"Reckon not." David looked over at his friend and forced a grin. "I saw an auction with Pa once in Mobile, but we didn't git this close."

"It's sad that they have to split up the mothers from the young'uns, but Pa says it's like weanin' piglets. They git over it," Jake said, looking back at the commotion.

David wondered if Mr. Kimball was right. He hoped that, for the Negroes' sake, he was.

"At what point, then, is the approach of danger to be expected? I answer, if it ever reach us, it must spring up amongst us; it cannot come from abroad. If destruction be our lot we must ourselves be its author and finisher. As a nation of free men we must live through all time, or die by suicide."

—*Abraham Lincoln*
Lyceum Address, January 27, 1838

Chapter Five

President Lincoln appointed his "Little Napoleon," George McClellan, to the position of general-in-chief of all Union forces on November 1. This followed the resignation of Winfield Scott, a hero in the Mexican War, who had acquired the nickname "Old Fuss and Feathers," but was now too old and too obese to continue in his current capacity. McClellan had graduated from West Point, in the same class as Thomas "Stonewall" Jackson.

Lincoln reportedly said to McClellan, "The supreme command of the army will entail a vast labor upon you."

To which the general replied, "I can do it all." His pompous, arrogant nature was overlooked, for he was adored by his men, and so he deemed himself worthy of the elevated position.

According to newspaper reports, the USS *San Jacinto* stopped the British ship *Trent* in international waters, and arrested two Confederate ambassadors: J. M. Mason, the commissioner to England, and John Slidell, the commissioner to France. The men were taken to Boston and imprisoned, but when the news broke, public outcry prevailed, so Lincoln felt compelled to release the two captives, excusing his disregard for foreign policy by saying only, "One war at a time."

The North instigated the Revenue Act of 1861, which placed a federal income tax on all its citizens in order to pay for the increasing war debt. It also established a three percent tax on annual incomes exceeding $800, which was far more than what most wage-earners made.

By mid-November, winter in north Alabama made itself known. The ground hardened, the first frost transpired, and hardwood trees dropped their leaves. Several days of gray, gloomy, drizzly weather set in. To occupy their time indoors, Caroline cooked, the girls read voraciously, and the womenfolk sewed clothing for the troops, but David was too restless. When he wasn't tending to farm chores, he spent his time cutting wood, riding Cotaco around the neighborhood, or working with

Renegade on a lead rope. He couldn't wait until the day he could ride him, and anticipated the adventures they would embark on together.

Two of their five hogs had been slaughtered, and hung in the smokehouse, drying. The three cows had been bred, and were expected to produce calves in the spring. As far as the rest of the livestock was concerned, everything was well tended to and accounted for. David kept a close eye on the chickens, the number of barn cats they had at the moment, and of course, his two faithful hounds. Hunting was fruitful, and he frequently returned from day-trips with a deer or wild turkey carcass.

Jake expressed David's unease one day in early December while they sat in his front parlor playing chess. "I wish there was somethin' more excitin' to do than this," he muttered. "Checkmate!"

David moaned. "What did you have in mind?" he growled, annoyed by his loss.

"Oh, I don't know."

Suddenly, they heard a vehicle coming. They looked out through the lace-curtained window to see a carriage approach. It came to a stop in front of the house, and the Negro coachman jumped down. He opened the carriage door. Out stepped a young woman Jake and David's age, who was wearing a flowing red dress with an embroidered burgundy shawl draped over her shoulders. She climbed the steps to the veranda, and rapped on the door. Jake sprang to his feet to answer it.

"Why, Jake, darlin'!" she greeted him enthusiastically as she whisked into the parlor. She gave him a mock kiss on both cheeks, sashayed across to David, and gave him the same treatment. "How have y'all been?" Her sultry belle air surrounded her like glowing embers.

"Jist fine, Miss Callie," said Jake, "but we're mighty bored with the state of things."

"Well, I have a remedy for that." She winked at David, who blushed. "Is your mother here?" she asked, handing Jake her shawl. Removing her bonnet, she let her long blond hair fall freely. She withdrew a fan from her dress pocket and promptly began fanning herself, fluttering her eyelashes as quickly as she fluttered her fan.

"She's in the kitchen with Isabelle," Jake responded. "Want me to fetch her?"

"Oh, no! Don't bother. I'll tell y'all myself, and you, Jake, darlin', can inform our intentions later on."

She took a seat on the floral velvet sofa. David noticed that, for once, she wasn't wearing hoops.

"My folks are hostin' a Christmas party, and I'm here to give y'all a proper invitation to our grand soirée."

"When is it?" David timidly asked.

She fluttered the fan at him suggestively, motioning him to her. He obeyed by taking a seat beside her on the sofa.

"In two weeks, on the twenty-first," she said softly. Her mesmerizing blue eyes gazed into his. "It's the Saturday before Christmas. You will attend, won't you, Mr. Summers?"

"I ..." David's voice trailed off. He couldn't help but be hypnotized by her opulent demeanor.

Jake giggled and came to his rescue. "He'll be there," he volunteered, "and so will I. We'll all be there!"

"Why, that's jist splendid!" Callie exclaimed.

Reaching over, she gave David's knee a squeeze, which made his darkening eyes widen with surprise. Callie rose to her feet, closed the fan, and stuffed it into her pocket. "Well, I must be off." She gave Jake a quick kiss on the cheek, and took the shawl from his hand. "Come rarin' to dance, but don't bring a partner, because y'all will be dancin' with me!" She laughed melodically.

"Two dance partners at once? Why, darlin', how will you manage?" Jake grinned as he escorted her to the door.

Reminded of his manners, David sprang from his seat and followed them out onto the veranda.

"The same way I'll marry the both of you!" she teased. "One at a time!"

Jake chortled, amused by her flirtatiousness, but David was too stunned to react. He watched while Callie's footman helped her into the carriage, climbed up onto the driver's seat, and slapped the reins upon the haunches of two bay horses. The carriage lurched into motion. Callie's white handkerchief fluttered out the window, waving at them as she rode away.

Shaking his head, Jake chuckled. "That Callie Mae Copeland," he remarked. "She sure is a firecracker!"

David couldn't find words to express his opinion, for he was too awestruck by the creature who had just whirled in and out. Surprisingly, even though he had known her since childhood, Callie always had the same effect on him. She was intimidating and intriguing all at once. The dance would make him self-conscious, he knew, but he wanted to go anyway, if only to be in her presence and receive her attentions. The thought made him woozy.

The week drifted by, and the weather grew so cold that David could see his breath when he went outside. He wished to travel, but knew he was confined to the farm, so he occupied himself by creating Christmas gifts for his family. His father had taught him how to whittle, and he had to admit to himself he was getting pretty good at it. The intricate details he included in his carvings were incorporated into his mother's and siblings' gifts, consisting of wooden hair pins, broaches, and bangles. For his father, he made a wooden shelf for his musket, to place over the fieldstone fireplace. That way, when Hiram returned, he wouldn't have to leave it on the mantel, which was now occupied by a tintype of his likeness in uniform, and a clock gifted to Caroline by her beloved on their wedding day.

Rena found her brother in the barn one evening, diligently working away by the light of a kerosene lantern. The topic came up, and she expressed her desire to leave as well, telling him to keep it a secret from their mother, so as not to upset her.

"Someday, I want to jine a singin' troupe, like the Christy Minstrels," she confessed, "or be an opera singer. For now, though, I reckon I'm obliged to stay home and finish school, and maybe go on to college after that."

"I'd like to go to college myself," he stated.

"Oh? Which one?"

"I was thinkin' Auburn. Then I could be a doctor … or a journalist."

She giggled. "That's a mighty strange combination!"

"I ain't made up my mind yet," he said with a grin. "Maybe I'll be an animal doctor."

"Well, you are good with horses," she observed. "Renegade follows you around like he's a dog!"

David chuckled. "I reckon Renie jist knows I have sugar in my pocket."

The following Tuesday, he took Joe Boy over to have him re-shod before the Copeland's Christmas event. There he found the blacksmith, John Moss, who was busy pounding horseshoes over an open flame.

"Have you heard from your pa?" John asked while prying off one of Joe Boy's old shoes.

"Not recently. I'm right worried about Ma. She gits too nervous, and she even lost a tooth the other day."

John threw a glance at him, his blue eyes glistening over his stark white beard. "Sorry to hear that."

David nodded. "I hope the war ends soon, so she won't git so upset."

"Well, I do, too. Say, did you hear about poor ole Senator Crittenden?"

"Who?"

"Crittenden, from Kentucky. My kinfolk live up that way, and told me all about it." He paused, but hearing no objection, continued. "The good senator tried his darnedest to make those humbugs up in Washin'ton come to their senses." Seeing David look at him questioningly, he elaborated. "He proposed a bill that would entitle each new state to vote if it wanted slavery, and for the plantation owners to be compensated for their slaves, should their niggers be set free. But ole 'Rail Splitter' Lincoln and his cronies in Congress shot down his bill. Now the poor senator has one son fightin' for the North, and the other one fightin' for the South."

"That's right awful," David said.

John shook his head, his long beard flowing with his movement. "It's a wonder what this here world is comin' to."

David wondered himself, but dispelled any bad notions, deciding to concentrate on Christmas instead. Things could only get better.

Caroline received another letter from Hiram the following week, informing her that the 4th Alabama had established their winter camp in the Virginia wilderness. He apologized, but didn't foresee the possibility of returning home for Christmas. Hiding her disappointment, she put on a smile, told her children that their brave father was staying in Virginia for the holidays, and carried on as if it didn't affect her. Deep down, however, her heart was breaking. She knew he was defending their homeland, but although it was honorable and noble, she missed him desperately. Every day was more of a struggle, trying to keep up with the farm. She was thankful for her children, and the neighbors who supported her, but it still seemed daunting. Hopefully, the war would end after the first of the year, so that the grand Confederacy would be allowed to secede and become its own country.

The day of Callie's Christmas party arrived. Rena and Josie had primped for a week, repeatedly trying on the five dresses they owned between them, until they finally came to a decision. David didn't give it much thought, since Callie's charms had worn off with time, but he did carve a beautiful broach for her.

They reached the Copeland's as dusk was setting in. It was an unseasonably warm evening, and Caroline remarked about how the weather seemed to be cooperating with the party. Pulling into the yard, they saw several other carriages and wagons parked outside. David directed Joe Boy to an open area. He jumped down, tied the draft horse to a shrub, greeted Percy, who was tending the horses, and after assisting his mother and sisters down from the wagon, he escorted them up the steps to the house. The stylings of festive violin music floated through the air. Caroline tapped on the door. Momentarily, Mr. Copeland answered, dressed in a waistcoat with matching black trousers.

"Why, there y'all are!" he greeted them happily. "Please do come in!"

Extending his hand to David, the two shook and followed the ladies into the parlor, which was aglow with glittering lights. Candles flickered on brass candlesticks, reflecting off blown-glass decorations that adorned an enormous pine Christmas tree regally standing in a corner. The women were attired in festive, colorful dresses, and the men wore fine suits. David thought the entire sparkling room was enchanting.

Josie and Rena saw some friends, so they went off to mingle. Mr. Copeland took Caroline's arm and led her over to his wife, leaving David awkwardly alone. He gazed around for a familiar face, and finally found one. Jake ambled across the room in his direction, with Callie on his arm. She was radiant in a shimmering, bronze-colored, hooped gown. Her golden hair was drawn up and confined within a snood that matched the hue of her dress. Jake appeared similarly attractive in his best suit.

"Glad to see you could make it!" he exclaimed, giving his friend a playful punch on the arm.

"Y'all knew we couldn't miss this."

"Well, I should certainly hope not!" exclaimed Callie. "Everyone knows mine is the most extravagant party in the county this season. And we have cause for celebration, this bein' the first yuletide since the start of the war." Releasing Jake, she clamped onto David. "Jake, would you be a darlin' and go fetch me some punch?"

"It would be my pleasure, Miss Callie," he said with a smile. Giving David a wink, he strolled off into the crowd.

"Now, Mr. Summers, if you please, I would like you to come with me," she said, giving his arm a tug, so he obediently followed along like a puppy.

The violinist, joined by a pianist, delved into a tender rendition of "Silent Night." Callie stopped momentarily to listen, so David took his opportunity.

"Miss Callie, I made you a token," he bashfully admitted. Withdrawing a small wrapped package from his pocket, he handed it to her.

"Well, I do declare! David, darlin', you shouldn't have!" She tore open the wrapping and pried open the box, revealing the broach he had painstakingly carved for her. "Why, it's absolutely breathtakin'." She pinned it onto the front of her gown. "I shall wear it always."

Taking his hand, she leaned over to give him a gentle kiss on the cheek, barely missing his mouth.

He shied away, embarrassed. Clearing his throat while his face flushed, he muttered, "What did you want to show me, Miss Callie?"

"I would like to present you to some friends who are out back."

He followed her to the garden, but immediately wished he hadn't, for as soon as they were outside, he saw several faces he recognized.

"David, you know Owen Ridgeway, and his brother, Lemuel."

"Hey, Summers," said Lemuel in a friendly manner, but his older brother only glared.

"Hey, y'all," David responded genially, for Callie's sake.

Jake arrived, and handed Callie a glass filled with sparkling red fluid. Seeing the tension, he said, "Zeke, go on in and git yourself some punch."

"Don't mind if I do," he said, taking his chance to escape the scene. He knew Callie was unaware of the conflict, but he was riled, and he didn't wish to spoil her party, so he went inside to the food table.

The spread temporarily distracted him from a possible confrontation. Ham, turkey, stuffing, cornbread, pickles, garden vegetables, bread pudding, and assorted pies were displayed on gold leaf china. His mouth watered as he absorbed the sight.

Rena appeared beside him. "Are you enjoyin' yourself?" she asked, taking a plate.

"I was, till Callie took me outside. That scoundrel Owen Ridgeway is here."

"He is?"

"Yeah, and so is his brother. I don't have a quarrel with him, though."

"Jist avoid him, David," she advised.

He looked over to see the seriousness in her gaze. "I'll be on my best behavior for Ma's sake, but if he tries to make a fuss, well …"

"Jist don't." Rena glared insistently at him before moving on.

Once he had filled his plate, he walked across the kitchen, sat at the table, and began eating. Soon, several guests joined him, and struck up a conversation about his father. Isabelle scurried about to accommodate the partygoers, as did the Copeland's five slaves, and a few others the neighbors had brought along to help support them.

After lingering for half an hour, David excused himself. He walked into the parlor, where he saw Jake and Callie talking to Alice Walker, so he joined them.

"Oh, David, Miss Alice has jist informed us of the most dreadful news!" Callie leaned against Jake for support.

"What is it, Miss Alice?" he asked.

"We're movin' to California," she announced. A broad smile spread across her young porcelain-like face.

"Californee is a right far piece away!" Jake exclaimed with a chuckle.

She nodded. "My pa has an uncle out that way who struck it rich, so we're fixin' to go next year sometime. Perhaps after spring thaw."

David smirked through a flash of jealousy. "I wish I could go out to Californee and strike it rich," he muttered.

Callie smiled at him. "Perhaps we can all go out for a visit later on," she suggested hopefully. Turning toward the wall, she decided to change the subject. "David, have you seen the paintin' my ma jist acquired?"

"No." He drew closer to have a look.

"Pa bought it for her for Christmas. Ain't it magnificent?"

"It surely is." He gazed at the landscape, noticing how the bluish-purple colors of twilight were accurately represented.

"My ma says that it's right fittin' and all. She says that this paintin', *Twilight*, symbolizes the transitions we've all been goin' through—the new Confederacy and two new presidents, talk of freein' the slaves, and the country splittin' in two. It's like the dawnin' of a new day."

David stared at the painting, reading her description into the swirls left by the artist's brushstrokes, and reckoned she was right.

Mrs. Copeland's high-pitched voice cut through the din. "May I have your attention, please?"

Callie's father tapped on a crystal champagne glass with a piece of silverware, causing it to ring out. The participants grew quiet.

"We would like for all of our guests to please assemble out back in the garden!" she exclaimed, and motioned invitingly, so the partygoers followed her.

As David walked outside, he noticed the entire backyard had been redecorated. Paper lanterns strung across the length of the yard illuminated the setting, and musicians were gathered on a platform near the back. The violinist had transformed himself into a fiddle player. He was joined by a banjo player and a percussionist, who sat poised atop a stool with spoons in his hand.

"For our first song," the banjo player announced, "we're playin' a fine tune by Stephen Foster, called 'O Lemuel.'"

Owen guffawed at the reference, jabbing his little brother with his elbow. The music started, and the crowd coupled up. Walking out into the center of the straw-covered yard, they began swirling to the music. The chill in the air seemed to dissipate as the dancers moved in synchronized harmony across the makeshift dance floor.

David watched while a schoolmate, Thomas Halsey, escorted Rena. Jake and Callie took to the floor, as did their parents, even though Mr. Kimball's injured leg prevented him from dancing with much elegance. Like he usually did at gatherings such as these, David partnered with his mother and younger sister, dancing to the lively melodies of "The Yellow Rose of Texas" and "Jim along Josie." He danced with Alice, and once, timidly, with Callie, who complimented him on his stylish grace. When the music changed to a waltz, she stated that she thought he would easily fit into high society with his fancy footwork.

After the musicians took a break, he strolled into the house for refreshment. Owen followed, confronting him in the kitchen.

"Think you're quite the rooster, don't you? Dancin' with every gal at the party." He stared provokingly with penetrating green eyes, his blond hair tussled atop his head.

David whirled around to face him. Owen had always been a showoff, and was constantly teasing him because he was left-handed, and trying to outdo him at every opportunity.

"That ain't none of your concern. Savvy?"

Owen snorted. "You're worthless. You ain't nothin' but a weasel. All you can do is hide behind them skirts!"

Rena entered to see her brother bristle at his adversary. "David ..." she warned.

"Not now, Rena," he growled back.

"Recall what we discussed." She could see from across the room that her brother's eyes were darkening from hazel to brown, which to her was a bad indication.

"I want to have a word with you out on the veranda, Ridgeway," David stated.

He tromped off through the house. Owen grinned, traipsing behind. David heard his mother's voice as she entered the kitchen.

"What's goin' on in here?" she asked.

"Dere's 'bout to be trouble out front, Miss Caroline," Isabelle explained as she gathered a trayful of dirty dishes.

"It's Owen Ridgeway again, Ma," added Josie.

Caroline growled, "I'll put a stop to this."

"No, Mrs. Summers," Jake intercepted. "Allow me." He sauntered through the house as voices outside escalated, and went outside to see David and Owen glaring intensely while throwing verbal spears at each other.

"I know it was you who killed my dog last winter!" David roared. "You did it jist to spite me, because you were jealous!"

"Why would I be jealous of you?" Owen mocked a laugh.

"Because I'm smarter than you, and you know it."

"You cheated on those school exams so you could graduate! You lied about your pa fightin' at Manassas, too! You're spoiled and soft!"

"I'll have you take that back!"

"Now, boys," Jake interrupted, "there ain't no need for—"

Suddenly, Owen lurched at David, who threw a punch into his attacker's face. They were immediately wrestling on the veranda, tumbling over each other while grunting, cursing, and yelling. Members of the party dashed outside, alarmed by the commotion. Jake managed to break the two apart, and held his friend's arms behind his back. Lemuel seized his brother in the same manner. The two opponents snorted like bulls, their faces red with vehemence. A trail of scarlet blood trickled from Owen's nose.

"Take it easy!" Jake hollered.

Mr. Copeland stepped in. "What is the meaning of this?! I will not have you two behave this way at my gatherin'!" He stomped over to Owen and took him by the ear. "I'm throwin' you out, young man! You're no longer welcome here!" Leading Owen to the steps, he thrust him toward the yard. Lemuel meekly scurried after his brother. "Off with you now, and don't come back!"

The brothers staggered toward their wagon, climbed in, and rode off down the lane.

Turning toward David, who was panting to catch his breath, Mr. Copeland sighed. "David, I thought better of you than this." He walked past him and went inside.

The words stung more than any expulsion could. Frowning, he looked at his startled family, at Jake, who simpered at him, and at Callie, who scowled at him. He knew what he had done, although it was unintentional, and he felt deeply ashamed. He had ruined Callie's Christmas party.

Soon, the family decided it was best to leave. Barely speaking to each other, they returned home and retired to their bedchambers. The next morning, on their way back from church, Josie broke the silence.

"How come Owen Ridgeway don't like you?" she asked straightforwardly.

David shrugged. "He never has, and I don't cotton to him, neither."

She chuckled faintly. "I reckon you would if he was nice to you."

He shrugged again. It was a situation he assumed he would likely never know.

On Christmas Eve, he hitched Joe Boy to the wagon before leading him into a thicket. With much consideration, he chose a pine tree that would suit his family, cut it down, tossed it into the wagon bed, and drove down the hill to where the saddlebag house sat nestled in the valley. The sun shone brightly, giving no indication it was a winter's day, other than the fact that the hardwood trees were bare.

He arrived home, extracted the tree, and struggled to carry it into the house. Wrestling it through the door while it poked him with pine needles, he finally squeezed it through. He set it in the stand he had prepared, and stood back to admire his accomplishment. The tree was glorious. In his eyes, it rivaled Callie's. Freshly cut pine instantly scented the air.

The family proceeded to decorate it, using what few ornaments they had accumulated over the years, most of which were handmade from wood, as well as strands of dried berries. They placed tiny candles in tin holders on the boughs and lit them. The tree glowed with inviting luminosity.

"I wish your pa was here to see this," Caroline sighed.

She gathered her clutch into the front room, where she read the story of Christ's birth from the Bible, just like Hiram did every Christmas Eve. As she drew to a close, her voice broke, and she sniffed back tears.

"It'll be all right, Ma," David assured her, gently stroking her arm. "Pa's thinkin' of us right now, too, I reckon."

She nodded in agreement. "Well, let's git to bed. Santa Claus won't be able to come if y'all are up late."

The children sniggered. They had been told the truth about Santa years ago, but they played along for their mother's sake, and promptly went to their rooms. David lit a fire in the fireplace and crawled into bed, but he couldn't sleep. He tossed and turned, staring at the gauze-covered window. Pale moonlight cast an eerie glow, enticing him to investigate. He arose and peeked out into the empty yard, but it was too dark to distinguish anything, so he climbed back into bed, folding himself in the covers. He thought of past Christmases spent with his family, and imagined what his father must be going through, camped in a tent in the middle of nowhere.

At least Bud is there with him, he thought. Finally, he dozed off.

In the morning, he awoke to a loud commotion, and sprang from his bed to investigate. He rushed across the breezeway to the front room. His younger sister was jumping up and down in her nightgown, clapping her hands, while Caroline and Rena stood by, smiling.

"What is it?" he asked, shaking the grogginess from his head. He rubbed his eyes to clear his vision, and discovered a box had been opened in the midst of the few others. Something was moving around inside.

Kneeling down to extract the box's contents, Josie withdrew a tiny black kitten. "Ain't she jist the purtiest li'l' kitty y'all ever did see?" she squealed, hugging the little creature, who mewed, to her delight.

"We all know how much you wanted one of your own to keep in the house, so I found you this one," Caroline explained. "She's quite friendly."

"Ma," Josie stated, a questioning tone in her voice, "you always said we couldn't have critters in the house." She gave the kitten a kiss on its tiny head.

"Well, I reckon I changed my stance on that. We need a good mouser in the house." She smiled at her. Turning toward her son, she said, "David, why don't you pass out the rest of the presents?"

"I'd be happy to, Ma."

He squatted beneath the drooping limbs of the pine and extracted the gifts, calling out his siblings' names as he distributed them, and finished with a small box for his mother.

"Before we begin," said Caroline, "I would like us all to give thanks for this day that the Lord has provided us in honor of His Son's holy birth."

She delved into a lovely prayer, and all said "Amen."

They tore into their presents at once. His sisters and mother opened the gifts he had made for them, after which they thanked him with praise for his artistry. Caroline received hand-sewn items from her daughters, and they received hand-sewn items from her in return. Rena and Josie opened gifts Caroline explained were from their father, who had purchased them before his departure. They discovered new bonnets inside. David opened his gifts, finding homespun clothing from his siblings and mother. In another box were a new halter and bridle meant for Renegade. Caroline held one small box in her lap, smiling at her children until all the other gifts were opened. Rena coaxed her, so she opened it. Inside was a wooden box with beautiful inlay across the top in various woods. She gently pried the box open, and music began to play.

"It's a tiny music box!" Josie said in awe.

Caroline put the back of her hand to her mouth, stifling a sob. The music box continued to play a haunting, melancholy melody. She closed the lid.

"Pa made it last spring," David explained. "He bought the li'l' player when we went down to Mobile, and he said for me to give it to you for Christmas if he wasn't back from the war yet to do it himself."

She smiled. "It's as though he knew he wouldn't be here."

"I reckon he was plannin' ahead, jist in case," Rena assured her. She stood and walked across the room. Taking her mother's hand, she said, "Come on, Ma. I'll help with breakfast."

"Me, too," added Josie. Loping over to David, she handed him her new pet. "Watch after Kitty for me," she instructed, depositing the miniscule fur ball into his hands before trotting off.

David grunted. He placed the baby feline on the floor. It scurried around in the discarded paper, making him chuckle with amusement. Deciding it was time to start his farm chores, he returned to his room, changed into his work clothes, and went outside. The morning was fresh, clean, and bright. He hoped it was an indication, like the painting he'd seen at Callie's. The war would be over soon—he was sure of it.

New Year's Day was cold and drizzly. David hadn't seen the sun in a week, which made him grow more agitated. It seemed twice as difficult to conduct his chores in foul weather, although, in reality, it took the same amount of time. He looked forward to school starting again, just so he could deliver his sisters. At least it would give him something to do for a few hours every day.

Winter dragged by. David named the hogs, something he didn't ordinarily do, but since they were down to three, he was growing quite fond of them. The biggest sow he named Pork Pie, the smaller sow was Ham Hock, and the runt he called Chitlin.

School resumed, but classes were intermittent, since the weather dictated participation and attendance. Josie brought home a new grammar book, which focused on the war effort and Confederate superiority over the Northern invaders. The new readers were also chock-full of anti-Yankee sentiment. David found them amusing, as did his little sister, although the propaganda they exuded was somewhat disturbing, in that they promoted the murder of Yankees.

By the end of January, everybody was ready for spring. No one had received word from the troops, but David's neighbors quelled his concern by stating it was simply the weather interfering with mail delivery. He managed to make his way to Jake's on a weekly basis, attempting to relieve his cabin fever, but upon his arrival, he discovered there wasn't much to do at the Kimball's house, either. Time drifted by slowly. Routine became so tedious and mind-numbing that it made him ache.

January seeped into February without much change. David spent his days reading and making up stories about heroines in distress who were saved by knights in shining armor. Josie suggested he try to write with his right hand, making his script more legible, but he found it too difficult. He was naturally born to write left-handed, and took exception to anyone who criticized him, even though he knew it made him extraordinary.

One afternoon in early March, he rode Cotaco over to Ben Johnson's mercantile. As he entered, he saw a few familiar faces hovering around the wood-burning stove.

"Did you hear about ole Abe Lincoln's son, Willie?" Mr. Foreman asked the group. "Died of typhoid about two weeks ago. He was only eleven years old."

"That's mighty sad news," said Mr. Banes. "Even if I don't take to that Lincoln feller much, I hate to hear such terrible things as that. 'Specially when it happens to a young'un."

The men somberly agreed.

"I learned yesterday the federal government is printin' off legal tender notes," Mr. Garrison said to no one in particular. "Can y'all imagine usin' paper money? Wonder how long that will last."

"Not long, I don't reckon," interjected Mr. Foreman. "Never lasted long before."

"Our new government jist passed a law allowin' plantation owners and overseers to be exempt from the fightin'," Kit informed the others. "They're callin' it the Twenty Negro Rule."

"Why are they exempt?" David inquired, taking his place among the others.

"Because the overseers are the best civil police system we have, and if they go off to the war, there won't be anyone standin' in the way of insurrection."

"Do you really think that would happen?" asked David.

Kit retorted, "I don't see why not."

"It's my understandin' that Lincoln issued an order for Yankee forces to attack us on the birthday of our foundin' father, George Washin'ton,"

Mr. Skidmore told the gathering. "But it never happened. McClellan don't have the courage to stand up to us!"

"Grant does, though," Mr. Banes said dolefully. "He's captured Fort Henry and Fort Donelson up in Tennessee, and word is, he's headed this way."

"They're callin' him Unconditional Surrender Grant," added Ben Johnson. "U. S. Grant for short."

"My younger cousin, Henry, is first lieutenant of Company H, which has been organized right here in Morgan County," Joseph Ryan proclaimed. "Soon as they git to Tennessee, they'll whip ole U. S., and send him back up North where he belongs!"

David pondered Mr. Ryan's statement. The Union troops were encroaching, that much was certain. How close they would get was unknown, but it was still very unsettling. If they did come down to Alabama, he would have to invent a plan to protect his family and possessions. Suddenly, he felt strangely alone and vulnerable, even though he knew he was surrounded by friends. His pa was too far away, and if Yankees came to the farm, none of his neighbors would be close enough to help, either. He had to find a way to fight them off by himself. The thought made him shudder.

"These are well-established principles of war, and the people of the South having appealed to war are barred from appealing to our Constitution, which they have practically and publicly defied. They have appealed to war, and must abide its rules and laws. The United States, as a belligerent party claiming right in the soil as the ultimate sovereign, have a right to change the population, and it may be and is, both politic and just, we should do so in certain districts."

—*William Tecumseh Sherman*

Chapter Six

The weather had been typical, although Hiram, Bud, and the rest of their regiment thought differently, since they were unaccustomed to Virginia's snowy winters. General Joe Johnston's Army of Northern Virginia established their winter quarters, and the camp sprawled from Fredericksburg southwest into the Shenandoah Valley, with the 4th Alabama constructing their site near Manassas Junction at Dumfries.

Most of the dwellings consisted of tents with chimneys, but Hiram and Bud, as well as a few other men, had cabins, which were made by slave labor from logs, earth, and cracker barrels. Makeshift stoves, created from bricks and fieldstone, occupied the centers. Bud and Hiram named their humble abode, "The Jameson Hotel," after an elaborate hotel in Decatur, and hung a sign above the door with their cabin's chosen name painted on it. Other comrades named their cabins "Home Sweet Home," "The Madison Boarding House," and the "Soljers Rest."

Bud and Hiram shared their home with two others: Hugh Oakes and Hugh Douglas. Bud referred to them as the two Hughs, while Hiram took it one step further, calling them "Blue" Hugh Oakes, because of his sky-blue eyes, and "Orange" Hugh Douglas. They constantly asked him, "Hey, orange Hugh Douglas?" To which the young soldier would happily reply, "Why, yes, I am." This sent the men flying into fits of laughter, since they were easily amused after months of confinement.

The soldiers spent their days drilling, constructing corduroy roads, and tending to what little livestock the camp contained. A few of the men acquired pets, including dogs, a goat, and a few chickens. Those who were fortunate enough to secure Confederate currency used their hard-earned cash on overpriced luxuries provided by sutlers' row, or "robbers' row," as they referred to it.

Out of sheer boredom, some infantrymen played practical jokes on their comrades. One such fellow, Enoch Campbell, whom Bud and Hiram met upon their arrival into the army, was appointed barber. For his own entertainment, Enoch frequently shaved half of his patrons' faces before walking off to leave the other half unshaven. A few of the younger, more irresponsible men planted gunpowder near their messmates' bedrolls, finding great fun in exploding it while their friends lay sleeping, until they were severely reprimanded by their superiors. Some unruly soldiers were disciplined for their disruptive behavior by spending time in the "bullpen," or guardhouse, and given just bread and water to sustain on. Other offenders were paraded around camp to the tunes of "Yankee Doodle" and "Rough's March," wearing only barrels, with signs around their necks that read "liar" and "thief." Several were ordered to carry out extra sentry duty, or were refused their pay, although the Confederacy had yet to compensate any of its defenders.

Deserters were fitted with a ball and chain around their ankles, and a few were tied to rails which, to Hiram, resembled Christ's crucifixion. The most degrading discipline for wrongdoing was a shaved head. Because of cold weather and the length of time it took to grow back, lack of hair was a humiliating, long-term form of punishment. A group of the rowdier soldiers played cards, gambled, or drank, but their behavior was frowned upon, although only a small number of them were whipped or branded as punishment.

The 4th Alabama's commanding officers had either returned or resigned. Captain Tracy had been transferred and promoted in August. Major Scott, a typical old Southern gentleman, returned home to recuperate, and was replaced by Captain Bowles. Lawrence Scruggs was appointed captain of the North Alabamians.

The war started to revive. Robert E. Lee had been defeated at Cheat Mountain, but the Rebels came out victorious at Balls Bluff. Two more states joined the Confederacy—Missouri and Kentucky. By March, Johnston moved his army to the Rappahannock River. The Alabamians were anxious for a fight.

Hiram offered his writing services to his closest comrades, and he frequently transcribed dictation that amused him.

Per Blue Hugh's request, he wrote:

> May those Northern fanatics who abuse their Southern neighbors,
>> Approach near enough to feel the point of our sabers;
>> May they come near enough to hear the click of a trigger,
>> And learn that a white man is better than a nigger.

He tried keeping a daily journal, but soon ran out of ink because the pokeberries and oak balls had all disappeared beneath the snow. It was painful as well, for each time he wrote, he thought back to young George Anderson, who had met his fate on the battlefield at Manassas. The recollection saddened him, in that the young soldier reminded him of his own son, David, not so much in appearance, but in age. He wondered about his own family's well-being and missed them dreadfully at Christmastime. At least some of the men received packages from home to share with their comrades, with delicacies included, such as brandied cherries. All were given a special indulgence, eggnog made from the officers' whiskey.

In early spring, some officers and reenlisted men were sent home for sixty days to secure recruits. By March, they had returned, and the regiment was once again replete of its losses. Meanwhile, some of the remaining Alabamians suffered from another epidemic, yellow jaundice, for which the common treatment was enemas.

The 4th Alabama received word that Stonewall Jackson had attacked Union forces in the Shenandoah Valley, forcing the Yankees to rush back to Washington and defend the city from a possible Confederate attack. They also learned Nathan Bedford Forrest's men were on the move in Tennessee, and great concern arose over the possible invasion of Alabama by Union troops. A significant battle had taken place at Pea Ridge, Arkansas, with triumphant Union troops seizing control of the Missouri River. And at the mouth of the James River, the CSS *Virginia*, the first of its kind, called an "ironclad," met its equal with the Union's ironclad, the USS *Monitor*. Both ships fired upon each other throughout the day of March 9, but neither was victorious. The *Virginia* was unable to penetrate and destroy the Union blockade.

General Johnston relocated the 4th Alabama to join with the main army south of the Rappahannock and moved it in the direction of Richmond. In early March, he learned McClellan was encroaching, so he hastily transferred his troops from Centreville, leaving behind half-cooked food and property belonging to the Confederate army. He moved his men south of the Rappahannock, but not before leaving Quaker guns behind in empty earthworks to deter his rival. The "guns" were actually logs that had been cut and painted to resemble cannon snouts.

With the advent of April, the Rebels were informed McClellan was gathering his Union troops in preparation for a march on Richmond, and they knew it wouldn't be long before they were called upon for defense. It was just a matter of time.

David spent his seventeenth birthday quietly with his family, who showered him with treats. They had little money for gifts, so instead they gave him sheet music to songs they thought he would enjoy: "Annie Laurie," "Pop Goes the Weasel," and "Goodnight Ladies." His mother was astounded by how much he had developed musically and wept when he obeyed her wish to serenade her, but he felt guilty for upsetting her, so he set his guitar aside. Coaxed by his sisters, he blew out his candles and indulged in an apple pie Caroline had baked in his honor. Following the subdued festivities, he announced his plans to attend Auburn the following year, to which his family responded with accolades.

A few days after his birthday, Rena received a letter from a schoolmate, Thomas Halsey, who had enlisted the previous month. He wrote that he was assigned to an Alabama battalion under General Braxton Bragg, and although the weather was predictably rainy, he was in good spirits. He then informed her that he had fond feelings for her. She brushed the sentiment aside, considering it to be nostalgia, and showed the letter to her brother, who flushed upon reading it. David knew Thomas was two years his senior and had more obligations to enlist, since he had a brother and four cousins who were Confederate soldiers. Regardless, he was envious, and although he obediently performed his duties at home, he still wished to be a soldier.

The family learned three days later about a great battle taking place in Tennessee, near Shiloh Church, which was only about eighty miles from Huntsville. Reports of the battle were carried in by courier. David eagerly hovered around Ben Johnson's in anticipation of incoming telegrams, and while he was there, a courier rode in. According to the messenger, some twenty thousand troops were converging on the area, and the fighting was bloody. Confederate General Albert Sidney Johnston had been killed, and the Union army had been chased back to Pittsburg Landing on the Tennessee River. From the looks of things, the Rebels were victorious, according to the dispatch rider, who immediately set off toward Huntsville to retrieve more information. Waving his hat in the air, he let out a whoop and rode away.

A few days later, on Thursday, April 10, Jake accompanied David to the mercantile, where they received terrible news. The Yankees had won the battle, forcing the defeated Confederates to retreat south. Rumor had it that the Federals were giving chase by also heading in their direction. The boys rode home to inform their parents, and all braced themselves for the worst, hiding valuables and preparing extra food, just in case they had to escape from invading Yankee soldiers.

Ormsby Mitchel's Union army marched into undefended Huntsville early the following morning. Once David and Jake found out, they couldn't wait to investigate. They finally found the opportunity to sneak off early one crisp spring morning a week later.

Devising a plan, they told their parents they were staying at each other's homes for two nights, thus buying themselves extra time for their adventure. With Jake on Stella and David on Cotaco, they stealthily made their way up to Huntsville. Once they arrived at the outskirts of town the following day, they were awed by the spectacle that lay before them. Union soldiers were everywhere, like blue ants on a picnic, swarming about the city streets. No civilians were in sight. David and Jake tied their horses behind a shed half a mile out and headed into town. They slinked past sentries, cowered behind wagons, barrels, and buildings, and hid in the shadows, making their way toward the courthouse. As they crouched behind a cluster of budding shrubs in front of an enormous white Greek revival house, peering out at a patrol of Yankees marching down the street, they muttered to each other in hushed tones.

"Lookee, there, Zeke," Jake said, pointing his index finger. "That must be a general. See all them bars on his sleeve?"

"He ain't a general," replied David. "He looks too young. Maybe he's a corporal."

"Is that a rank jist below a general?"

"Reckon so. I dunno."

"Yoo-hoo!"

The boys both jumped in astonishment. Whirling around, they saw a young woman, attired in a pastel-colored calico dress, standing in the doorway of a house. She reacted to their wide-eyed surprise by stifling a snicker.

"Come here, boys!"

Sweeping her arm toward herself, she motioned for them to approach, which they did with anxious enthusiasm by quickly bounding up the steps of the portico.

"Miss, how-do," said Jake. Removing his slouch hat, he swept it across his body, taking a bow. "How may we be of service?"

"What are y'all doin' lurkin' 'round my mother's rosebushes?" she asked, thrusting her fists onto her hips in obvious irritation. "I wish you Yankees would jist—"

David and Jake threw glances at each other.

"We ain't Yankees!" exclaimed Jake. "Whatever gave you that notion?"

She stared at them for a moment before her expression softened. "Oh, kind sirs, beggin' y'all's pardon, but all I've been seein' this past week is Yankees. I thought y'all might be out of uniform."

"No, miss," David said kindly. "We came up to Huntsville because we heard the Yankees took over the town."

"Well, in that case, please do come in."

They followed her through the doorway, and once inside, David took in his surroundings. The receiving room opened up with high ceilings, and stained-glass windows occupied the upper echelon. A dark oak winding staircase, complete with an elaborate banister, spiraled upward. Overstuffed red velvet furniture filled the front room, and the floor was draped with oriental tapestries. On the walls were scenic paintings. Brass candlesticks, crystal chandeliers, and dried floral arrangements displayed under glass bell jars accented the décor. The room-length paned windows, framed by heavy burgundy velvet drapes, allowed bright light to beam in. He noticed a box piano in one corner and wondered if the elegant swan in female form standing before him ever graced its ivories.

"Have the Yankees caused y'all much trouble since they arrived?" he innocently inquired.

She nodded mournfully. "That they have." Unexpectedly, she let out a little sob.

"Don't cry, miss," said Jake reassuringly. "I'm sure everything will be all right."

She forced a smile. "Thank you … Oh, please do forgive my inhospitality. My name is Emily Levinsworth."

She held out her slender hand, so Jake graciously took it, and kissed the back of it while she watched his movements.

He released her. "I'm Jake Kimball, and this here's David Summers."

Taking his cue, David kissed her hand as well.

"We came up to see what y'all have had to tolerate," Jake explained.

"Please, come on into the kitchen. I'll fix y'all some sweet tea and tell y'all about it," she said in invitation.

They cordially followed her. Once David entered the kitchen, she requested he take a seat at the long cherry table with his friend. Emily busied herself momentarily before carrying over a tray with a pitcher and three glasses. She set them on the table, filled each glass, and distributed them.

Taking a sip, Jake complimented her in gentlemanly fashion and asked, "When did the Yankees arrive? We heard it was last Friday."

"Those beastly men!" Emily's face turned red with frustration. "They are everywhere! The dreadful brutes even trampled down some of my mother's rosebushes, but I chased them off with a broom."

Jake chuckled, but seeing her annoyed glare, he quickly ceased.

"They got here at first light on the mornin' of the eleventh," she said forlornly. "It was a surprise to us all."

David frowned. He had been warned of the impending danger. Why hadn't the civilians of Huntsville?

"It all started with their takin' the trains over at the depot," she explained. "One train got away, but they wounded the poor nigger fireman. We were soon isolated, because the telegraph lines were cut. There were about a hundred and fifty wounded men on one train who had been at the battle at Pittsburg Landin', and the Yankees took them all prisoner. Can y'all imagine? Those poor boys already sufferin', and along come the Federals to keep them from their medicines."

"That's horrific," said Jake dramatically. "How dare they!"

"The poor souls couldn't even defend themselves. Well, y'all can imagine how mortified they were!"

"Yes, miss. We surely can," David agreed.

"They were kept in the depot for over a week, until those heathens finally decided to send them off to Yankee-land, to wither away in some Godforsaken prison."

"That's right awful," David sympathetically remarked.

Emily shook her head in disgust. "Those horrid rascals played 'Yankee Doodle' when they came into town." She angrily scowled. "They marched right past our house in all their mud-splattered glory, and ended up yonder at Court House Square. Some of them even had the audacity to gloat about our capture!"

"Shameful!" exclaimed Jake. He flashed a glance at David, who raised an eyebrow.

"And then they took down our beloved flag, and hoisted up those atrocious stars and stripes." Emily shook her head in abhorrence. "I only hope the good Lord in Heaven will spare us any more afflictions."

"Why don't y'all jist leave?" asked David.

"My father wouldn't hear of it!" she exclaimed. "Some of the more prominent citizens in town ran off. But we want to stay and try to protect that which is ours."

Suddenly there came an abrupt knock at the front door. "Is anyone in there?" a brusque male voice inquired. "Open up immediately!"

Emily's eyes flew wide with panic. "They've come to steal us blind!" she cried. Hurriedly, she gathered her family's silverware box from a lower drawer of the dining room sideboard and thrust it into Jake's hands. "Please, Mr. Kimball. Keep this safe from those despicable men!" She motioned toward the back door, and scurried off to answer the front.

David and Jake glared at each other. Having no other plan of recourse, they exited out the kitchen door to the back alley, with Jake concealing the awkward bundle inside his coat. They made their way to their waiting mounts and galloped away from the infested town. After traveling a fair distance, they crossed the Tennessee River and continued south for about a mile. Selecting a group of sweetgum trees, recognizable by their star-shaped leaves, the boys dismounted, stepped off thirty paces east from where the trees were clustered, and buried the silverware box. Nightfall was upon them, so they made makeshift beds from horse blankets on the hard, cold ground, dozed for a few hours, and rode back home, exhilarated by their escapade.

By the time they arrived at Jake's, it was evening. As quickly and quietly as they could, they entered the warmth of the Kimball home. Without disclosing the details of their exploits, they hungrily devoured the meal Isabelle prepared for them and hurried upstairs to Jake's room, where they lay sprawled out on the bed, rehashing their excursion. They vowed to return the silver to Emily once the threat of enemy invasion had passed, but when that would be, they couldn't predict. The Yankee occupation had arrived.

Hiram's regiment, which was camped at Yorktown, reorganized on April 21 because the one-year commitment many soldiers gave upon their enlistment expired. William Rivers, whose cousin, James Alexander, had been killed at Manassas, opted to resign his position. He was so heartbroken over the loss of his cousin that he deemed himself worthless as a fighting soldier, and so, after bidding his company farewell, he departed for home with several others.

New officers were chosen. Ivander Law was reelected as colonel, and Charles Scott as major. In all, twenty-five officers were replaced. It wasn't surprising to the men that Law retained his command. He had become close to Confederate General John Bell Hood as a strategic career move and had also positioned himself favorably with influential military personnel and politicians. The remaining North Alabamians reenlisted for three years, hoping their service wouldn't be needed for that duration.

Some of the soldiers managed to secure newspapers, which reported that Lincoln had been pressured to relieve Grant of his duties at Shiloh. The president was quoted as saying, "I can't spare this man; he fights." Therefore, Unconditional Surrender Grant still remained in command, and he won the battle, as Lincoln predicted. The president also signed into effect the abolition of slavery in the Yankee nation's capital.

Meanwhile, the Confederacy passed the Conscription Act, which required all men aged eighteen years and older to enlist. Many felt the law was a contradiction to state sovereignty, which was what the Confederacy had been founded on. Newspapers reported the fall of Fort Pulaski, located at the mouth of the Savannah River, and Union forces captured it by using rifled cannon. They also printed that, on April 12, what was being called the "Great Locomotive Chase" took place. Several Federal volunteers had attempted to steal the Confederate locomotive *General*, but were discovered as they headed north from Big Shanty, Georgia. The Confederate crew of the *Texas* chased the *General* with their train in reverse, and finally captured it north of Ringgold. The story made great fodder for adventure-seeking readers. Hiram knew it wouldn't be long before dime novels exploited the event, which meant his son would eagerly devour it. Still waiting to embark on an adventure of their own, the men of the 4th Alabama sat poised on their haunches, impatiently waiting for another battle. They learned Huntsville had become occupied and vowed vengeance in whatever capacity they could manage, be it when they returned home on furlough, or sooner.

The situation was worsening in Huntsville, as Union soldiers went on a rampage. Their commander, Ormsby Mitchel, turned a blind eye to his soldiers' pilfering. Federal gunboats patrolled up and down the Tennessee River, shelling towns and settlements along the banks. The Yankees burned, plundered, and foraged from the poor displaced souls, and raiding parties became more frequent. When David learned of the abomination, he considered joining up with a local group of Rebels who were retaliating. These guerrillas, as they were known, were a force to be reckoned with, for even though their group was small, they were fiercely lethal.

Rumors ran rampant. Huntsville was being humiliated beyond comprehension. Although David's ire was riled, he knew deep down he was incapable of preventing incidents around him, which frustrated him all the more.

On April 24, he rode to Jake's, where he observed his friend riding bareback out in an open field, so he galloped Sally over.

"En guard!" Jake hollered, riding straight at his imaginary foe with a long stick pointed at him. He galloped by as David maneuvered Sally away from the blow, reining her hard, so that she whirled around to face their aggressors.

David grinned. Knowing Sally could outrun old Stella, he kicked his mare and galloped away. Jake rode frantically to catch him, but was soon left in the dust, so he gave up the chase.

Turning back, David rode up to him and laughed. "What's the matter with you? Attackin' an unarmed man!"

"Jist joustin' with you!" Jake slid off Stella's swayed back while the old mare began to graze.

"Well, next time, why don't you make it a fair fight?" David dismounted and gave Sally free rein to graze with Stella.

"Let's go out yonder and sit under that old oak tree," Jake suggested.

They walked a short distance to their "talking oak," as they called it, and sat down upon the new spring grass. The day was sunny and warm, with a soft breeze whispering through the vibrant green leaves, causing the canopy of Spanish moss hanging from its branches to sway gently above them.

"I heard the Yankees ain't been able to cross the Tennessee on account of our fellers chasin' them off," Jake remarked, leaning back against the trunk.

"I heard that, too. Reckon we're lucky to be this far south, or they'd come and take away all our worldly possessions."

"Not without a fight." Jake flashed a cunning smile at his friend. "What do you say we go explorin' tomorrow?"

David glared at him. "You mean ride back up to Huntsville?"

He nodded with a devilish grin. "We can visit purty Miss Emily again."

"If she's still there." Hesitating, David glanced over at the horses. "What if we git caught this time?"

"We won't git caught! How will our folks ever find out?"

He shrugged. "Okay. I'll meet up with you here at daybreak."

Jake snickered, his brown eyes sparkling with anticipation of their upcoming adventure.

When David arrived home, he was distressed by the reception he received.

"Darlin'," his mother said to him as he entered the front room, "we've been waitin' to talk to you."

She stood from her chair, set her pipe in the ashtray, and sashayed into the dining room. Rena and Josie were seated at the table, constructing something out of paper.

"What's goin' on?" he asked warily.

Rena looked up at him with weepy eyes. "We received word that poor Thomas Halsey was killed at the battle up in Tennessee," she sniveled. A trickle ran down her cheek. She wiped it away.

"Thomas was killed?" Stunned, David sank into a chair. He knew soldiers were dying, but this was far too familiar. Someone he actually knew wouldn't be coming home. "That's right awful."

"Yes, it surely is," stated Caroline. She sat down beside him. "We're makin' condolence cards for his kinfolk."

He reached across the table and took a piece of paper. "I'll make one, too," he volunteered.

They took turns passing around the inkwell and pen, writing heartfelt inscriptions on their notes, and when they had finished, they said a prayer for the preservation of Thomas' soul into Heaven.

"Honey, there's somethin' else I've been meanin' to tell you," Caroline said as she arose.

"What's that, Ma?" he asked.

"Auburn has closed. It won't reopen till the threat of Yankee invasion has passed."

"Oh. Well, that's all right," he remarked with a shrug. "This will all be over by the time I'm ready for college, anyways." He grinned at her reassuringly.

"I do hope you're right," she replied, returning the smile.

Before sunup, he completed his chores, saddled and bridled Sally with his new tack, and stole away after leaving his mother a brief note as to his whereabouts, stating he would be at Jake's for two days, and probably wouldn't be home until later in the week, making up an excuse about bow-hunting for deer. He rode down the familiar dirt road, making his way in the dark, but didn't pay it any mind, because he was so accustomed to the trek he could do it with his eyes closed. As the sun peered above the horizon, casting a pink hue across the cobalt sky, birds began twittering in the trees. He arrived at the Kimball's, and once Jake saddled up, they were on their way, traveling through intermittent sprinkles, bedding down that evening in a makeshift shelter, and continuing on until they arrived at the Tennessee River. To their dismay, several Union pickets were stationed at the bridge.

"How are we gonna git across?" asked David.

Jake glanced up and down the river. "Follow me," he instructed, turning Stella away from the bank.

They rode upstream for a couple of miles, until they discovered a boat tied to a long pole. Spotting a barn about half a mile down a nearby road, the boys led their horses over. They found it to be empty, so they confined their steeds in stalls, carried some hay over that they found piled in a corner, secured the barn door shut, and returned to the river, where they slid down the slope to the water's edge. The canoe was weathered but sturdy. They climbed in and began rowing. Reaching the other side, they hid the vessel in the reeds and clambered up the embankment. Without horses, they knew the trip would take much longer, but they were determined to reach their destination, so they set out on foot.

By the time they had walked the eight miles to Huntsville, it was late afternoon. Like before, they slithered through town undetected until they reached Emily's home. Cautiously, they bounded up the steps and knocked on the front door. There was no answer. They knocked again, but still no response came. Deciding to go around to the back, they went to the kitchen door and pounded on it. This time, a face peered out the window. The lock on the door rattled, and finally, the door creaked open. A young boy stood in the doorway, glaring at them.

"Who are y'all?" he asked boldly.

"We're friends of Miss Emily," replied Jake. "Is she here?"

The boy looked them up and down. "Wait here." He disappeared inside.

Jake and David stood awkwardly, glancing over their shoulders to see if there were any Yankees approaching to pounce on them. After several minutes, Emily emerged.

"It's y'all," she breathed. She reached out, took Jake by the hand, and pulled him in. David timidly followed. "Why, I can't believe y'all came back!" She smiled happily. "It's been a might lonely these past two weeks, bein' shut up in the house most all the time."

"Sorry about your circumstances, Miss Emily," said Jake. "We risked hide and hair to git here."

"Gracious sakes!" Her genuine concern became apparent. "Come in and sit down at the table for a spell."

They did so, and Emily saw to it that their thirst and hunger were soon satisfied.

"Luckily, those Yankees haven't been here to raid our pantry," she said smugly. "My father is quite affluent, so I reckon they're avoidin' us because of it."

"That's a reassurance," responded Jake. His gregarious nature compensated for his companion's painful shyness, so he carried the conversation. "What's happened in these parts since our last visit?"

Miss Emily shook her head. "It's been horrible," she stated blatantly. "The Confederate soldiers who were hidin' in town have all run off. My li'l' brother and I can't attend school, and the businesses have all closed. The *Huntsville Democrat* has been taken over, and those heathen Yankees have renamed it the *Huntsville Reveille*."

"Why did they do that?" David wondered aloud.

"Because their president is a Republican. They don't take to us Democrats," Jake stated, to which David nodded in agreement.

"They've moved into the train depot, the Female Seminary, and the Green Academy for boys," Emily went on. "They've stolen and robbed from anyone they can, and they go out of their way to frighten us. They even steal from the poor niggers, who are learnin' to hate those thievin' Yankees as much as our Southern brethren do. The freed slaves come to the soldiers, who jist tear up their freedom papers, whip them, and send them back home."

"That is an atrocity, I'll admit," declared Jake, shaking his head in disgust.

"The Yankees decided that they're tired of dealin' with the niggers, so they merely shoot them when they approach," she added. "They've shot several of the poor souls already."

David and Jake looked at each other and frowned, for they had no idea how to remedy the dire situation.

"Has anyone else been hurt?" asked Jake.

"No. But there is one funny story to come of all this," she said. "Do y'all know where the First Presbyterian Church is?"

"Yeah," said Jake. "Our mothers came up to sew uniforms and socks for the soldiers there."

"Well," said Emily, "Reverend Ross allowed Mr. Samuel Coltart to hide his mule down in the furnace room of that church, so the Yankees wouldn't steal it. Needless to say, durin' the prayer, the mule started brayin' like he was prayin', too!"

The threesome giggled.

"That is funny!" said Jake.

"It was. Till the Yankees had Dr. Ross arrested for offerin' prayers for the success of the South."

The boys groaned.

"We saw where they burned some of the bridges and cattle guards on the way up here," David stated.

"It's a wonder y'all didn't git caught," she said. "So take extra care on y'all's way back home."

"We will, Miss Emily, and we'll bring y'all's silver back when we can," Jake said as he stood, and David did the same. "We'd best be headed home now. We've got a long ride ahead of us."

Emily escorted them to the back door. "Mind what I said. It ain't safe comin' up here."

Jake grinned, took her hand, and kissed the back of it. "Fair maiden," he said whimsically, "till we meet again." He strutted out the door.

Following suit, David said, "M'lady," gave her a polite nod, flopped on his slouch hat, and sauntered after his friend. Turning back to see her standing in the doorway, he noticed the mournful expression on her pretty face, and felt his heart sink at the sight. Her predicament was disconcerting at the very least. He hoped the Yankees would leave her alone.

The boys made their way back through town. They avoided a cluster of Union soldiers near an intersection, but overheard some of their conversation while they cautiously went around.

"I've set my sights on some fine gals in this town," one of them was saying as he tilted the kepi back on his head and lit his pipe.

"I saw one down that street," said another, pointing toward the thoroughfare Jake and David had just come from. "She's a rapturous beauty!"

The men chuckled.

David and Jake glanced at each other, wondering if they were referring to Emily. Jake motioned for his friend to follow, so they slinked around the corner of a building, barely taking cover as another group of soldiers marched past. Hesitating momentarily, David gaped at the Yankees, not sure of what he was seeing.

"Jake!" he whispered loudly. "Lookee there!"

Jake looked in the direction of the passing soldiers. "What?"

"That's Owen Ridgeway!"

He squinted. "Are you sure?"

"I think so. Let's git around them and have another look."

David led the way this time. They dodged between buildings, scurrying to get ahead of the company until they reached the end of the block, where they peered around the corner of another building. The soldiers marched toward them. Their boots thudded in time on the dirt road, stirring up a small cloud of dust.

"It *is* him!" Jake said in amazement.

A few of the Federals heard his voice. They turned to look, but David and Jake quickly backed into the shadows to avoid being detected. The Union soldiers filed past.

"I told you!" David whispered.

The company marched off down the road until they were gone from sight.

"What's he doin' jinin' up with the Yankees?" Jake wondered out loud.

"He's a traitor!" exclaimed David. "And it don't surprise me one bit."

Jake sighed. "Come on, Zeke. It's almost dark out. We'd best git a move on."

They made haste out of town. The sun had set, and dark shadows surrounded them. At last, they reached the river. The black, foreboding water swooshed and gurgled as it rushed by. Without a lantern, they struggled to find the canoe, but finally did so after an hour of searching the riverbank. They quickly rowed across, hoping they wouldn't be carried downstream or discovered, until they reached the other side. Surprised once again by their good fortune, they found the long pole that the canoe had been tied to, secured the boat, climbed away from the river, and started along the road.

"I still can't believe we saw Owen with those Yankees," panted Jake while they walked.

"Are you fixin' to tell Miss Callie?" David asked breathlessly.

"I don't reckon there's a need for that."

They continued on in the dark, listening for approaching soldiers.

David's heart pounded in his ears. Suddenly, a terrible thought came to mind. "I hope our horses are still there."

"They will be," Jake stated confidently. "Or we'll be walkin' all night."

At last, they saw the empty barn where they had left their steeds. Making their way to the door, they pulled it back. To their relief, the two horses blew, and whinnied in recognition. Without hesitation, the boys mounted, setting off toward home, for they were still too close to danger. Once they traveled several miles, they dismounted.

Jake withdrew his pocket watch. "It's already after eleven," he said. "We should find a place to sleep."

They looked around at their surroundings, but couldn't make anything out in the dark. Raindrops started pelting them, accelerating until the droplets turned into a steady downpour. Climbing back onto their horses, the boys continued their journey, cursing the rain while they rode. After another hour, they saw a shed near the road, so they took refuge, leaving the horses tied outside. Huddled together in the dark for warmth, they finally dozed off.

David jolted awake, realizing it was daybreak. Chilled to the bone, he shivered as he stood, and went outside. Jake was nowhere to be seen. Alarmed by his absence, he looked in every direction, and saw Sally standing under a coppice of trees, so he ran over to her, oblivious to the cold rain that whipped against his face. The mare's reins were tangled in the undergrowth. Her front forelocks were bloody from cuts she had acquired while trying to pull free. Distraught by the sight, he untangled her, sprang up onto her back, and turned her toward the shed.

"Jake?" he screamed. "Jake! Where are you?"

The rain came down harder, pelting like hail. He struggled to clear his mind, trying to decide what to do next as he yelled at the top of his lungs, until he thought he was losing his voice. Riding for a few miles, he hollered out, all the while becoming more panicked.

"Jake! Answer me, damn it!"

Noticing a farmhouse down the road, he rode toward it. A large, furry dog barked manically as he approached, but refused to leave its shelter under the porch. David dismounted, stepped up onto the porch, and knocked on the door. An elderly woman answered.

"Yes?"

"Ma'am. If you please, I seem to have lost my way, and …"

"Is that you, Zeke?"

David frowned at the familiar voice. "Jake?"

His friend appeared from behind the woman. "Get on in here!" He motioned, and the woman let him by.

"Why did you leave me out there?" he asked, containing his rage.

"I was comin' right back. I didn't think you'd wake up so early. Reckon I gave you a fright, huh?"

He exploded into laughter, but David didn't think it was so funny, and scowled at him.

Jake contained himself. "Mrs. Ward here has made up some fine viands for us to dine on while we ride home."

The elderly woman handed Jake a basket covered with a cloth napkin. "Try not to git too wet out there, boys!" she said with a cackle, exposing several missing teeth.

"I'll fetch Stella," Jake said. He walked past his friend and trotted out to the barn.

"Thank you kindly, Mrs. Ward," David said, attempting to be cordial, even though he felt like punching his partner. "We're much obliged for your hospitality."

"My pleasure, young man," she responded. "Y'all have a safe ride back."

She waved from the doorway as David mounted and Jake rode up. They galloped toward home. Thankfully, the rain tapered off to a light drizzle.

While the boys ate the provisions given them, David muttered, "Sure could go for a cup of coffee with this," but realizing his throat hurt, refrained from speaking any further.

After they had ridden for a while in silence, Jake asked, "You ain't still riled, are you, Zeke?"

He hesitated, but then replied, "Naw. Reckon not. It was jist a misunderstandin'." His throat was raw, he assumed from all his bellowing, but the damp weather didn't help, and as they neared Jake's house, it felt like it had swollen shut.

"Come on up to the house for a spell," invited Jake.

"I think I'll jist head on home," said David. "See you later."

They parted ways. He continued on until he saw his family's familiar dogtrot house snuggled in the valley. His head throbbed with pain, and felt like it might explode. He rode around the house to the barn, where he unsaddled Sally, dried her off with a towel, and gave her a nosebag full of oats. Allowing her to munch while he attempted to wash her cuts, he knew he'd have hell to pay when his mother found out. Once he finished tending to the mare, he oiled his saddle, recalling how his father had beamed with delight upon presenting it to him. The thought made him smile through his discomfort.

Temporarily satisfied with his cleanup, he dragged himself to the house, and walked through the breezeway. Entering the sanctuary of his room, he shed his wet clothing, left it in a heap on the floor, pulled on a dry pair of drawers, socks, and a shirt, and climbed into bed, thankful for the quilts his mother had piled on. He hoped he wasn't getting sick, but knew otherwise, because his sore throat had now become unbearably painful, and he felt feverish as well. He croakily called for his mother.

This is all Jake's fault, he grumbled miserably to himself.

The thought occurred to him that his father might be suffering in a similar fashion, but he dismissed it, taking pity on his own affliction instead. Getting no response from his mother, he closed his eyes, and soon drifted off to sleep.

"We knew there was some game at hand then, for when General Jackson ordered knapsacks to be left behind he meant business."

—*Private John Casler*

Chapter Seven

The end of April brought more misery to the citizens of Huntsville David learned of their predicament on May 5 while he conversed with several locals at Ben Johnson's mercantile store.

"There has been a rumor floatin' around that two hundred and fifty of our boys ambushed a Yankee detachment of infantry at Paint Rock Bridge," said Mr. Skidmore. "But we all think General Mitchel invented that story to make his own men look good."

David thought of Owen Ridgeway, and wondered if he had been in on the deception. Knowing the kind of showboat Owen was, he most certainly had.

"Captain Frank Gurley and his band of cavalrymen have been tormentin' General Mitchel for weeks," stated Mr. Foreman as he casually lit his pipe. "They cut telegraph lines, fired into departin' trains and tore up railroad tracks. So in return, Mitchel arrested twelve of Huntsville's most prominent citizens, jist last week."

Mr. Skidmore elaborated by explaining to David, "We heard all the details from Billy Ryan, whose cousin snuck out of Huntsville and came down here to tell him."

"Which fellers got arrested?" asked Kit, who had remained in Alabama since the Yankee invasion.

"Dr. Fearn is one," replied Mr. Skidmore. "And Attorney William Acklen is another. He's the grandson of Huntsville's founder."

"Who else?" Kit insisted.

David wondered if Emily's father was one of the detained.

"McDowell, Bishop Henry Lay, and some other fellers whose names don't recall," responded Mr. Foreman. "You know any of them?"

"No, don't reckon I do," Kit grumbled. The men stared at him compelling him to share more information. "I was hopin' it wasn't anyone my brother and I do business with, is all."

"Not that you could anyway!" exclaimed Mr. Garrison. "Nothin's goin' in or out of Huntsville, thanks to those damn Yankees."

"They attacked Athens on the second," Mr. Powell informed the men, referring to the nearby town. "Soldiers from Illinois came down from fightin' at Shiloh Church, went in, and sacked the town. From what we were told, that Yankee Colonel Turchin walked into the town square and hollered out at his troops that he would shut his eyes for two hours. That gave them the go-ahead to loot the town. They set fire to it, raped the servants, verbally abused the womenfolk, and pillaged the rest. They even caused one young lady to miscarry her baby, which resulted in both their deaths."

Ben Johnson shook his head in abhorrence while standing behind the counter. "If you ask me," he said, "they ought to hold General Mitchel accountable. It's intolerable for such terrible behavior to take place, even if they are Yankees."

"It's ironic, too," Mr. Powell interjected, "because Athens flew the stars and stripes longer than the rest of the state in protest for not havin' secession submitted to the popular vote. They wanted to stay in the Union, and now they're bein' attacked by it."

"The Yankees are closin' in, it seems to me," Mr. Foreman said stoically. "They've taken New Orleans, and God only knows what else will fall."

Uncontrollably, David shuddered. He glanced around at the solemn, downturned eyes, glad that they didn't see his involuntary reaction, and wondered if his father's army was faring any better. Deciding it was time to leave, he bid everyone good-day.

On his way out, Kit seemingly sensed his thoughts, pulled him aside, and said blatantly, "If somethin' should happen to your pa, I don't want you to fret about anything. I'll take care of it."

"What do you mean by that?" he asked with a frown.

"Jist that I promised your pa I'd look after y'all." Kit turned his head and spat into the grass.

"I can take care of my own kin," David said earnestly.

Kit simpered, showing yellow, tobacco-stained teeth. "All right, boy. If you say so." He strolled back inside.

David scowled. He knew Kit was up to something, but just what, he couldn't be sure. One thing was certain, though. Kit was crafty, and he most likely was only interested in his own good fortune. Letting out a sigh, he decided it wasn't worth his concern. His father would return home soon enough.

McClellan's army occupied Yorktown. Hiram's regiment was bivouacked among George Washington's old breastworks, which were still plainly visible. Many expressed pride in fighting for their liberty, just as the patriots of the Revolution had done. Because they were without utensils, the men resorted to cooking "Indian style" by placing dough on peeled hickory bark and setting it over their campfires to bake bread, or skewing their food on sticks and holding it over the open flames. They managed to acquire a good amount of oysters, which they relished with delight. The regimental pets had dwindled down to only a few dogs. Mysteriously, the chickens had disappeared, although Hiram and Bud knew they had all been eaten. The goat, it was discovered, had developed an appetite for kepis. He too vanished soon after, most likely into a stew.

Their relatively comfortable existence was soon disrupted, however, because they were ordered to march up the peninsula to Richmond. Before they reached Williamsburg, which was only twelve miles from Yorktown, the 4th Alabama was moved ahead of Johnston's entire army, along with the Third Brigade, the 18th Georgia, Hampton's Legion, and General John Bell Hood's Texans. The troops proceeded to West Point on the York River, but the going was slow because of ankle-deep mud and heavy rain. Exhausted and without rations, the men marched until late into the night. When they could go no farther, they fell upon the ground to sleep. Hearing artillery fire coming from the direction of Williamsburg, they knew McClellan was hot on their heels, but they had left a surprise for him there—land mines.

The following morning, they learned a regiment of Union soldiers had gotten ahead of them in an attempt to cut them off. General Whiting, the brigade commander, galloped past them on his steed, his hands clasped and his face raised to the sky in prayer while he rode to the front. Later on in the day, General Hood managed to push the Yankees back, prompting some of the men to comment on how General Whiting's prayers had been answered. One of the North Alabamians, Orderly Sergeant Hartley, and a private from Company A, were sent out as scouts later that evening, but when morning came, only the private returned. Sergeant Hartley had been shot, and the private brought back his bullet-pierced roll book to prove it. Hiram and the rest of Company I once again felt sorrow, for although Hartley had been from Connecticut, he was well liked, and a true Confederate patriot.

Inexplicably, Union forces backed off, so the Rebels were able to continue unmolested until they reached the outskirts of Richmond. They camped there for three weeks. During that time, the men managed to obtain news. On May 15, the CSS *Alabama* had been launched from England, and five days later, the Homestead Act was signed into law. Before the war, Southern states had opposed the act because of its anti-slavery sentiment, but now there were no Southern states represented in Congress to contest it. The act allowed settlers to occupy, improve, and farm 160-acre parcels of land in the Western territories for five years, but without the use of slaves. If, after that time, the farmers were successful in establishing a farmstead, the land was theirs to keep.

The Alabamians learned Thomas "Stonewall" Jackson had been victorious in Winchester, driving General Nathaniel P. Banks' Union forces north, and had captured scores of Yankee soldiers, as well as their supply wagons. Because of it, the Rebels were referring to the Union general as "Commissary" Banks. Hiram happily contrived a song about their revered general that soon caught on in camp.

"Jackson's in the valley, Stonewall is on the loose,
Jackson's in the valley, all hell's a-breakin' loose!"

After a while, the 4th Alabama became restless, with nothing to break up the monotony of their inactivity, except for their artillery, which fired halfheartedly at the Union army's observation balloon. Hiram's messmates expressed their discontent about being idle as well, and Blue Hugh complained the most, living up to his nickname. Hiram expected the man's cynicism to dissipate once spring set in, but instead, Blue Hugh just became more sarcastic.

"I wish we'd git to fightin' so's we could whip them Yankees and go on home," Blue Hugh grumbled while the men cooked their midday meal.

"Reckon we all wish that," remarked Bud with a smirk.

Blue Hugh glared at him. "I'm sick and tired of livin' like this. I'm sick of the mud, and I'm sick of the food. When in the hell are they fixin' to git us new uniforms?"

"Hopefully, soon," said Hiram. "Ain't your wife sent you any clothes?"

"No. She's bedridden most of the time."

Hiram was afraid to ask why. "With the weather warmin' up, it shouldn't be long before we see some action."

"I'm all for that!" exclaimed Orange Hugh with a smile. "No offense, fellers, but it is a mite dull around here. I'd like to end this war so I can git on back home and tend to the crops."

Bud nodded in agreement. "We'll all be home soon, I reckon."

"Well, don't matter either way," growled Blue Hugh. "I'm only in it for the pay, anyhow."

His three messmates exchanged glances. Theirs was a nobler, higher cause, but that wasn't the case for Blue Hugh, and they knew it. With any luck, Bud's wish would soon come true.

On the evening of May 30, Hiram's regiment was ordered to march a few miles east of Richmond, where they bivouacked in a grove of oak trees. The men of Company G, the Marion Light Infantry, stacked their guns against one of the oaks, and went to sleep beneath it. During the night, a terrible electrical storm blew in. A bolt of lightning hit the tree, destroyed the guns, killed one soldier, and injured forty-six others. The 4th Alabama expressed sadness for losing their comrades before they were ordered to march. Hiram wondered if such a great loss was a terrible indication of what was to come, but he kept his daunting thoughts to himself.

Early the following morning, the Alabamians traveled eight miles to the beat of their drums toward Seven Pines and their foe. The Stars and Bars, St. Andrews Cross, the regimental colors, and the Bonnie Blue Flag all flew gallantly above the advancing Confederates. Once they arrived, they saw the Union army had been driven out, for all that remained were their empty tents. Throughout the course of the day, the 4th was maneuvered to different locations, but still didn't see any fighting. By evening, they had been placed on the Richmond and York River railroad tracks. The empty camp was in a patch of woods to their left, and an active Union battery was in front of them.

Chaplain Chaddick recited scripture to inspire the men. "Be not afraid of sudden fear, neither of the desolation of the wicked, when it cometh. For the Lord shall be thy confidence, and shall keep thy foot from being taken."

As soon as the men took their position, Union soldiers opened fire. The Alabamians were forced to endure an unmerciful bombardment, since no other regiment appeared to support them. While they lay in wait, tolerating the shelling, General Johnston slowly rode up to them. He sat upon his mount, staring off at the advancing Union army. Suddenly, a piece of shell struck him in the shoulder, knocking him off his horse. As rapidly as he had fallen, a group of litter bearers besieged him and carried him off the field.

Because the position of the regiment was on open ground, it moved at twilight toward the cover of trees and the abandoned Yankee camp, but before the men reached their refuge, another shell exploded in their midst, killing several. Agonized screams pierced the air, and the survivors yelled and cursed as they fled. Union soldiers advanced toward them in the dark. Their voices carried across the field, so the Alabamians could tell they were being pursued. Hiram and his comrades turned and fired upon their adversaries. The Yankees returned the volley. Fighting continued for several minutes until the Federals retired.

While the men were regaining their composure, President Davis appeared on his horse. After congratulating them for their valor in warding off the enemy by making a bold and determined stand, he rode off.

The battlefield grew quiet, except for the distant moans and cries of the wounded. The men bedded down in the abandoned camp, and partook of what fresh water and provisions had been left. A few wandered back to the battlefield in the darkness, trying in vain to find their fallen comrades.

At daybreak, the Confederates waited for the battle to resume. Word spread throughout camp that General Johnston had been replaced by General Smith, who hesitated in bringing on an advancing attack. The men wondered about this proxy, because they knew General Smith was in ill health. Talk of the wounded reached the North Alabamians, who were saddened to learn one of the casualties was Gus Mastin, the color bearer for the Huntsville Guards. The same silk flag that had been given to him during the presentation ceremony, featuring the name of the Huntsville Female College, had been taken from his lifeless body by a Union soldier.

While the hours ticked by, the soldiers grew restless, but knew there was nothing they could do. Early in the afternoon, General Lee arrived.

The men soon learned he had been given control of the Confederate army, and General Smith was relieved of command. Lee promptly renamed his soldiers. What had previously been known as the "Army of the Potomac" became the "Army of Northern Virginia." For his first act of authority, he commanded his troops to "strike the tent," and returned them to Richmond. The 4th Alabama had lost eight of their own, and nineteen were wounded. General Whiting was placed in command of the division, while Colonel Law was designated as brigade commander. The men had "seen the elephant" once more, and speculated about when the beast would reappear to rear its ugly head.

Because death had come knocking again, Hiram didn't feel as invincible as he had a year ago, so he and Bud made a pact. Hiram would write a letter to his wife, Bud would keep it for him, and vice versa. That way, if something were to happen to either one of them, the survivor would deliver the message home. It seemed like a feasible plan, albeit a morbid one. Chances were, they agreed, the letters would never need to be delivered.

As summer approached, David learned of events igniting the region. Frank Gurley and his cavalrymen, who were being referred to as his "Seven Immortals," became more active in their attempts to aggravate General Mitchel in Huntsville. At McDavid's Mill, they captured four sutlers' wagons and ninety-six bales of cotton that Northern buyers were preparing to ship north. They also made several attacks on the Union garrison at the railroad bridge over Flint River. On one occasion, they killed a Federal soldier and captured another. Annoyed with their constant harassment, the Union army burned the town of Whitesburg to the ground in retribution. Local businessman, "Uncle" Billy Ryan, distributed supplies to Gurley and his men, as well as to needy families in the area. *Harper's Weekly* printed a story about General Mitchel's success in capturing north Alabama down to the Tennessee River, which included Huntsville. The article, embellished with a beautiful painting of the town, enraged David when he saw it.

On June 27, a Friday, he rode Cotaco over to Jake's house, and was promptly greeted by Isabelle, who seemed happier than usual. This sparked his curiosity, so he asked Jake about it.

"She told us yesterday that she's with child."

"Her and Percy? Havin' a baby?" Dumbfounded, he had never considered their starting a family together.

Jake laughed. "That's right. Isabelle and Percy." He motioned for David to follow him into the barn and out of earshot. "What do you say we ride up to Huntsville and see what's been goin' on?"

David shook his head. "I don't know, Jake. I heard at Ben Johnson's mercantile Captain Gurley has been causin' trouble up that way, and the Yankees are all riled up about it."

"So?" Jake grinned devilishly, his brown eyes twinkling.

"It might mean trouble for us, too," said David.

"We won't meet up with trouble. The Yankees are too busy frettin' about ole Captain Gurley to give us any mind."

Hesitating, David finally relented. "Okay. But you're ridin' home with me first to make sure it's all right that I'm gone for two nights."

Jake agreed.

The boys mounted up and rode to the Summers' farm. David asked his mother for permission, but avoided giving her details about their plans. To his guilty delight, she granted his request. He decided to take Sally, since he didn't want trouble from an unruly stallion, so he quickly relieved Cotaco of his worn saddle, placed it on the mare's back, and bridled her. After gathering food and sleeping materials, the boys set off for Huntsville. Regardless of a slight breeze, the day grew hot. They rode north for several hours. Deeming it necessary to rest, they chose a spot in the shade of a catalpa tree.

"Sure could go for a cup of coffee with this," David remarked while he munched on a sandwich. Changing the subject, he said, "I heard at Ben Johnson's that the Yankee Congress banned slavery in the Western territories. The slave owners ain't gettin' paid, neither. They have to give up their slaves, and the government won't compensate them."

"That ain't right," remarked Jake. He took a deep swig of water from the flask he had brought along. "They should at least git paid for them. It's like Pa says, if the Yankees would jist be willin' to work with us, this war would never have happened."

"Reckon that's so," David agreed. "I heard England paid its slave owners for their slaves before they were all set free."

117

"And Pa says we have every constitutional right to secede. But ole Abe Lincoln don't see it that way, so here we are." Jake pulled out his pocket watch. "It's purt near three. Reckon we'd best git a move on."

They climbed up onto their horses and rode toward their destination. Once night fell, they camped out, resuming their trek early the following morning, and after several hours of riding, they reached the familiar barn. Upon entering, the boys saw that it was still abandoned, so they confined their mares, and walked down to the river's edge. The canoe was right where they had left it nearly two months ago. They paddled across, tied the boat, and set off on foot. Noticing a group of Union soldiers nearby, they took cover in some scrub oaks and waited until the bluecoats walked off. Finally, the boys arrived in Huntsville, but the town seemed deserted of civilians. Only Union soldiers occupied the streets.

David's heart leaped into his throat. "I've got a bad feelin' about this," he muttered to Jake as they stealthily made their way around the soldiers.

"Don't fret," Jake assured him. "We'll be at Miss Emily's in no time."

They squatted behind a stack of barrels, waiting for several soldiers to pass. The guards talked raucously with German accents. A few freed slaves followed them, keeping a short distance behind. They were dressed in tattered clothing, and had no shoes on their feet. One of the Negroes glanced over. Noticing the two boys peering out from behind the barrels, he put his index finger to his lips, chuckled, and went on.

David and Jake made their way through town, cautiously ducking behind obstacles to avoid being seen. After what seemed like hours, they finally reached Emily's. The house took on the appearance of neglect, for weeds knee-high grew in the previously manicured lawn, and its curtains were drawn. The boys went around to the back door, but before Jake could knock, David stopped him.

"Wait!" he whispered insistently.

Hearing low voices coming from within, he peered into an opened kitchen window. He stepped back, his face pale, and his wide eyes clouding from hazel to dark umber.

"What is it?" Jake whispered.

"The house is full of Yankees!" David softly uttered in awe.

118

They glared at each other for a second, and then ran as fast as they could, away from the dwelling. Once they reached a church at the end of the street, they stopped to catch their breath.

"What do you suppose happened to Miss Emily?" Jake asked mournfully.

"I don't know, but she ain't in there." David motioned for his friend to follow.

The soldiers had congregated farther away, so the boys started walking toward the edge of town. Two women attired in day dresses appeared, scurrying down the street.

Jake decided to intercept them. "Pardon us, ladies, but would y'all know what happened to Miss Emily Levinsworth?"

"She and her kinfolk left town," one of the women responded. "You boys had best git out, too, before they catch sight of y'all." The women started to walk away.

"Wait!" Jake hollered.

They stopped and turned around to face him.

"Would y'all know where they went?"

"Haven't a clue," said the other woman. "But everyone's leavin' who can. That tyrant General Mitchel is keepin' twelve men hostage, and usin' Mr. McDowell's house for his headquarters. He has his desk set up in the front parlor so he can keep an eye on what's goin' on outside."

"Those Yankees have been holdin' their vile dances in our houses. They're makin' their selves at home, and takin' whatever they please," said the first woman. "I can't stand them!"

"Come along, Tess," the second woman coaxed. As the two shuffled off, she turned and said, "Heed our warnin'. They'll force y'all to jine up for their cause." They bustled down the street and disappeared around a corner.

Jake chuckled. "Let's head on home, Zeke."

The two boys made their way out of town without being noticed. They reached the canoe as dusk was setting in, and rowed across the Tennessee River, surrounded by glittering fireflies. When they reached the other side, they tied it to the pole like before, and walked to the barn. Entering the dark structure, they looked inside the stalls. Their horses were gone.

"Somebody stole them!" exclaimed Jake.

"Let's go over to that old woman's house," David suggested. "Maybe she knows who took them."

"She ain't gonna know anything!" Jake cried. "And besides, she's two miles down the road!"

At a loss, David became alarmed to see his friend near panic, something he rarely witnessed. His heart thumped so loudly in his ears he could barely hear his own breathing. Suddenly, a thought came to mind. "There was a group of soldiers on the other side of the river when we got here. Remember?"

"Yeah. So?"

"I'll wager they saw us and took our horses."

Jake snorted. "How are we gonna find them in the dark?"

"They couldn't have gone too far. And they can't git the horses across the river without crossin' the bridge. Come on!"

Sprinting to the road, they saw hoofprints in the dirt, and followed the trail toward the bridge, which was about two miles downstream. As they neared, they saw campfires flickering from the opposite side.

"How will we git over the river?" Jake whispered while they slinked toward the soldiers. "They'll see us cross the bridge."

"I dunno. Do you see our horses over yonder?"

The boys both squinted, but it was difficult to distinguish black horses in the dark.

"They have to be there. Let's go!" David said.

As quietly as possible, they made their way across the bridge. Suddenly, a picket noticed them.

"Halt!" he ordered. "Who goes there?"

The boys held up their hands to show they were unarmed.

"We're here to enlist!" hollered Jake.

David glared at him.

The picket approached, saw they were harmless, and relaxed his weapon. "You boys want to fight for the Union army?"

"Yessir. That's right," said Jake. He elbowed his friend, who hesitantly agreed.

The picket spit out his tobacco. "How old are you?" he asked, eyeing them suspiciously.

"We're both eighteen," David lied.

"Why are you out here in the dark?"

A BEAUTIFUL GLITTERING LIE

"Because someone stole our horses. We were fixin' to ride in, but we had to walk instead."

The picket stared at them. He pushed his kepi back on his head. "Humbug," he muttered.

"We're tellin' the truth," insisted Jake. "We intend to jine the cavalry, and capture Captain Gurley."

The boys could see now that the picket wasn't too bright. He seemed to have difficulty comprehending them.

"What makes you think you can catch him if our own fellows haven't been able to?" he asked.

"Because we know where he hides out," said David.

"Humbug," the picket said again.

"It's true," David replied. "We have a score to settle with him, so we don't have a problem trackin' him down for y'all."

The picket seemed to believe this nonsense. "I know where your horses are," he stated.

David and Jake stared at him, avoiding reaction.

"I seen them come across earlier today. Two black mares, right?"

"Yessir," said Jake.

"I'll get your horses ... for a price."

Jake glanced at his companion. "What did you have in mind?"

The picket grinned. "You get me something for my trouble, and I'll see to it your horses are returned."

"We don't have—"

Jake interrupted his friend. "You'll be here in the mornin'?"

"That I will."

"We'll be back then."

Curiosity got the best of him, so David asked, "Do you know Owen Ridgeway?"

"Who?"

"Have a pleasant night!" Jake said. He wheeled around, pulled David by the arm, and set off across the bridge.

When they reached the other side, David freed himself. "What are you doin'?" he asked.

"Why did you ask him if he knew Owen?"

He shook his head. "I dunno. It jist popped into my head."

"Owen ain't gonna help us out of this fix. We have to do it ourselves."

"How?"

"Remember that silver set Miss Emily gave us?"

David's eyes grew wide. "We can't use that! We promised we'd return it!"

"I don't see how that's possible now. She's gone, and no one knows where she is."

"Well ... I reckon it's the only way we'll git our horses back."

The boys set off for the place where they had buried the silverware. Fortunately, the moon provided some light as they walked a mile to where the treasure was hidden. They found the familiar clump of sweetgum trees, counted off thirty paces, and using two thick sticks, started digging, all the while complaining about their hunger. Finally, after two hours of hunting, they discovered the box, so they pulled it free from the soil. Elated they had actually found it, they sat down in the damp grass and sighed with relief. Suddenly realizing their exhaustion, they decided to take a nap before heading back.

David awoke at sunrise. Alarmed that it would be daylight soon, he nudged his friend, and picked up the silverware box. They immediately set off toward the bridge. By the time they arrived, it was daylight. The picket had been replaced by another.

"What do we do now?" asked Jake.

Before David could respond, a brusque voice startled them. "Turn around with your hands up!"

They whirled around to see a dark-eyed soldier holding them at gunpoint.

Obeying his command, David said, "We ain't armed."

"I can see that." The soldier looked them up and down. He eyeballed the silverware box David was holding. "State your business."

"We're here to enlist," Jake responded, hoping the same ploy would work on him.

"Are you the two who were here last night?"

"Yessir," replied Jake.

"I heard about you. Come on across."

He motioned with his rifle, so the boys walked ahead of him over the bridge. When they reached the other side, they saw the picket, who glared at them.

"We've got everything ready for you boys," the dark-eyed soldier said.

He led them to a nearby tent, where several other soldiers were lounging. David looked over at a group of horses tied beneath some nearby trees, and spotted their two mares. His head throbbed from trying to come up with a way to escape their predicament. They entered the tent, and couldn't believe what they saw.

"Owen Ridgeway!" exclaimed Jake.

The boys both gawked at him.

Owen laughed. "So y'all are the ones who were askin' about me." He stood from the wooden folding chair he had been sitting on, but remained behind the table. "Private Boyle says y'all want to enlist."

"Yeah. That's right," Jake said with a grin. "But we want our horses back."

"Why should we give them back?" Owen sneered at David, who scowled, noticing the three-striped chevron on Owen's sleeve.

"Because we can't chase deserters or Frank Gurley without them," Jake reasoned.

"Your mothers know about this?"

"Why, of course they do!" Jake exclaimed. "We want to do our part by preservin' the glorious Union!"

"Is your brother, Lemuel, a Yankee, too?" David asked.

Leering at them, Owen said, "He's in my regiment."

"Well, we can't wait to be Yankees, either!" Jake interjected cheerfully.

Owen seemed convinced. "All right." He pushed two sheets of paper across the table. "Sign these here enlistment papers."

Jake looked at David, and winked at him without Owen seeing. He bent down to draw a large X on the signature line. David followed suit.

"Why, if I didn't know better," said Owen, "I'd swear y'all could sign your own names, especially you, lefty. In fact, I've seen y'all do it at school."

"Now, lookee here, Owen," Jake said in a low, threatening voice. "We signed your papers. It's your turn to live up to the bargain."

Owen snorted. "Come with me." He led them out to the tied equines, and the dark-eyed soldier followed. "Which one is yours, Kimball?"

"This one here," Jake said, taking hold of Stella's reins.

"Summers?" Owen asked.

"This one." He started toward Sally, but Owen stepped in front of him.

"Fine-lookin' mare," he snidely remarked. "What's in that box?" He snatched it from David's grasp, opened it, and eyed the silverware. "This should be enough to pay for one of y'all's horses." Closing the lid, he handed it to the soldier, who carried it away. Owen stepped in closer to them. "I know what y'all are up to," he hissed. "But since Kimball's ma is friends with mine, I'll let it slide this time. Take that ole nag and git on out of here."

"I ain't leavin' without my horse," David said defiantly.

"I'll shoot you if I have to, and I won't have no trouble doin' it." He stared hard at David, who stared back.

"Come on, Zeke," Jake said, stepping between the two.

David's face grew red hot with rage, but he knew contesting Owen was useless. Reluctantly, he followed Jake, who led Stella toward the bridge.

"Tell your mothers I said hello!" Owen hollered after them. He laughed, causing some of the other soldiers to chuckle.

David couldn't help himself. Rebelliously, he started whistling his favorite song, the "Bonnie Blue Flag." The soldiers stopped laughing and stared.

Once the boys had crossed the bridge, they climbed up on Stella's swayed back, and trotted toward home. Shocked by their narrow escape, they said little until they reached the turnoff for Jake's house.

"You can let me off here," David said.

"Are you sure?"

"I need to walk ... and clear my head."

Jake pulled back on Stella, allowing him to slide off. "What are you fixin' to tell her?"

"I don't know, but I can't tell her we were in Huntsville."

"You're gonna make up a lie?"

He sighed. "I'll see you later, Jake. If I'm still breathin'."

Setting off toward home, he heard Jake ride off behind him. After walking a few miles, he arrived home well after dark, and entered the front room to see his mother sitting in her favorite chair, reading. She looked up as he entered.

"Well, it's about time you came home. It's way past suppertime." She smiled, but after seeing his expression, her smile quickly faded. "David, what is it?"

The concerned look on her face overwhelmed him. Suddenly overcome, he started to sob. "I'm sorry, Ma! I didn't mean for it to happen!"

She rushed to him, taking him in her arms. "What's wrong, honey?"

He had considered every option on his walk home, but came to the resolution that he couldn't lie, so he confessed everything. Stunned, she released him, and stared at the floor for several minutes. David bit his lower lip, waiting for her wrath to fall.

"Go tend to the other three horses," she finally said.

At a loss, he did as he was told. His head throbbed so badly it nearly blinded him. His guilt was all-consuming. Somehow, he had to find a way to get Sally back, but he didn't know how. Owen would certainly shoot him if he got the chance. He loathed Owen with every ounce of his being, and wished he could shoot him first. But his scorn and frustration, he knew, weren't Christian-like. He couldn't let his fury control him. He had to think rationally in order to come up with a viable solution.

After he tended to the horses, he sat down in the straw beside Renegade. The colt turned his head, walked over, and nuzzled him. David reached up to stroke his muzzle. For some reason, he missed Sally terribly. Horrendous thoughts raced through his mind about the mare's fate. The burden was too much to bear. His self-blame finally overpowered him. Unable to contain his self-loathing any longer, he silently wept.

"Our home was the regiment, and the farther we got from our native state the more we became attached to it."

—*Private William Watson*
3rd Louisiana Infantry

Chapter Eight

General McClellan moved his vast army to the south side of the Chickahominy River in an attempt to confront Lee below Richmond. While he was there, the commander of Robert E. Lee's Confederate cavalry, General J. E. B. Stuart, received fame by riding around McClellan's troops. Originally ordered to reconnoiter the Army of the Potomac's movements, Stuart and his cavaliers decided to risk their lives by going around, instead of returning to Richmond the way they had come, and their successful exploit awarded them the capture of 170 prisoners and 300 horses and mules. According to one the report, cavaliers slowed down only to accept bouquets and kisses from admiring women.

On June 17, General Lee sent the 4th Alabama and Hood's Texans to the Shenandoah Valley to support Stonewall Jackson, while Union General McDowell was ordered to defend Washington against Jackson's advance. Hiram's regiment marched 150 miles, and was allowed to rest for only one day during the journey. Eight days later, the men bivouacked near Ashland, twelve miles from Richmond. Circling around McClellan's army, they were now behind it. The following morning, General Lee pursued the fleeing Federals.

In the early morning coolness, Hiram marched alongside his comrades, noticing his surroundings as he traveled. Mockingbirds sang from overhanging tree limbs, as did orioles, flickers, and red-winged blackbirds, while they flitted above in the shimmering leaves. He heard soldiers singing behind him, as well as the echoes of clomping boots and horses' hooves. The dew-covered grass smelled fresh and clean. At 10:00 a.m., the Rebels reached a bridge that had been partially destroyed by Union pickets, who were now on the opposite side, felling trees to impede them.

Confederate General Whiting rode forward, and soon the bridge was repaired, enabling the men to cross. The Confederates shelled the woods to make sure no Yankees were waiting to ambush them, and then they cautiously proceeded, clearing debris from their path while they forged

127

ahead. Generals Ewell and A. P. Hill joined them, taking one road, and the Alabamians took another. On June 27, they reached Cold Harbor, but only after considerable effort, because obstacles and sharpshooters hindered their progress.

At one point, while the men sat by the roadside, waiting for their scouts and pickets to clear the path ahead, an ambulance drawn by a pair of fine bay horses pulled up. The driver realized too late he was in the midst of the enemy. Soldiers piled into the ambulance, relieving the driver of any foodstuffs he had. Soon the road was cleared, the men marched on, and the stunned driver, who was with Union General Porter's corps, was taken prisoner.

The Alabamians heard heavy fighting ahead, and knew they were headed for a hornets' nest. They passed General Porter's abandoned camp. Everything was still intact, including tents, officers' tables, and chairs. It appeared as though the Federals intended to return once the threat had passed. General Porter, it was learned, fell back to Gaines' Farm, which was about a mile from Cold Harbor. Before the 4th reached the firing line, Captain Robbins of Company G requested the men to kneel. He then delivered a heartfelt prayer.

General Jackson ordered his troops to support A. P. Hill's Virginians, who arrived first, and had been engaged in battle for over two hours. The Alabamians, who were on the far right beside the 11th Mississippi, hesitated upon seeing the open field they were expected to cross in order to reach the Virginians.

"Forward, boys! Charge them!" their commander, Colonel Law, encouraged.

They advanced across. The stench of smoke and sulfur rose up to meet them as they fell victim to the waiting Union artillery and small guns. The roar was nearly deafening, and several men fell screaming to their deaths while the regiment progressed. Smoke was so thick and suffocating that the Rebels choked and coughed. They could barely see ten feet in front of them, but they knew they had to persevere. The Alabamians advanced to find a brigade of A. P. Hill's Virginians lying in front of the enemy's lines. Hill, in his distinctive red shirt, rode up and down the line, immune to the shelling. Out of ammunition, and too exhausted to move, the Virginians were forced to endure the shower of bullets and shrapnel that hailed down upon them.

Lieutenant Colonel McLemore, who had been promoted to the 4th Alabama in May, appeared at the front of the line. Marching backward, he faced his Confederates and loudly ordered the march: "Guide center, keep in step! One, two, three, four! One, two, three, four!"

The 4th Alabama responded, as if they were in a dress parade, until they passed the Virginians. Given the command, the Rebels charged, bounding toward their foe with a shrill, screeching yell.

Caught in the whirlwind, Hiram charged fearlessly. Men dropped around him like flies, the thud of bullets sinking into them before their bodies exploded with blood. The Alabamians kept running until they reached a ravine. A line of Federals welcomed them with a hail of gunfire, but Hiram and his comrades were oblivious to the death that surrounded them. Bullets whistled and whizzed by. Colonel McLemore fell wounded, and was quickly replaced by Captain Scruggs.

The Confederates jumped into the Union breastworks, stampeding like cattle. In response, the Federals broke and ran as the Alabamians thundered up the ascent to the second line of defense. The Yankees from the first line swept through the second, and all turned tail. The Rebels kept shrieking, cursing, and running in pursuit. They attacked the third line that waited at the top of the hill. The Union soldiers panicked and fell back, retreating at a run to avoid the charging Confederates, who fired a successful volley into the fleeing enemy. Before the Federals could remove their artillery pieces, the Rebels captured fourteen of them. As the Alabamians watched their enemies escape, their voices rose up in triumphant cheers, which spread through the ranks.

Hiram stopped to catch his breath, watching the smoke clear. He looked around for Bud until he finally saw him walking toward him. The two congratulated each other amidst their shouting, jubilant comrades. As darkness fell, the Yankees escaped across the Chickahominy. General Lee was rewarded with his first victory. The Confederates' shock tactics had proved to be successful.

It was discovered the following day that the 4th Alabama lost twenty-three, including Captain Armistead and Captain Price, and 109 were either wounded or missing. Jim Harrison of Company D received admiration for his ability to capture twenty-three men and an officer. In the excitement of battle, he had unintentionally jumped into a trench filled with Federals, so he shot one and took the rest prisoner. Among the Yankees captured by the Confederates was Colonel McLemore's old regiment, the 8th U.S. Infantry, which he had resigned from at the onset of the war.

The Alabamians spent the day tending to their dead and wounded, and repairing the bridge across the Chickahominy, which the Federals had destroyed upon their departure. Bud and Hiram volunteered for bridge repair, since they preferred to evade the morose task of burial duty.

On June 29, the Rebels crossed the bridge and followed the retreating Union army to Malvern Hill, where McClellan made a stand. The 4th Alabama was subjected to heavy artillery fire while they supported their batteries. As darkness fell, they were forced to endure a heavy thunderstorm.

In the morning, it was discovered the Federals had run off, leaving their casualties behind, as well as a few artillery pieces and some small arms. Wails from thousands of wounded men rose up from the fog. Once it had lifted, a horrible scene played out before the Alabamians. At least five thousand dead or wounded soldiers were sprawled across the field. A third of the victims lay still in death, but the rest were alive, crawling over the battlefield like maggots on a carcass. Only two men of the 4th Alabama were killed, but thirteen were wounded.

The injured Confederates were carried to Richmond, where nearly every house was a hospital, and every woman served as a nurse. General McClellan retreated to his gunboats on the James River, while General Jackson moved his troops to Harrison's Landing. They arrived on July 3, and remained there for five more days, until General Lee ordered his army back to Richmond, and restructured it into two corps. The 4th Alabama fell under the command of Generals Lee and Longstreet, and General Jackson led the other corps. General Whiting was transferred, so General Hood took his command. While camped at Richmond, the men acquired new clothing, cooking utensils, kettles, frying pans, and "spiders," or skillets.

Orange Hugh received a gift of admiration from a young Richmond woman named Betsy. They had struck up a conversation one morning when she came to deliver clothing and food to the "orphans," a nickname the North Alabamians had acquired because they were without correspondence from their loved ones, due to the Yankee occupation in north Alabama. Betsy felt sorry for the young man, so she gave him a small white dog to keep him company, and to remind him of her. Orange Hugh named the canine Bo, and the two became inseparable.

The Union army was far superior in numbers and rations, although McClellan had been fooled into thinking otherwise. The Rebels realized they had an enormous task before them, but they were willing to accept the challenge, because they adored "Bobby" Lee and Colonel Law. Their loyalty ran deep, even though the men were all too familiar with hunger, as well as discomfort brought on by rain and vermin. Despite new clothing, their shoes were wearing thin. Regardless, they still intended to keep their vow to the Confederacy.

Hiram was no different. He fully intended to see the thing through, because his conscience wouldn't allow it any other way. It was his duty to remain.

On July 1, 1862, President Lincoln signed the Pacific Railroad Act, which laid the foundation for completion of the transcontinental railroad. The track would run from Omaha to Sacramento. Because no Southern state officials were present in Congress, Lincoln took the liberty of having the railroad built through Northern states, thus accentuating their economic prosperity. Once word spread to Ben Johnson's mercantile, the men who frequented the establishment were, of course, outraged. But one bright spot appeared: General Mitchel was recalled from Huntsville to Washington, and charged with failing in his duty to repress pillaging and plundering, and for allowing illegal shipments of cotton to be sent north.

Colonel Turchin's men had been having a field day in Athens. Aside from their uncontrolled outrages against the citizens, the Yankees singled out a slave named Matthew Gray. They forced Gray and a captured Confederate soldier to mount a mule, and after tying their feet together under the animal, they drove the mule into the Tennessee River. Fortunately for the victims, the mule swam to the other side, and the two men managed to free themselves instead of drowning, as was the intention. The townsfolk were ecstatic when Turchin, as well as his superior, General Mitchel, was finally removed from command.

Although Mitchel was gone, his family, who had arrived on July 12, remained in Huntsville. According to Billy Ryan, they could be seen riding around town in their carriage as though flaunting their presence in enemy territory. On one occasion, they cut off the funeral procession of a murdered Confederate picket. The Mitchel's were disliked from the start because they helped themselves to anyone's property they desired. The citizens couldn't be rid of them soon enough, but it took several weeks for them to get their wish. In the meantime, Mitchel was replaced by Major General Lovell H. Rousseau, who was more easygoing than his predecessor.

Union sympathizers arrived in Decatur and made it their mission to report Rebels who were hiding in the hills. Union Colonel Abel Streight decided to pursue the offenders, so he took a regiment of infantry and one company of cavalry into the mountains to hunt them down. The cavalry was attacked by Confederate scouts, so they returned to Decatur but the infantry was successful in capturing the fugitives, and forced them to enlist with the 1st Alabama Cavalry. On July 10, they were inducted into the Union Army.

News arrived that Lincoln was immensely dissatisfied with "Little Mac's" reluctance, so he replaced him with General John Pope. In typical political style, he also promoted Colonel Turchin to brigadier general on July 17. Congress passed the Revenue Act of 1862, which placed a tax on luxury items, tobacco, alcohol, and playing cards.

On the morning of July 31, Caroline awoke to hear the dogs barking frantically outside. She quickly arose and came out of her bedroom Walking across the dining room and through the front room, she peered out the window. Two riders approached up the lane. It was still too dark for her to make out who they were. She rushed over to the gun rack, took down the shotgun, and walked out the front door to the porch. As the riders neared, she was able to make out their identities.

"We don't want no Yankees comin' 'round here!" she hollered at the top of her lungs, taking aim.

The riders came to a stop in front of her.

"Ma'am," one of them said, touching the brim of his kepi, "we've been sent to scout the area, and if you have anything the Union army deems necessary, it is our lawful right to confiscate it."

He started to dismount, but she cocked the trigger, so he wisely decided to stay in the saddle.

"Your lawful right? Y'all ain't got the right to take anything of mine!"

The dogs stood on either side of her, baring their teeth and growling menacingly.

"We beg to differ, ma'am," the other Union soldier said cordially. "We don't want any trouble, but if you make a fuss, we'll have to send for assistance."

"Git off my land! You hear?"

David was startled awake at the sound of voices coming from beyond his bedroom window. He peered out around the curtain. "Yankees!" he said softly to himself. Springing from bed, he pulled on his trousers, quietly snuck out of his bedroom barefooted, and bolted to the barn.

"Now, listen here, madam," the first bluecoat said, noticing her wedding band, his voice strained as though she was trying his patience, "we have our orders. You might as well make it easy on all of us and just ..."

Suddenly, his eyes bulged in horrified shock. He grasped the shaft in his side. Another arrow flew through the air past Caroline, making a whispering sound as it traveled, and seated itself into the other Union soldier's thigh. Before he could react, one more arrow flew by the first Yankee. Another pierced through the second man's forage cap.

"We have Injuns up in these hills!" exclaimed Caroline, still pointing the rifle at them while she improvised through the situation. "They were supposed to go on the Trail of Tears, but some of them stayed. They don't take kindly to invaders like y'all!"

An arrow whisked through the air, lodging in one of the horses' flanks. The chestnut reared in surprise, screaming with pain. Both horses panicked. Their riders could barely control them. The first soldier saw what direction the arrows were coming from. He drew his pistol and fired a shot into the nearby trees, but it was still too dark to make anything out in the shadows. Before he could react, an arrow flew into the arm he was holding up. He cried out, dropping his weapon.

"Let's get out of here!" he shrieked.

"We'll be back with reinforcements!" hollered the second man.

The two soldiers galloped off on their horses into the brightening dawn.

Caroline turned toward the woods. "Who's out there?" she called, daring the archer to show himself.

"It's me, Ma. Don't shoot!" David rode out of the trees, bareback on Cotaco.

Seeing who it was, she lowered her weapon. "Land sakes, child!" she gasped, trying to slow her racing heart. "What were you doin'? You could have been killed!"

David slid from his mount's back, grinning. "I knew they might come around here, so I invented a plan." He bent down to pick up the soldier's discarded handgun. "And now we've got this here pistol!"

"*David Ezekiel Summers!*"

The tone in her voice made his smile instantly vanish.

"What in tarnation were you thinkin'?"

"I had to chase them off, Ma, or they'd jist rob us blind."

"Who's to say they won't come back here and do that anyway?"

He frowned. "Well, this buys us more time if they do."

Josie and Rena came out the front door.

"Ma?" Josie asked sleepily. "What's goin' on?"

"We thought we heard a gunshot," said Rena.

"We had some early mornin' visitors," Caroline replied, aggravated.

"Yeah, unwelcome ones," added David.

"What do you mean?" Rena inquired.

A rooster crowed from the henhouse, which aroused Caleb and Si' curiosity, so they loped off.

"Yankees were here," he replied.

Rena gasped in reaction.

"Don't fret," he assured her. "I have an idea. Go git changed, and I'll show y'all."

While he waited for his mother and sisters to dress, he rehashed the morning's events until he could feel his loathing boil up inside him. The sight of those thieving Yankees infuriated him, so he made a resolution. He would protect his family at all costs. It was what his father would expect of him; it was what his father was doing right now. Clenching his jaw in conviction, he knew what he had to do. There was no way any damn Yankees would take what was rightfully his by inheritance. He would kill them all if he had to. He would fight to the death … but an alternative method, he realized, would probably be more effective.

When the womenfolk were ready, he led them to the barn, where Joe Boy was waiting, already hitched to the wagon. David drove to the cave he and Jake had discovered a year earlier.

"We can hide our valuables in here until the Yankees are gone," he explained.

With no other alternative, Caroline agreed, so they spent the day transporting their livestock, silverware, the family Bible, and anything else they deemed valuable and could carry to the cavern. In case the Yankees returned, they wouldn't find anything worth salvaging. David had even devised a plan in case they torched the farm. His family would simply relocate into the McGovern house. He had spent the last two weeks tending to the abandoned property, and had made enough minor repairs to render it somewhat livable. It wasn't easy, since Caroline had been watching him like a hawk to ensure he didn't trot off to Huntsville again.

Leaving his family there, he returned to the farm. He waited alone as night fell, watching stars shower overhead in the dark sky, and recalled the same occurrence a year ago, when he and Jake had lounged upon the Kimball's veranda, contemplating the war and their trip to Huntsville, where they first caught sight of Wheeler's Confederate army preparing for war.

The following afternoon, just as he was about to conclude it was safe to bring his family home, a band of Union cavalrymen thundered up the lane. Hearing the horses' pounding hooves announce their arrival, he hid in the safety of the trees, watching and waiting while he held his breath in anticipation. The men dismounted. They walked into the house and around the premises. To his amazement, they mounted back up and rode off. His plan had worked.

As he rode to the cavern to collect his kin, he thanked God for His blessing, and for not allowing the Yankees to set fire to their home. He prayed over and over, hoping to reinforce his thankfulness, so that the Almighty would protect them, just in case they might need it again later.

The sweltering summer wore on. Every day remained hot and muggy. David rode to the mercantile on the afternoon of August 9, determined to inform his neighbors of his close encounter. However, some of them, he discovered, had already been visited by Yankee invaders. The men made a promise to protect each other's property if it was in their power to do so, since the threat of Yankee soldiers, looters, and deserters was becoming more ubiquitous. Not surprisingly, Kit the coward had disappeared. *Some protector*, David thought to himself. Kit had always been unreliable, but still, it irritated him that the man had volunteered to look after his family, when he knew Kit couldn't be depended upon. He knew Kit knew it, too.

"I heard Captain Gurley got arrested," said Mr. Skidmore.

"*No!*" responded Ben Johnson in alarm.

"Yup. Billy Ryan says he was in a runnin' fight with a large force of Yankee cavalry and got caught. They arrested him for the murder of that Yankee general, McCook, even though his death was an accident."

"Is that a fact?" asked Mr. Powell.

"Reckon so. I was also told that five hundred freed slaves were sent by train to Nashville," Mr. Skidmore went on.

"Why?" Ben asked.

"To erect Yankee fortifications. From what I was told, they didn't want to go, and more ran off and hid in the hills than went."

"It's my understandin' the Yankees don't want to fight for slavery. Most could care less," Mr. Garrison informed the men. "If it comes down to that, they'll quit and go home."

David stood silently listening, and thought of Percy, surprising himself by feeling a twinge of pity. No one seemed to want the blacks, North or South. How the slaves could ever be freed remained a mystery to him, because even if they were, they wouldn't have any place to go.

General Lee's Confederates spent July and the first part of August recuperating. Jackson moved to Gordonsville, where he encountered Pope, and deceived the Union general by lighting numerous fires to make his forces appear larger than they were. This stratagem proved effective, because Pope retreated, but not before Jackson captured a portion of his army. Meanwhile, the 4th Alabama repositioned from Richmond to Gordonsville to support Jackson. After spending three months in Richmond, they were more than happy to be back on the march. Hiram and Bud joked between themselves as they tramped along, and Bo the dog obediently trotted behind Orange Hugh.

By August 20, both corps joined together, and continued on across the Rapidan River toward Culpeper Court House. Pope discovered their advance, so he withdrew across the Rappahannock. Once the Rebels arrived, the people of Culpeper came out to greet them, cheering and waving flags in welcome. Some told horror stories of how they had been abused by Pope's Union army. Others described how Pope's own men despised him because of his arrogant, pompous nature, and how Pope's bombastic braggadocio deflated his troops' morale.

By now, many of the Southern soldiers wore tattered clothing and were without shoes. All had little rations, since the Seven Days Battles had depleted Virginia of crops and livestock, which had been taken by both advancing armies. Because of heavy rain and exposure to the elements, numerous men fell victim to fever. Bud was no exception. He tried to hide his ailment, but Hiram knew him too well.

"You're goin' to the hospital, whether you like it or not," he insisted.

"But who will look after you? And keep you in line?" Bud croaked as sweat trickled down his fevered brow. He forced a smile, but Hiram could see he was suffering.

"Don't fret about that," he said. "Our messmates and I will look after each other. You jist git yourself well."

Bud was taken to Dr. Hudson, who left him, adjutant R. T. Cole, and several others behind with the kindhearted citizens of Culpeper to convalesce.

Two days later, the Rebels continued their pursuit of the Federals. They reached the Rappahannock, and moved upriver under constant shelling from their adversaries. The 4th Alabama was ordered to the front of the advancing Confederates. They charged, driving the Yankees into the river. As a result, many who couldn't swim drowned, while others were killed or captured.

Jackson's corps crossed the Rappahannock in an attempt to flank the Union army, while General Lee's portion stayed behind to keep Pope occupied. The Alabamians learned of Jackson's departure a few days later, but didn't flinch in their determination. The fact that they were immensely outnumbered didn't deter them.

Making their way through intermittent, intense humidity, one-hundred-degree heat, and drenching rains, General Lee's corps advanced across the Rappahannock on August 26. Over the course of three days, they ventured through the abandoned towns of Orleans and White Plains, all the while being harassed by enemy fire, until they reached Thoroughfare Gap in the Bull Run Mountains. The Alabamians took up the rear. After marching for a few miles, the corps came to a standstill. Finally, their progression resumed.

The North Alabamians came to a crossing, where they discovered what had held them up. A young man in full Confederate uniform, but without shoes, dangled from an overhead branch, his lifeless body swaying at the end of a horse's reins.

"That's somebody's darlin'," Blue Hugh remarked sarcastically while they passed, referring to the popular, melancholy song.

Information about the dead man filtered back through the ranks, and it was discovered he was actually a Union spy who had paid for his infraction with his life.

Late that evening, the corps' two brigades were positioned to advance through the narrow gap, which was only wide enough to allow for railroad tracks and a road. The steep, craggy sides prevented the Confederates from seeing in any direction but straight ahead. They chased the retreating Yankees, firing their rifles and muskets continuously while they pursued, the clatter of their guns echoing through the gap. The 4th was directed to climb the slope in an attempt to flank their retreating enemy, and after much difficulty, they succeeded at nightfall. The men bivouacked, where they sustained themselves on hardtack and tobacco.

In the morning, they discovered Pope had escaped during the night, so they resumed their march, traveling nine miles to join up with General Jackson. They continued on through Gainesville, and ended up at the Warrenton Pike, where they turned toward the Stone Bridge over Bull Run River. The terrain was familiar, for the men had fought their first battle there a year prior. When they finally reached Jackson, his corps welcomed them down the line with hearty cheers. Hiram saw Jackson himself, sucking on a lemon as he sat atop Little Sorrel.

The Confederates continued to drive the Yankees until they were close, and then waited for their artillery to arrive. Once positioned on the field, the cannons exploded into the Union soldiers.

The men were forced to tolerate heavy artillery fire and skirmishing until 4:00 p.m., when the fighting started in earnest. Hiram knelt to load his musket, stood, and fired on command with his comrades, who were positioned in a line. The veterans continued pouring shot and shell into their foe, some falling randomly to the ground as they were hit. He heard a gun go off behind him, and a man down the line from him fell dead. A group of soldiers behind him started yelling, creating a commotion.

One of them ran up to the deceased man. Realizing it was his comrade who had been hit by friendly fire, the soldier cried, "Damn it, Martin! You shot him!"

Hiram slowly shook his head in anguish while the body was carried off. He was glad Bud hadn't been there to witness it, because he knew how his friend would react. The sight would influence Bud's patriotism, no doubt causing him to question his comrades' capabilities.

The effusion of blood raged on. Jackson's right brigade pressed the Yankees, and managed to capture one of their three-inch rifles. At six o'clock, a large portion of the enemy's artillery, as well as their infantry, started up the turnpike toward the Alabamians, who were ordered to charge. The Federals reacted by firing their artillery into the advancing rebels. Members of Colonel Law's brigade were blown to pieces, their appendages torn from their torsos, and their broken bodies hurled through the air. Blood splattered down like a rapid downpour, mixed with dirt and shrapnel. Several others were hit by flying metal, and screamed in agony as they writhed to the ground.

Blue Hugh marched up the incline, indifferently saying, "Goodbye, Bill. Goodbye, Sam," to each fallen comrade he passed.

Fortunate enough to avoid the bombardment, Hiram kept on with the advance, hastily brushing dirt from his face while he marched alongside his fellow soldiers. Glancing over, he saw their faces and hands were burned by gunpowder, and realized his were, too.

Quickening their pace, the men of the 4th Alabama ran hunched over, and reached the cover of a hill, where the belching cannons had no effect. Seeing that they were being overtaken, the Yankees fell back, but not before some members of the 4th managed to wrestle a sponge staff from one of the artillery gunners and take his howitzer. The Alabamians continued pressing the Federals until darkness prevented further pursuit.

Colonel Law ordered his men to halt. He then positioned them across the pike, but at 1:00 a.m., General Hood, Law's superior, ordered them to abandon their position, along with the captured howitzer, and return to their original position. Through the course of the night, they obtained little sleep, because the loud banging of guns, roar of cannons, and tramp of infantrymen prevented it. By the time the sun rose on the morning of Saturday, August 30, all of the Rebel corps had reached the field, extending from Groveton across the pike to Bull Run below the Stone Bridge.

The day progressed in much the same way as the preceding one, and again at 4:00 p.m., the skirmishing amplified to heavy fighting, which involved troops close to the Alabamians. Because the regiment was located on an elevation, they were able to see the entire battle play out before them in panoramic view.

The Federals advanced a column of infantry out from the woods toward Jackson and his men, who lay in wait within a railroad cut. They retaliated by firing into them. The two opposing forces clashed in hand to-hand combat until the Yankees finally retreated. Pope marched out one column after another, only to have each one repelled. Jackson's men used all of their ammunition, so they had to fight off the advancing Union soldiers by hurling rocks. The 4th Alabama continued to observe until they were called upon, along with General Longstreet's men, to support Jackson. They rushed to his rescue, and the Yankees were finally forced to retreat, leaving their dead and dying on the field. All the while, artillery from both sides continued firing canister and grapeshot. Billowing smoke hung over the infantrymen as opposing sides shot at each other. Like the previous day, the Confederates again drove their enemies, until nightfall hindered them.

The men made their way back to their bivouac on Bull Run, knowing they had secured yet another glorious victory. General Lee rode up. His soldiers crowded around to shake his bandaged hands, offer congratulations, and stroke his horse, Traveller.

"Bless Marse Robert!" they exulted. "God bless General Lee!"

It was learned the next morning that the combined armies lost five times more men than they had a year ago at the First Battle of Manassas and the most of any battle thus far. Over the course of two days' fighting the Alabamians lost twenty, with forty-three wounded. One of the casualties was Matthew Curry, the farmer from Lawrence County whom Bud and Hiram had met before their enlistment. When Hiram learned of his demise, he felt heartsick, and struggled to hold back his emotions. His exhaustion played a part in his reaction, he knew, but the loss still seemed more personal than some of the others.

Later in the day, a soldier from Company A returned to camp explaining how he had been captured by Sigel's Dutch, who were really Germans. In the Federals' haste to depart, he was left behind. The Confederates were fed better rations than they had been given since leaving Richmond. Musicians in Hiram's company, Foggarty, Halsey, and

Hickey, celebrated the victory by playing Irish music with instruments they found abandoned on the battlefield by the Union army. That evening, Bud and several others returned to camp. Happy to see his friend had recovered, Hiram greeted him enthusiastically, and the two exchanged stories of their exploits.

After telling Bud about his meeting with Robert E. Lee, Hiram wondered out loud about the general's bandaged hands.

"Oh, I heard he got them injuries from his horse," Bud said.

When Hiram questioned him, he explained that the general had fallen while trying to control Traveller, who had spooked. Bud then changed the subject, and went on to describe how he had stayed at the home of Miss Madeline Smith, who lived with her elderly parents. Lieutenant Colonel Scruggs, who had also fallen ill with fever, was staying at a nearby residence. Dr. Hudson had prescribed Fowler's Solution to all of his patients, which Bud obediently guzzled down, finding it to be flavorless. Miss Smith then told him about several hams she had hidden inside her chimney to protect against the marauding Yankees. She cheerfully invited him to partake in dinner with her once he was well, but alas, it was not to be, for Colonel Scruggs ordered the recuperated soldiers to return to duty.

"Doggone a soldier's luck," he muttered.

Hiram agreed.

Four days later, Jake arrived at the Summers' farm. Directed by Caroline to the barn, he sauntered across the yard, and heard his friend whistling the "Bonnie Blue Flag."

"My sister, Jenny, told me General Butler is chargin' anyone who sings that song a twenty-five-dollar fine," he declared as he entered, referring to the Union commander who was ruling New Orleans with an iron fist.

David straightened from mucking stalls. Leaning on his pitchfork, he asked, "Why's that?"

"Because he thinks it's too inspirational. He even arrested the song's publisher!"

They laughed at the ridiculousness of his action.

141

"Is this all you've been up to?" asked Jake. "I ain't seen you around for purt near a week."

"I decided to stay close to home in case the Yankees come back."

Jake grinned. "I don't reckon you'll have to fret about that from now on."

"Why not?"

"Because last Sunday, the Yankees left Huntsville!"

David's eyes grew wide in amazement. "They did?"

"Yessiree. They jist up and left. General Braxton Bragg's army is gettin' too close, and they ran 'em off!"

"That's dandy news!" David exclaimed.

"Frank Gurley escaped. He and his Seven Immortals rode in, and the townsfolk placed laurel wreaths on their heads," Jake continued. "The darkies were all dancin' around in the streets with the young'uns, and John Withers Clay got his newspaper back."

"Who?"

"The ex-governor's son. His father was one of the twelve hostages those two ladies in Huntsville told us about."

David nodded as he recollected the conversation. "So the *Huntsville Democrat* is back in business?"

"Sure is. Except now it's called the *Huntsville Confederate*."

"That seems right fittin'."

"And the Unionists in town left with the Yankees, too. Reckon they were afraid of what might happen to them if they stayed."

"That's understandable."

David hesitated, letting the news sink in. He smiled and sighed contentedly with relief. His family was safe once again. Things were starting to look up after all.

"People who are anxious to bring on war don't know what they are bargaining for; they don't see all the horrors that must accompany such an event."

—*General Thomas "Stonewall" Jackson*

Chapter Nine

General Pope bragged that his "headquarters were in the saddle," but the Rebels teased that his headquarters were where his hindquarters ought to be. With the advent of September, Pope proved their philosophy was accurate by retreating back to Washington. General Jackson, in hot pursuit, soon caught up to the Union general. The Alabamians, who were trailing behind, heard the report of cannons ahead as Jackson and Pope confronted one another.

Struggling forward in the mud and pouring rain, one of Hiram's comrades, Dump Sterling, hollered, "Come on, boys! Ole Jack's got 'em treed!"

The 4th bivouacked between Centreville and Chantilly, cold, exhausted, and soaked to the bone. In the morning, they resumed their march, but once they made Chantilly, General Lee decided to give up the chase, so he turned his troops toward Leesburg. On Saturday, September 6, the Alabamians crossed the Potomac into Maryland, leaving behind surplus wagons, their baggage, broken batteries, worn-out horses, and unnecessary gear. They continued north to Fredericktown, and by September 10, they approached Hagerstown after crossing South Mountain at Boonesborough Gap.

On strict orders to respect the citizens, the Rebels were on their best behavior, and didn't disturb anything. Upon entering Maryland, they received an icy reception, which was not at all what they expected. The Marylanders had heard from Union sympathizers in Europe that Lee expected to conscript all able-bodied men for his army. This wasn't the case, but because of the rumor, their sentiments were equally divided. Hiram overheard a few spectators who were observing their march from open second-story windows.

"I can't distinguish the generals from the enlisted men, because they are all in filthy tatters," commented one Marylander.

General Lee ordered his regimental bands to play "Maryland, My Maryland." His men cheered while they marched through, but they were ter disappointed, for they were unable to successfully recruit enough oldiers to replenish their depleted ranks.

One man they did recruit, however, was Bernard Kelton, who ubstituted for his brother. He was a stocky young man with a pleasant isposition, and because of it, Bud and Hiram took to him right away. nother was Dozier Downs, a thin, scruffy-looking character with shifty yes.

"My brother's wife jist had a baby," Bernie explained while the men rudged along, "so I volunteered to take his place."

"That was mighty nice of you," remarked Bud.

"I'll make certain he returns the favor," Bernie joked.

"I'm in it for the bonus," Dozier apathetically stated.

Bud mumbled, "So much for pride and valor."

Hiram understood what he meant. Soldiers forced to fight had no atriotic motivation whatsoever, and Dozier was just one example of nany. "They say war can make heroes out of cowards," he replied with a nrug, repeating what he had heard other men in the ranks proclaim.

"Yeah, but it's the exact opposite case for some fellers," Bud added arcastically, glancing at Dozier, who he knew was out of earshot.

The men made their way through unfamiliar terrain, weighed down vith haversacks, bedrolls, cartridges, weaponry, and whatever cooking tensils they deemed essential. Many were barefooted. They were also icking in equipment and numbers, thus making their Maryland campaign niserable.

The Confederates heard that General Pope had been replaced by one other than McClellan, who had turned his Grand Army of the otomac away from Washington, and was headed back in the direction of redericktown. The Alabamians reached Hagerstown, where they waited news from Jackson. While there, they discovered the Maryland ountryside had been left virtually untainted, unlike the ravaged ndscape of Virginia.

Their reprieve was short-lived, for the next morning, September 14, ney were ordered to hurriedly prepare rations and march back to oonesborough Gap. The men learned their sudden turnabout was due o a blunder made during the previous week. A copy of Confidential pecial Order No. 191, wrapped around three cigars, was discovered by a 'nion soldier in Fredericktown, and given to General McClellan. The rder outlined Lee's intentions, so McClellan reacted by attempting to cut off the Confederate army, which was scattered from Harpers Ferry to Hagerstown. The Alabamians raced to the aid of General Hill, who was subjected to protecting the gap with his small army until reinforcement arrived.

After struggling through a fourteen-mile march, the Alabamians arrived between three and four o'clock that afternoon, exhausted from their strenuous excursion over the mountain. The 4th was immediately put into action, commanded to attack the enemy to the left of the road with fixed bayonets. They were then ordered to their right. The men charged through an apple orchard overladen with fruit. Starving, yet unable to pick any because time wouldn't allow for it, they forged ahead with the Texans and the rest of Colonel Law's Third Brigade. Night fell before they could reach their opponents, so they positioned themselves in a sunken road for protection. The enemy continued firing into laurel trees which stood several yards away, but to no avail, for the pelting of their bullets whacked into the trunks. At one point, Colonel McLemore climbed up on a nearby wooden rail fence to reconnoiter, but he was hit in the shoulder.

The firing tapered off, and soon Hiram and his comrades fell asleep. Around midnight, they were ordered to quietly go down the road, one at a time, in an attempt to sneak past the enemy. Carrying Colonel McLemore on a stretcher, they managed to escape, and continued on until they reached the Antietam River near Sharpsburg at noon the next day. They learned that General Jackson had successfully captured Harpers Ferry because McClellan was too slow to prevent it. The Alabamians found the opportunity to wash their ragged butternut clothing and take much-needed baths.

While they stood in waist-deep water, waiting for their clothes to dry, Bud said, "I don't know if y'all have noticed, but it seems to me that the Yankees jist don't run out. They keep on comin' like an endless tidal wave."

Hiram dunked his head under the cool water. Letting it rivulet down his face and through the stubble on his chin, he replied, "I have noticed. We're up against Goliath, I'll wager that."

"Maybe we'll whip them before year's end," said Orange Hugh optimistically.

"It's my understandin' that if we win another battle, Europe will pay us notice, and possibly come to our defense," said Hiram.

"That's all well and good," Bud remarked, "but what if we don't win? Our troops and ammunition are runnin' low."

Hiram and Orange Hugh looked at each other. "We'll win," Orange Hugh defiantly said with a grin.

Hiram hoped he was right.

That evening, the regiment was ordered to position itself on the Sharpsburg and Hagerstown Pike, about a mile from Sharpsburg near the Dunker Church, which was a simple, small, whitewashed, one-story structure sans steeple. The men learned it was named after German Baptist immigrants, who baptized their brethren in the creek, thus acquiring the nickname "dunkers." The soldiers remained there under heavy shelling throughout the next day until sunset, when McClellan sent a force across the Antietam River, so they moved forward to meet it. They marched through an open field while a cyclone of shells burst around them, and along with the clatter of their musketry, created such a ruckus that their commanders' orders were lost in the din. Few were hit, however, and as dusk set in, the explosion of colors set off by the shells gave a spectacular display.

Around nine o'clock that night, the North Alabamians were moved to outpost duty at a worm-and-hole fence, isolated from the rest of their regiment. Lieutenant Stewart directed them to draw back on their weapons in order to conserve ammunition. The men did their best to make themselves comfortable, although a drizzle had started, and the constant noise of moving caissons and artillery kept the hungry, exhausted Rebels awake. About an hour later, the sound of tramping boots came toward them. Captain Scruggs, who had replaced Colonel McLemore, gave the order to fire. Every gun exploded in a flash of fire at the same instant. The sounds of retreating footsteps and moaning wounded persisted for several minutes. After a while, everything grew quiet again. Not even a cricket chirped, which Hiram and Bud agreed was spooky. They sat in silence, straining to hear if more Yankees were approaching. Hiram's heart beat wildly with anticipation, and his breathing became erratic.

"They know our location," Bud whispered. "You reckon they'll send another advance?"

"I don't know," Hiram responded.

The men were too terrified to speak further. After what seemed like hours, a regiment of Georgians showed up to relieve them of their post. Learning that General Jackson had arrived on the field, the Alabamians returned to Dunker Church, partook in a few rations, and tried to sleep.

"Have y'all seen Dozier Downs today?" Bud whispered.

"He showed up about an hour ago," Blue Hugh grumbled.

"I think he's a skulker," remarked Orange Hugh, cuddling his little white dog.

"Well, if that's the case," said Lieutenant Stewart, "if I can't force him to fight, I'll shoot him myself."

Hiram hoped that wouldn't happen. His mind drifted to his wife. For a moment, he saw her radiant face smiling at him before he surrendered to sleep.

At 3:00 a.m., the men were awakened to the sound of McClellan's army attacking the Georgians, who had come to their relief the previous night. For an hour and a half, the battle raged, until General Hood was called upon for assistance. He brought his two brigades to the front, one of which included the 4th Alabama. As they were ordered to line up, Orange Hugh approached his messmates in a panic.

"Have y'all seen Bo?" he asked. "I woke up, and he was gone."

"Nope. Ain't seen him," replied Blue Hugh with a smirk. "He might be buzzard food by now."

"Don't pay him no mind," said Hiram. "Bo will show up. He's likely just hidin' somewhere."

"I surely hope so," replied Orange Hugh. "We're both anxious to git back to Richmond so we can visit Miss Betsy!"

Blue Hugh chuckled. "Don't be such a skylark. We ain't headed back there. I heard tell General Lee wants us to march up to Harrisburg."

"Is that a fact?" inquired Bud.

"It's what I heard."

The men were instructed to advance toward their enemy. They audaciously marched across an open field in front of the church, in perfect alignment, while a hailstorm of Minié balls rained down on them. Because it was still too dark to see, the men could hardly determine who was shot, except for random screams that came across the field both near and far, and they were unable to distinguish between blue and gray

148

uniforms. Solid shot cracked into skulls and bones, which sounded like breaking eggshells.

They stumbled along, making their way to a grove of trees. Hiram heard Lieutenant Stewart and his comrade, Lieutenant King, yelling at someone. He could make out that it was Dozier, who had fallen down and was refusing to get back up. The officers grew frustrated, so they kicked the young private before they continued on and left him behind. Springing to his feet, Dozier sprinted back toward the church.

The Confederates advanced into the trees, skirmishing with their enemies as they drove them out. Captain Scruggs, who fell wounded, was quickly replaced by Captain Robbins. Realizing they were at an advantage, the Rebels shot down scores of Yankees while concealing themselves in the cover of trees, fighting savagely despite their extreme hunger and fatigue. Other regiments of their brigade, the Texans, South Carolinians, and Georgians, were out in the open on their left, and suffered because of it. As dawn began to lighten the sky, Hiram noticed a Union general riding around the field on a large white horse.

"Who do you reckon that is?" he asked, to no one in particular.

Smoke billowed across the field, but the white horse still remained visible.

"That there's Fightin' Joe Hooker," Lieutenant King informed him. "He's makin' himself an easy target, ain't he?" The lieutenant laughed at the Union general's absurdity.

Yankee artillery fired into General Hood's right flank and rear, causing the Rebels to fall back. The ground was scattered with bodies, most of which were clad in blue. Many Confederate soldiers had exhausted their ammunition when Lieutenant Stewart informed them they had been fighting for nearly three hours straight. Fearing the enemy would chase after them, they quickly re-formed, but discovered their haste was unnecessary, as the Yankees failed to respond. The Alabamians took much needed time to replenish their ammunition and catch their breath.

General Hood directed his men back to the church to retire. Suddenly, a shell flew by, blowing off the top of Lieutenant King's head. The body dropped limply into a pool of blood and brain matter. Bud and Hiram looked at each other, dazed, their faces blackened by gunpowder. They turned and walked away, putting the horrific sight behind them, both knowing there was nothing they could do for the man.

Finally, Hiram said, "I won't ever git used to seein' that."

"I've gotten used to it," Bud remarked indifferently. "I know it's a terrible thing to say, but after a while, those boys jist look like dead animal carcasses to me."

Hiram glared at him for a moment, shocked by his callousness.

"Life is uncertain, but death … is certain," Bud added under his breath.

While they walked across the field, which was strewn with bodies, they tried not to look into the pinched faces, whose eyes stared vacantly up at the sunny morning sky. Young men not more than eighteen, their cheeks once rosy with the blossom of vigor and manhood, lay cold and still, bathing in their own hearts' blood. Some didn't even look human, while others were missing heads, arms, legs, or torsos. Several members of the regiment scurried around the battlefield, placing the wounded on stretchers. The victims cried out in anguish, their blood leaking from their broken bodies like fractured wine bottles as they were carried away. Bud heard a persistent whimpering sound, so he followed it, and walked around an enormous oak tree, its trunk riddled with bullet holes.

"Hiram! Y'all had best git over here!"

Hiram and Blue Hugh walked over to see what Bud was gawking at. They went around the tree, and saw Orange Hugh with his little dog, Bo, sitting on his lap. The young man seemed to be asleep sitting up, his body leaning back against the trunk. Bo whined pathetically, and licked Orange Hugh's face like he was trying to wake him.

"Dear Lord," said Hiram under his breath.

"It's a damned shame," remarked Bud, slowly shaking his head.

Blue Hugh stared down at his comrade for a moment. "Reckon he's seen his last fight," he blurted. "Good-bye, Hugh." He turned and walked away.

Hiram frowned, appalled by the man's insensitivity.

Returning to the church, the Alabamians settled in, and sustained on what meager rations they had left: half an ounce each of beef and green corn. Noticing Bo wander into their bivouac, Bud took the little dog into his arms. One of the men said that after the 4th had started across the field that morning, he saw Bo climb out of a hole from under the church.

As artillery blasted away in the distance, Bud and Hiram reflected on the day's events, sadly conveying their regret for losing such a fine young friend and soldier as Orange Hugh.

150

Intentionally changing the subject, Hiram remarked, "Strange how all
the wildlife knows when there's a battle brewin'. They all high tail it out
of there. Even the bugs vanish."

"I've noticed that myself," said Bud. "I'm right glad for it, too. I hate
seein' innocent critters suffer, like those poor warhorses with their legs
blown off."

Hiram grunted. "It bothers you to see dead horses, but not dead
soldiers?"

"Of course it bothers me. I've jist built up a tolerance for it, is all.
Except when it comes to someone I know. That's different."

With a sigh, Hiram said, "They all remind me too much of David. I
don't reckon I'll ever build up a tolerance for that."

"It makes you not want to git too close to any of them," said Bud.

Hiram grew solemnly quiet, considering his own mortality.

An hour passed. McLaws' Division arrived from Harpers Ferry, moved
to the front, and immediately became engaged, while the 4th Alabama
was held in reserve. The fighting was intense, until darkness finally
interrupted it, with neither side emerging triumphant. Soon the
Alabamians fell asleep from utter exhaustion, but were roused in the
middle of the night, and marched across the Potomac to the Virginia side.

During the following days, reports came in that the battle was declared a
draw, although General Lee pulled his troops back onto Confederate soil.
The cornfield that the Alabamians had marched across was mowed down
by bullets, as though cut with a scythe. The 4th Alabama came out better
than most, with only eight dead and thirty-six wounded. Hood's Texans
lost nearly 80 percent of their troops, as well as their colors. The battle
was the bloodiest single day since the war's start, the casualties so
excessive that both sides called a truce at one point to clear the field of
their dead. One of those killed was Union General Phil Kearny, who had
been close friends with A. P. Hill. Another was Bernie Kelton, the man
who had volunteered to enlist in place of his brother. Hiram wondered
how the brother would take hearing the news, once he learned Bernie
sacrificed his life for him. He felt a wave of pity for the new father who
had lost his brother, and who most certainly would feel responsible.
Dozier Downs had simply disappeared.

"I wonder what became of him," said Bud as the men sat around their campfire.

"He most likely ran back home," Blue Hugh remarked cynically. " wouldn't be surprised if he signs up again in the future, jist so he can g another hundred-dollar bounty."

Hiram and Bud glanced at each other, shaking their heads in disgust.

"Why ain't you done that?" Hiram asked.

Blue Hugh hesitated for a moment. "I considered it," he said finall "but I'd jist as soon do my tour and be done with it, once and for all. Throwing an angry, fleeting glance at his comrades, he sauntered off.

Stories of young heroines who came to the mercy of wounde soldiers filled the warriors' hearts with adoration. One such woman wa referred to as the "Angel of the Battlefield." Serving on the Union sid during the recent battle, she dared to assist her fellow man in the mid: of all the fighting. It was rumored Miss Clara Barton narrowly escape death herself.

McClellan attempted to chase after the Rebels, and some of hi troops captured four Confederate cannons. On the morning c September 20, the Federals were driven back across the Potomac, wher they remained. Apparently, McClellan was satisfied with himself enoug to sit back on his laurels.

The Alabamians camped in the valley of the Opequon Creek, wher they recuperated from their hard campaign. During their hiatus, the me received letters from home, discovering that ties had been restored, du to the departure of the Union army from north Alabama. They waited i anticipation to hear their names called out by Quartermaster Georg Washington Jones, and went up to answer the post. Hiram and Bud bot received letters, and after reading to themselves, they shared them wit one another.

"'Dear husband,' mine says," Bud proclaimed with a wide smile o his scraggly face. "'The Yankees were finally chased off Sunday last o August thirty-first.'" He glanced at his audience. "That was nearly thre weeks ago," he stated.

"Keep readin'," prompted Blue Hugh.

"'We are all doin' fine, and ain't had a lick of trouble since. Most c the neighbors got together to celebrate, although there ain't a lot c money to go around. I am gettin' on fine and will send you a large parc of essentials when I git the chance. All my love.'" Bud folded the lette and slid it into his pocket, tears welling up in his eyes. "The missus is doin' jist fine," he reiterated with a sniffle.

"Glad to hear it," said Hiram. He produced his letter. "Mine says, 'Dear Hiram. You will be happy to learn that we have been liberated from Yankee domination. We had a scare a month back, but your ingenious son found a way to distract the Yankees from our home. We are managin' all right, but one of the hogs went missin', and some of the chickens have disappeared. Mr. Skidmore was kind enough to give us a few lambs and pigs, but they are scrawny at best, and most likely won't survive. I would like you to consider sellin' your stallion for the well-bein' of the children. Times are hard, and I am fretful the Yankees will steal him should they return. They have already secured my mare.'" Hiram scowled with concern.

"They stole Sally?" Bud asked, without getting a response.

"'I do believe we can git by with jist David's colt and Joe Boy. If I fail to hear back on the subject in three weeks' time, I will assume it is all right by you. I have a buyer who is interested, and would take fine care of Cotaco. In the meantime, I will send you more socks, underwear,'" Hiram blushed slightly, to which his comrades chuckled, "'and readin' materials if I can secure any. Your children send their love, as do I. May the good Lord find it within His power to bring you safely home to us soon. Caroline.'"

Hiram felt his throat tighten. Like Bud, he struggled to contain his tears as his homesickness swelled. Folding the letter, he said with a broken voice, "Sounds like they're all gittin' on fine, too."

"Reckon she's gone and sold Cotaco by now," Bud stated.

"Reckon so," replied Hiram.

Lost for words, the two stared at the ground, overwhelmed with melancholy.

Two days later, on September 22, Abraham Lincoln announced his Preliminary Emancipation Proclamation, freeing slaves in Confederate states, but not in Union or neutral states. No blacks were allowed into Lincoln's home state of Illinois, and the president didn't contest it. The Rebels thought him a hypocrite, since he was freeing slaves he had no jurisdiction over, but the ones he had the power to liberate remained enslaved. Eight days later, the men learned their beloved commander, Colonel McLemore, had died after a prolonged decline. The next day, they moved their camp to a location between Bunker Hill and Winchester, where they remained until the latter part of October, living on captured provisions and food they obtained from local farmers.

The soldiers were eager to hear news about the war, and of battles that had taken place elsewhere. One such battle, an artillery fight at Little Bear Creek near Tuscumbia, Alabama, took place between General Roddey and Sweeny. After Roddey drove the Yankee invaders back to Corinth, Mississippi, he engaged the Federals at Barton Station, where he again drove them back.

On October 8, the Battle of Perryville took place, which was Kentucky's only major battle thus far, between Union General Buell and Confederate General Braxton Bragg. Because the Republicans thought Buell was proslavery for wanting to protect Southerners' property, he was relieved of his command. On October 9, General Longstreet was promoted to lieutenant general. A day later, so was General Jackson, and on that same day, General Stuart began his raid into Pennsylvania. The troopers rode up to Chambersburg, where they helped themselves to fresh horses and newly harvested fodder. They continued on around the Union army and returned to Virginia, completing Stuart's second ride around McClellan.

David learned of Lincoln's proclamation to free the slaves, and was reminded of it again when he rode up to the Kimball's veranda. The day was warm for November 8, and on this Saturday, he had exciting plans.
Percy hollered at him from across the yard, capturing his attention. "Fine day, ain't it, Massa David?" he said with a smile as he approached. "Fine day, indeed!"

"That it is, Percy," he replied, although in his heart, he didn't mean it. He wondered if Percy would run off to find his freedom, taking his expectant wife with him.

"You here to see Massa Jake?" Percy inquired with his usual friendly demeanor. He took Renegade's reins and tied him while David dismounted.

"Yessir. We've been invited over to Miss Callie's for a harvest party."

"Da folks already gone ober dere," Percy explained, "but Massa Jake's been waitin' on you. I'll go fetch him." The cheerful man shuffled into the house.

David followed, waited in the parlor for Jake to appear, and once he did, made sure Percy was out of earshot before asking, "Did you hear about that proclamation ole Abe Lincoln made?"

"Sure did," his best friend responded.

Jake led the way out to the porch. Both boys climbed up onto the colt's back, and David started him at an easy walk down the lane.

"Do you reckon Percy and Isabelle will run off?"

"I dunno, but I surely hope not. Say, Renegade's lookin' right sound, and spirited, too."

"I'm fixin' to race him. I've been workin' with him a lot since Ma sold Cotaco."

"To who?"

"Mr. Walker. Ma says they'll be at the party."

They continued chatting until they arrived at the Copeland residence. Sliding from the saddle, David tied his colt.

"We won't be long, Renie," he said. "Behave yourself."

He gave his horse a pat on the neck, and Renegade winked a hazel eye in response. After greeting the menfolk, who were gathered on the front porch, he followed Jake inside, where he saw his mother and several other women seated on velvet chairs in the parlor, having a discussion.

"Mrs. Ridgeway received one jist the other day," Mrs. Copeland was saying.

"I was dreadin' the terrible black letter myself," Mrs. Samuels informed the other women. "But praise be, I got one from my man instead."

"I received one from Hiram, too," said Caroline. "Fortunately, he gave his consent, because I had already sold Cotaco."

"Well," said Mrs. Kimball, "I'm sure Mr. Walker will take fine care of him."

Eavesdropping, David's curiosity got the better of him, so he asked, "What did Mrs. Ridgeway git?"

Caroline looked at him with sorrowful eyes. "She got a letter from the government."

"And the envelope was sealed with black wax," added Mrs. Samuels. "You know what that means."

"No. What?" David asked innocently.

"It means there's been a death," said Caroline.

"Who died?"

"Lemuel. He got the pox and passed away to our Lord last week."

"Oh," David said, stunned. At a loss for further words, he went to find Jake and report the news. He found him in the kitchen with Callie.

"Why, there you are!" she said as he entered.

She was dressed in a festive orange gown, and crimson ribbon spiraled through her golden hair. Approaching him like a stalking feline, she immediately clamped onto his arm.

"David, darlin', tell Jake how radiant I look!"

Jake chuckled at David, who blushed and said, "Yes'm, Miss Callie, you look a mite glamorous."

"Jist a mite?" She stuck her lower lip out in a mock pout.

"Oh. Did I say mite? I mean right. You look right glamorous."

Accepting his explanation, she smiled slyly at her successful manipulation. "I hope y'all brought along your appetites," she said, "because Ma and I have been bakin' all mornin'!"

David had noticed the scent of baked goods, but because she mentioned it, the aroma made his mouth water. "I have," he admitted. His stomach growled loudly.

Jake and Callie laughed.

"Goodness gracious!" she exclaimed. "Why, Mr. Summers, you'd best fetch yourself some vittles, dear, before you starve!"

She led him to the dining room, where a table of food was displayed beneath a glittering crystal chandelier. Handing him a plate, she released his arm.

"Y'all help yourselves," she instructed. "I'll be back quick as a wink." She winked at David, turned, and flounced into the parlor.

Jake glanced at his friend, who was still blushing. Letting a snort escape him, he asked, "Are you all right?"

"She jist gits me flustered, is all," he replied. "Ever since last July, when we were down yonder at the swimmin' hole, and ..." He looked at Jake, who was frowning at him. Deciding to spare his feelings, he quickly changed the subject. "Did you hear about Lemuel Ridgeway?" he asked quietly while they heaped victuals onto their plates. "He died!"

"He did? Was he shot?"

"No. He got sick." David hesitated, and said, "I only wish it was his brother instead."

Jake sniggered. "You don't mean that."

"Hell if I don't! After all the trouble he caused us up in Huntsville?"

"Shhh!" Jake glared at him. "We don't want anyone to know about that."

"Why not? He's a traitor, far as I can tell. I've already told my kin, anyways."

"Well, I ain't told mine," Jake confessed.

David grunted. "He probably still has my ma's mare."

"Most likely. But they're all up in Tennessee now. There ain't nothin' you can do about it, unless you want to traipse up there to collect her yourself."

He shook his head in loathing. "If there's a God in Heaven, justice will come his way," he pronounced.

Callie returned. "How are my boys?" she asked, batting her eyelashes flirtatiously.

"Jist fine, darlin'," replied Jake. "Tell your ma this here persimmon pie is a treat for the taste buds!"

"Tell her yourself!" she responded, giving him a playful nudge, which almost caused him to drop his plate. She giggled at his reaction.

"All right, young lady, I will." He set his plate on the table and walked into the parlor.

David suddenly felt self-conscious. "Uh, Miss Callie," he said bashfully. "Did you hear about ole Abe Lincoln settin' the darkies free?"

"Why, yes, I did!" she exclaimed. "I do declare, when will those Yankees leave well enough alone and jist let us be?" She huffed.

"Makes me wonder if Jake's niggers will run off."

"Well, ours already have," she announced.

David glared at her.

She nodded her head enthusiastically, causing her pipe curls to bounce. "Uh-huh. All five of them run off Tuesday mornin'. Pa says if they git caught and dragged back here, he's fixin' to jist sell them. You can't trust a nigger who's run off once he's done it."

"No, reckon not." He stuck a forkful of pie into his mouth.

To his relief, in walked his sisters, saving him from further discomfort.

"Oh, Callie!" exclaimed Rena, who was dressed in a colorful calic print dress. "We are havin' such a wonderful time!"

"Glad to hear it, y'all!" she replied.

The two older girls sashayed off. Josie took up a plate as Jak returned.

"Miss Callie's slaves have run off," David informed them.

"So has Miss Kitty," Josie said somberly.

"Who's Miss Kitty?" asked Jake.

"She's my li'l' black cat. My li'l' miss priss!" Josie's voice cracked, a though she might cry.

"Don't fret, sis," David said. "She's likely jist off havin' her kittens."

"A black cat, you say?" Jake picked up his plate. "Y'all know wha they say about black cats?"

David rolled his eyes. "Here we go again," he muttered.

"If a black cat disappears on the blackest night of the harvest, means there will be snow on the way, and that winter will last tw months longer."

"Really?" asked Josie, her eyes widening.

Jake grinned. "Naw. I jist made that one up." He chuckled, dodgin her fist as she playfully tried to punch his arm.

"I'll help you look for her when we git home," David offered.

She seemed satisfied with his solution, so she bounded off to fin her sister. The boys followed, discovering that Callie and Rena wer conversing with Alice Walker. They sauntered across the parlor t participate.

"Miss Alice was jist tellin' us about her upcomin' plans," Calli informed them, taking Jake's arm.

"Do tell, Miss Alice," Jake prompted.

She smiled. "We will be departin' our great state of Alabama on week from this comin' Monday. My pa already has a wagon ready, an we'll be travelin' with two other families. We're takin' Cotaco with u David. I don't know if your ma told you."

"Where are y'all headed?" he asked. "Californee?"

"Eventually. We're goin' to my ma's cousins first. They live in S Louis. We should git there by Christmas, and we'll be stayin' till ne> spring."

"Have you ever been there?" Jake inquired.

"Never have. My brothers and I can't wait. We'll be seein' our cousins for the very first time!"

"That's splendid!" Callie exclaimed.

"Pa says next spring he's fixin' for us to go out west through Kansas, and he reckons we'll be in Colorado territory come early summer."

"Y'all are headed out to Colorado?" David repeated.

"Yessir. Pa knows some fellers who are miners. They say there are gold nuggets the size of your fist that sparkle and glow, and you can see them in the side of the mountain, so they're real easy to pluck out."

"Is that a fact?" Jake grinned at his friend.

David smiled through his twinge of jealousy. He longed for adventure, and going to the Rocky Mountains to dig out a fortune in gold sounded wonderful. He might even get the chance to meet his hero, Kit Carson. His mind wandered, and he envisioned himself scaling the mountains, sporting only a pickax, with Kit Carson trailing behind.

"You will, too, won't you, Zeke?"

The gathering glared at him.

"I will what?" he asked, suddenly pulled back to reality. Seeing them all staring at him, he blushed.

Callie rolled her eyes. "Daydreamin' again?" She snickered, released Jake, took Alice's arm, and led her off.

"Miss Callie asked if you knew Owen Ridgeway was headed back home, and I said I didn't reckon you did."

David frowned. "No. Course not."

"Then Miss Alice said she'd miss us, especially you, David, and that she'd be sorry to leave us, and Miss Callie said we'd all be sorry to see her go, and I agreed, but you didn't say nothin', so that's when I said—"

"Okay. I'll go tell her myself. Now what's this about Owen Ridgeway?"

"He's on furlough."

"And he's comin' here?"

"Yup." Jake squinted at his friend. "What're you thinkin', David?"

"Oh, nothin'. 'Cept I'd like to git back at him somehow."

"You'd best leave him be. He'll have you arrested if you give him reason."

"We ain't under Yankee rule. He can't do nothin' to me."

Glaring at him, Jake shook his head. "You know he'll jist lie abou bein' in the Union army. His ma thinks he and Lemuel jined up with ol Braxton Bragg."

"Well, maybe it's time we set the record straight."

Jake groaned. "You're askin' for trouble. Jist leave me out of it."

He walked away while David fumed. "I'll teach that traitor a thing o two," he said out loud to himself. Regaining his composure, he sauntered into the parlor to join the party.

"The muster rolls on which the name and oath were written were pledges of honor, redeemable at the gates of death. And they who went up to them, knowing this, are on the lists of heroes."

—*Brigadier General Joshua Lawrence Chamberlain, U.S.A.*

Chapter Ten

Once his family returned home, David fulfilled his promise by helping Josie look high and low for her missing cat, but they failed to find the feline. In an attempt to comfort her, he assured her Kitty must be at a neighbors' farm, where he was certain she was being fed a bowl of warm milk every day. Josie was saddened by her pet's disappearance, but with the approach of Christmas, she learned to accept it by redirecting her attentions.

David stayed informed by acquiring current editions of the *Huntsville Confederate*, which had been reduced down to only one sheet folded into two pages, due to the paper shortage. Major changes were taking place within both armies. As of November 10, Alabama had supplied over sixty thousand men to the Confederate cause. President Lincoln replaced McClellan yet again, this time with General Burnside, not so much because of Burnside's performance at the recent Battle of Sharpsburg, or Antietam as the Yankees were calling it, but because of his displayed abilities at First Manassas. Frustrated that "Little Napoleon" had refused to aggressively pursue and attack the Rebels by inaccurately assuming he was outnumbered, Lincoln was quoted as saying to him, "If you don't want to use the army, I should like to borrow it for a while."

It seemed obvious by what the press was reporting that, because of Lincoln's declared Emancipation Proclamation, the chances of Europe backing the C.S.A. were quelled. England and France had considered supporting the Southern states before the war became an issue of slavery, but now it was something they didn't want to get involved in. The Confederacy was completely on its own.

Coming across a recent copy of *Harper's Weekly* at the mercantile, David opened the publication to discover contents within it that alarmed yet intrigued him. Inside the pages were engravings, copies of photographs taken near Sharpsburg by a photographer named Alexander Gardner. Even though they were drawings, the pictures were disturbing nevertheless, and depicted crumpled corpses slumped together like potato sacks, laid out in front of a small white building, along with broken

issons, dead mules, overturned limbers, and more pictures of
Confederate bodies. It seemed to him there were no deceased Union
soldiers lying about in any of the pictures. Although he knew his father
wasn't among the casualties, he was still appalled by the drawings. He
had seen photos of corpses post mortem before, but nothing as
horrendous as the mangled bodies of slain soldiers left rotting on the
ground with dead horses. Setting the newspaper down, he came to the
conclusion that his mother had to somehow be prevented from seeing
them. It was apparent that the distant battles in Virginia were getting
closer all the time, which he found somewhat distressing.

He waited for word of Owen's arrival, but none came, so he assumed
he must have been misinformed. Even though he didn't like him
personally, he did wish Owen had enlisted with the Confederacy instead,
for then he would loathe his schoolmate a little less. He also wished he
could get his mother's mare back, but realized it was improbable.

Three weeks after Callie's party, Jake rode up the lane and quickly
dismounted. Without knocking, he strode into the familiar saddlebag
house to find his friend in the front room, helping Josie construct a
Christmas present for their mother.

Glancing up as he entered, David greeted him by saying, "Hey, Jake.
What brings you by?"

"Miss Josie. David."

The tone in his voice caught David's attention. "What's wrong?"

"It's Miss Callie. She's fallen ill and has taken to her bed."

"That's too bad," remarked Josie.

"I was wonderin' if y'all want to go check on her with me." For once,
Jake's lighthearted demeanor was replaced with concern.

David consented. "Of course we will."

They went out to the barn. David saddled Renegade, mounted, and
pulled his little sister up behind him. The threesome rode to the
Copeland residence. Once they arrived, Jake asked if they could visit
Callie. Mrs. Copeland consented, and led them upstairs to her daughter's
bedchamber. Hesitating at the threshold, David followed the others into
Callie's room, which was illuminated by warm, glowing embers from the
fireplace. Mrs. Copeland made her way to the window, and slightly pulled
open the blue velvet curtain, allowing a sliver of sunlight to filter through.

Callie stirred. "Ma?" she asked groggily from under the quilts of he canapé bed.

"It's all right, dear," her mother reassured her. "Your friends ar here."

Callie's eyes fluttered open. Squinting at first, with her pupils dilatec she finally focused on the visitors. "Jake?" Her blue eyes flitted ov David's and Josie's faces.

"Beggin' your pardon, Miss Callie," David apologized, suddenl feeling uneasy about invading her privacy. "We jist wanted to make sur you were all right." He gave Josie a gentle tug on her arm, and glance over to see Jake kneel down beside Callie's bed.

Taking her cue, Josie called out, "Please git well soon, Callie," as sh exited.

"Y'all can wait right here if you'd like," Mrs. Copeland offered, faintl smiling before she went downstairs.

David looked at his little sister, and she at him. Each knew what th other was thinking. It was intrusive, yet they didn't want to leave Jake c Callie, so they remained at their awkward position in the hallway.

Soon, Jake came out of the dimly lit room, and quietly pulled th door nearly closed. "She's restin' now," he informed them.

Josie and David followed him downstairs to see Callie's mothe sitting in the parlor sewing needlepoint.

"How is she, Mrs. Copeland?" Jake asked.

"She's improvin'," Callie's mother replied. "And I know y'all's beir here makes her feel a whole lot better."

"We surely hope so," responded Josie.

"Ma said she's been sick for three days straight," Jake said, h eyebrows furrowed. "But she didn't know what ails her."

"Doctor Thompson says its glandular fever. She has a sore throa and she's been mighty tuckered out," stated Mrs. Copeland. "She wa runnin' a fever, but that's passed. Now she has chills, but we're keepir the fireplace lit, and a hot water bottle at her feet to warm her."

"Did the doc say when Miss Callie will recover?" David inquire compassionately.

"He seems to think she'll be over it in a week or two."

Jake gave a tremendous sigh of relief, which made Josie snicker.

"No need to fret, honey," said Mrs. Copeland, noticing his worr "She should be good as new by Christmas at the latest."

"Good," he said. "Well, we'd best be gettin' on home now, ma'am. Sorry if we caused you any trouble."

"Y'all ain't no trouble at all, and Callie's right happy to know she has admirers." She led them to the front door. "Tell your mothers I said hello. We'll be expectin' to see y'all here in three weeks' time."

"What's in three weeks?" asked Josie.

"Our annual Christmas gatherin'. It will be on Saturday, December the twentieth, unless Callie takes a turn for the worse, but I'll keep y'all informed."

With that, she closed the door behind them. The boys and Josie walked out to their waiting horses. Suddenly, Jake stopped and stared up at Callie's bedroom window.

"What is it, Jake?" Josie asked him.

He sighed again.

"She'll be fine," David insisted. "The doc said so."

"I hope he's right," Jake replied seriously. "I came to understand somethin' while we were up there."

"What's that?" asked David.

"That I love her. I can't live without her."

"We all love her," Josie said with a smile.

Jake nodded. A serene expression crossed his face. "I'm fixin' to marry that gal," he proclaimed.

David stifled a chuckle.

Noticing his friend's smirk, Jake emphasized, "I am. I'll ask her right after New Year's. Next summer, we'll be man and wife. You'll see."

"We believe you," Josie assured him.

"Next summer, huh? You sure you want to take such a big step?" David teased. "And so soon?"

Jake mounted up. "I am now."

David and Josie exchanged glances, and he winked at her. Climbing up onto Renegade, they followed Jake down the road.

A few days later, David learned that Owen had indeed returned to Morgan County, so he devised a plan and summoned his courage. He knew the pistol the Union officer had dropped when he shot him with an arrow was stashed in Caroline's top dresser drawer. Attempting to be inconspicuous, he tucked it under the waistband of his trousers, and set off to confront his adversary. After riding for almost an hour, he recognized the small shotgun house, sitting in a glen off to the side of the road, so he turned Renegade onto the path leading up to it. The cabin looked similar to his own family's dogtrot, but smaller and more run down. A mangy mutt trotted out from under the house to meet him, forced a guttural growl, and slinked back to its haven-hole. David dismounted. A cold gust of wind blew through him, making him shiver. He looked over at the lifeless windows.

"Stay right here, ole pard," he muttered.

Renegade nervously stomped his front hoof in response.

David walked up onto the porch, his boots clomping on the pine boards as he approached the door. There wasn't a sound but for the breeze breathing through the empty trees. Cautiously, he rapped on the door. No one answered. He tried again. Still, no response came. Slowly turning the knob, he pushed the door open and went inside.

"Is anyone here?" he called out apprehensively.

He heard a cough originate from a back room, so he decided to investigate. Pulling the pistol from his waistband, he held it in his left hand, preparing to use it.

"Who's out there?"

He recognized the voice. Turning the corner, he peered around the door frame to see his old schoolmate.

"Ridgeway," he said, trying to sound as threatening as possible. "I've come to call."

Owen pulled himself up onto his elbows. "Well, that's mighty thoughtful," he said. "I surely didn't expect to see you here."

David frowned. This wasn't how he had envisioned their altercation at all. "Why are you still in bed?"

"Oh. I've been taken ill these past few weeks," he replied. Suddenly a coughing attack sent him into convulsions.

Waiting for the spasms to cease, David winced. "What's ailin' you?" he asked.

"The pox. My whole regiment came down with it. I reckon you heard about my brother."

"Yeah. Dreadful sorry."

Noticing tiny red spots covering Owen's face, he backed up slightly while shoving the handgun into his waistband, but Owen noticed.

"Whatcha got there?"

"Nothin'."

"Don't tell me it's nothin'. Were you aimin' to shoot me?"

"Course not!" David forced a chuckle, which sounded more like a hiccup.

Owen squinted at him. "If you ain't fixin' to shoot me, then why do you have that fire iron?"

"Uh ... Is your ma here?"

"No. Why?"

"Because I wanted to tell her how you and Lemuel turned traitor."

"She already knows we was fightin' for the Union, if that's what you mean."

"You're lyin'."

Owen grinned. "So what if I am? What business is it of yours, anyway?"

He scowled. "I jist don't like anyone who goes around killin' our boys for his own amusement. Savvy?"

"Is that what you think?"

Owen glared right through him, intimidating him like he always did. Feeling safer with the gun drawn, David pulled it back out. "I got this off a Yankee soldier," he said, feeling the need to explain, "and I was fixin' to tell your ma that it was yours, so she'd git upset."

The annoyed expression on Owen's face relaxed into a smirk. "That's the stupidest notion you've had yet!"

David bristled at the implication. "I wanted to git back at you, for takin' Sally."

"Who?"

"My ma's mare."

With a snort, Owen said, "I ain't got your ma's horse. And I don't know what happened to her. She's most likely been traded off by now, to some farmer up in Nashville."

Irritated by Owen's smugness, David shook his head. "Why do you have to be so damned infuriatin'?"

"What do you mean by that, Summers? You weren't invited here, and you shouldn't have gone up to Huntsville lookin' for trouble, either, because you found it. The look on your face when I took your horse sure did make it worthwhile, though," he gloated with a snicker. Suddenly, the snicker got caught in his throat. He burst out coughing.

David cringed in repulsion. "Reckon I should leave. You don't sound so good."

"I ain't good, you fool!" Owen lay back against the pillows. "Git o
out of here! And don't come back!" He rolled over onto his side, coverin,
his head with a pillow.

Clenching his jaw, David considered taking aim, but he suppresse
the urge. He spun around and stomped toward the door. Giving pause
he set the firearm on the kitchen table before departing.

Maybe Mrs. Ridgeway will see it when she gits back, he thought, *an
put two and two together.*

His hostility took control, so he slammed the door behind hir
bounded off the steps, and sprang up onto his horse.

"I hope you rot in hell!" he hollered maliciously. Turning his colt, h
galloped away from the dismal dwelling.

When he returned home, he was taken aback by his reception. Th
house was alive with celebration.

"What's goin' on?" he asked warily.

"I jist got word from your pa!" Caroline exclaimed. Still holding th
letter in her hand, she embraced him. "He's comin' home for Christmas!"

David smiled. "That's dandy news!" he exclaimed with a laugh.

Josie and Rena jumped up and down for joy, clapping their hand
and giggling excitedly. David's heart filled with elation. His father woul
be home in only three short weeks. Perhaps, with any luck, the wa
would be over by then, too.

Five days later, Jake arrived, looking as downtrodden as he ha
before. Caroline greeted him this time and directed him into the dinin,
room, where David was painting a wooden broach he had carved fo
Rena.

"Hey, Jake." He greeted with a grin. His friend's somber expressio
melted the smile from his face. "What is it?"

"There's been a death."

David's eyes grew wide. His heart leaped into his throat. Rising to hi
feet, he asked the dreaded question. "Is it ... Miss Callie?"

Jake looked down at the floor. He brought his brown eyes up to mee
David's and slowly shook his head. "No. Owen Ridgeway passed awa
yesterday. His funeral is this Saturday."

"Oh," was all he could muster. He hadn't seen that one coming. Eve
if he did detest Owen, he didn't truly desire his death. Surprising himsel
he was genuinely stunned. Suddenly, he recalled the last words he ha

ashed out at him—a curse, really—and a rush of nausea swept over him. Suppose some higher power had heard his wish? Ashamed, he felt like he was responsible somehow.

When Saturday came, his family attended the sad event. Saying little, he managed to convey his condolences to Owen's mother, who was draped in black bombazine. He felt so sorry for her that he wanted to hug her, confess his sin, and bear the burden of her sorrow. More than that, though, he desperately wanted to escape the depressing ceremony. She had tragically lost a husband and all three of her children, including an infant daughter, and now, both her sons. Even though he disliked Owen immensely, he didn't wish for such grief to be bestowed on his mother. His guilt was overwhelming.

On the way home, Caroline simply said, "That was a nice funeral."

David's mouth dropped open as he glared at her. "Poor Mrs. Ridgeway," he finally mumbled.

"Yes, it is a shame how she's suffered so." Caroline gave him a loving pat on the shoulder. "We are all so blessed, havin' only lost our dear little Elijah. I don't know how I could ever cope with losin' any more."

"Don't fret, Ma," said Rena peacefully. "You won't have to find out."

They exchanged smiles, knowing their sadness had passed, and they only had good things to look forward to. Beautiful Christmas would soon be upon them.

Hiram glanced around at his comrades, who were entrenched on either side of him, waiting for another Yankee advance. With time to reflect, he thought back to the previous month's events. The 4th Alabama had abandoned their encampment and moved to Culpeper Court House. They remained there until November 22, when Lee discovered Burnside was headed north from Richmond, so he assembled his troops near the quaint town of Fredericksburg. The Confederate army swelled to almost twice its size, due to returning soldiers who had become ill prior to their march into Maryland. Remaining on the south side of the icy Rappahannock River, the Rebels gazed at the church spires that rose up from the town like bony, skeletal fingers, reaching to the heavens for sanctuary.

They waited for Burnside to pounce, but their wait was long-lived, for he hesitated. Since the men were required only to attend dress parade and roll call, they idled away their time by staging snowball fights, some so zealous that several soldiers were wounded, and a few were killed. They also spent time exploring the town, as well as the terrain north of camp. Fredericksburg had been nearly evacuated, except for a few citizens who still remained, because their only other option was to camp in the snowy woods until danger passed. On a few rare occasions, the 4th Alabama was detailed to picket duty in town, where they stayed inside deserted homes that housed fine paintings, extensive libraries, and lovely furniture, or they stood guard outside on the piazzas, and in the immaculate sculptured gardens, gazing across the river at the Union soldiers' tents. They noticed how finely outfitted the Yankees were in their splendid blue uniforms, but the Confederates, in contrast, were clothed in ragged, tattered, dingy butternut.

Some of the Rebels managed to converse with the enemy, even though it was strictly forbidden, and exchange their tobacco for much desired coffee and sugar. After a while, though, a treaty was established and the Southerners sent across a plank, with a mast made from current Richmond newspaper. The Federals sent their "boat" to the Southern port, using a mast constructed from a Northern newspaper. Thus, the two sides stayed abreast of what the media was saying.

On several occasions, Hiram heard music float across the river. The Yankee bands played new songs he had never heard before. One sounded like "John Brown's Body," but the words had been changed. This, he learned, was the Union army's new anthem, "The Battle Hymn of the Republic." He didn't appreciate the lyrics, since they equated the Confederates to devils, but listened with interest, nonetheless. Another Yankee song they played repetitively was called the "Battle Cry of Freedom." He liked that one better, but it still didn't make his spirit soar like "Dixie" did. The Federals played "The Star-Spangled Banner" and "Hail Columbia," songs the Southerners once held dear, and waited for Confederate bands to reply, but no reprisal came. As if reading Hiram's mind, the Yankees rambunctiously played "Dixie's Land." Men on both sides of the river burst into cheers, which fell away to mutual laughter.

At dawn on December 11, the Rebels' heavy artillery report sounded the alarm: two shots fired in quick succession signaled the Union army's advance across the river. The 4th fell out and took their position in line. They heard heavy firing down in the town and learned McLaws' Division was shooting at the Yankees to prevent them from constructing pontoon bridges.

Chaplain Chaddick decided it was an appropriate time to delve into prayer, so he quoted from Corinthians, attempting to instill fearlessness into the men. "Oh death, where is thy sting? Oh death, where is thy victory? The sting of death is sin; and the strength of sin is the law. But thanks be to God, which giveth us the victory through our Lord Jesus Christ. Therefore, my beloved brethren, be ye steadfast, unmovable, always abounding in the work of the Lord, forasmuch as ye know that your labour is not in vain in the Lord."

At ten o'clock, the Yankees started to bombard the town, with each of their 367 guns firing fifty rounds. From their position, Hiram and his comrades saw Fredericksburg set ablaze. Hysterical citizens ran out into the streets, scattering into the nearby woods. Although the weather was mild for December, Hiram knew they would likely freeze come nightfall. The thought of those destitute women and children wrenched his heart. After some time, the Confederates' efforts to repel the Yankees proved futile. The Federals started over the river in boats and soon began filing across their pontoon bridges. By nightfall, they had taken the town. General Lee arranged his troops, comprised of the brigades of Jackson, Longstreet, A. P. Hill, and McLaws, as well as the divisions led by Taliaferro, D. H. Hill, and Early. Supported by General J. E. B. Stuart's cavalry and John Pelham's artillery, the men became entrenched at Marye's Hill. Their lines stretched seven miles, with eleven thousand men per mile, or six Confederate soldiers per yard. Over three hundred cannons were poised and ready to fire. The 4th was put into position behind an embankment that afforded them sufficient protection.

Early the following morning, the enemy began firing, but the Rebels held off so as not to disclose the locations of their guns. Hiram lay in wait, watching as General Jackson rode by, dressed in a crisp new uniform, followed by Generals Stuart and Lee. The day was a repeat of the previous one, and when darkness fell, the men returned to their winter quarters to secure rations, since their food supply had vastly improved upon their arrival to Fredericksburg. Warm and comfortable, most fell asleep right away, but Hiram stayed awake, penning a letter to his wife by firelight.

At sunup, the North Alabamians awoke to hear Federal band playing, and the Union infantrymen scuffling about while they moved However, they couldn't see anything due to heavy fog. The 4th marche back to their previous position, where they discovered brisk skirmishin and artillery fire taking place. Burnside had begun harassing th Confederates but was unable to accomplish anything.

The fog remained heavy until ten o'clock, when it lifted to reveal wave of bluecoats moving across an open field. The Rebels watched th spectacle in awe. Tens of thousands of Yankees moved like a slitherin blue serpent, sparkling with silver from sunlight glinting off thei bayonets.

The Federals marched at a double quick, loudly yelling, "Hi! Hi! Hi! and "Huzzah!" as they advanced, flattening fences and fields in thei wake.

They came up from the town as though on parade, and appeared t be unstoppable, like they would keep going over and through th Confederate line. With grape, shell, and shot, the Rebel guns immediatel began their deadly work, pouring a storm of lead into the advancing foe They blew holes into the dark, solid columns, which were filled in lik water rushing around a fractured dam. The thunderous salvos o cannonade shook the ground, retorted by the Yankees' counter-barrage The men in gray let loose a bloodcurdling Rebel yell and fired a storm o lead canister into the faces of their enemies as they approached, whic was enough to send the bluecoats reeling. They stumbled, taking cove behind the bank. A line of colorful Zouaves passed them, but they coul not withstand the Rebel onslaught either. They fell back in confusion.

The Irish Brigade advanced, hollering "Ireland forever" in Gaeli "Erin go bragh!" They bellowed in unison while advancing, but they wer forced to retreat under the murderous fire of the Confederate guns.

With his own comrades entrenched on either side of him, Hiram an the North Alabamians observed the fighting. Burnside reignited his attac in earnest at two o'clock by shelling another regiment of Rebels, wh stood their ground in a sunken road behind a stone wall. One advanc after another tried in vain to break the Confederate stance, but all wer unable to penetrate the line. The Yankees marched up the hill until ther were so many of their dead clogging the battlefield that the advancin Federals were unable to climb over them. The frozen ground in th sunken road gave way to mud and slush beneath the feet of hundreds o thrashing combatants. Some slipped and fell on grass made slick with the blood of their fellow soldiers. At last, twilight engulfed the battlefield, forcing the Yankees to fall back.

Exhausted, Hiram was vaguely aware of the suffering men around him, their moans and cries resounding in all directions. The voices of thousands of wounded soldiers rose up from the ground in an eerie, harmonious chorus. Injured men cried out in unearthly tones, begging for water; speaking to their loved ones, who weren't there to hear; and pleading for mercy from the Almighty as they awaited rescue or death.

"That's pitiful, jist pitiful," Bud repeated under his breath with a disgusted shake of his head.

Hiram was so aghast that he found it impossible to respond.

Icy coldness engulfed the Alabamians, who watched their own breath blow away with the stiff wind, and shivered in a feeble attempt to stay warm while the temperature dipped. They knew the wounded were bleeding and freezing to death, but there was nothing any of them could do. The lives around them were slowly ebbing out, drop by drop.

When at last the order was given to march, it was late afternoon. The men moved down the road at a double quick until they reached the front, where they formed a line of battle. Subjected to heavy shelling, the veteran Alabamians crested a hill to observe a newly formed brigade of Rebels retreat as fast as their legs could carry them, while the gunners, covered in powder from head to foot, frantically loaded and fired their pieces. All around, bullets whizzed, shells burst, and men yelled and cursed.

A young artillery officer suddenly rode up on his steed. "Don't come up here unless you will promise to support me!" he exclaimed.

Bud and Hiram's comrade, William Caldwell, spoke up. "Go back, Captain, to your battery! This is the ole Fourth Alabama!"

The officer smiled. "Thank God! I am safe!" He wheeled his horse and flew back down the hill to his battery.

The Alabamians ran behind the hill, dropping down as Company D was sent to the front. Immediately, they were engaged in heavy skirmishing. Bud and Hiram glanced over at each other, waiting in suspense for their line to be attacked. However, darkness soon fell, and the day's fighting ended. Stray bullets flew over the hill sporadically. While the men lay sleeping, William Caldwell, who was on his back, suddenly rolled over, blood spewing from his mouth. As quickly as the

men realized he had been hit, William died. They had little time to d
anything but helplessly watch.

Stunned by his comrade's death, which had taken place so close to
him, Hiram said quietly to Bud, "That could have been me."

"It could have been any of us," Bud responded. "But the good Lor
decided it was Bill's time to go."

Heaving a heavy sigh, Hiram withdrew the letter he had written t
his wife. "Here," he said. "Give this to Caroline, jist in case somethin
should happen to me."

Bud glared at him. "We already exchanged letters," he stated.

"I know. Give her this one instead."

"You can give it to her yourself, when you see her at Christmas."

"Please, Bud. Jist do as I ask."

With a solemn nod, he took the letter, stuck it into his coat pocket
and reclined against the dead, frosty grass.

At the advent of dawn, shelling and skirmishing resumed. Hiram'
regiment moved out into the open, near the edge of a wood. All fell eeril
quiet while they waited for the command. Noticing two captains and a
adjutant nearby, Bud decided to join in on their conversation, for he wa
curious to hear their plan of action. As he neared, a ball ricochetec
narrowly missed Hiram, and headed straight toward the threesome
Several men yelled out warnings, but one of the captains reacted to
late. He was struck directly in the chest, his torso turned into a mass o
jellylike flesh as he collapsed in a heap. Before the litter bearers coul
deliver him to the field hospital, he was dead.

A lull came in the battle. Colonel Bowles, who had been promote
from captain, approached his men, asking for volunteers to fill canteen
so Hiram accepted the challenge.

"You sure you want to go down there?" Bud asked him. "It's quie
now, but the fightin' could start up again."

He smiled. "I've outfoxed death twice in the past two days, an
we're holdin' the Yankees at bay. Besides that, we're at a vantage point.
reckon God is on our side." He sauntered off behind the cover of th
heights.

Bud looked over at his fellow soldiers, who were mostly dozing.
few were telling jokes.

"I overheard two officers talkin'. One was ours, and one was theirs. As they was discussin' the matters at hand, along comes ole Stonewall hisself, ridin' right past them. Well, the Yankee officer says, 'Who's that?' And our officer says, 'Stonewall Jackson. Had you known who it was, no doubt you would've shot him.' 'Oh, no,' says the Yankee officer. 'I'm in favor of keepin' him. We may, after whippin' you, need him!'"

Bud chuckled quietly. He looked back across the hillcrest to see Hiram make his way through the ranks. Deciding to join him, he sprang to his feet and rapidly caught up. Hiram gave him several canteens to fill. They cautiously went down the hill, made their way through a stiff, frozen cluster of reeds, and dipped the metal containers into the frigid water at the river's edge. While they squatted to fill the receptacles, they discussed the upcoming holiday, and how they excitedly looked forward to seeing their kinfolk, knowing that once the battle concluded, the winter campaign would be over.

Suddenly, three bluecoats burst from the shrubs, shooting. Hiram cried out as he was hit, and fell to the ground, writhing in agony. Another Yankee fired at Bud, who flinched as the bullet whizzed by his cheek.

"Surrender now, seceshes!" one of the Federals commanded, using a slang term for secessionists.

Before Bud could react, hot fire exploded behind him, and the Yankees fell back into the woods. He knelt to assist his friend.

"Git up, Hiram!" he beseeched, his voice riddled with panic.

Looking up at him with pain and confusion in his eyes, Hiram tried to hold his hand over the wound. Bud watched in horror as blood flowed over his hand, covering it in crimson, and saw that he had been shot through the neck.

The shelling resumed. Several of their comrades ran toward them.

"Come on!" yelled Blue Hugh. "They're comin' back!"

"I can't leave him!" Bud screamed.

He wrapped his arm around Hiram, attempting to pull him up before all the life flowed out of him, but his friend's body grew limp and motionless.

Blue Hugh grabbed hold of Bud, yanking him to his feet. "Leave him! There ain't nothin' you can do for him, Samuels!"

He succeeded, forcing Bud away.

Shells started flying at them, whistling and bursting all around. While they ran, shot and canister hit the ground, sending a torrent of dirt in

their faces, and creating huge craters they frantically zigzagged to avoid
The Confederates dashed up the hill, escaping the turmoil. Bud glanced
back over his shoulder. He saw a shell fly straight at Hiram. It hit him
Hiram's body exploded like a ripe tomato.

Bud helplessly gaped in shocked disbelief. "Dear God!" he uttered
nearly whispering.

The shell had done its work so completely that only a blood
splattered hole in the ground remained. There was no indication h
friend had ever been there, let alone, existed at all. He couldn't believ
his own eyes, and thought it must be a terrible dream. No one seemed t
notice, except for Blue Hugh, who stared at Bud, horror-stricken
Expecting him to cynically wish Hiram good-bye, Bud felt his gut roil, an
wretched in convulsive vomiting until his stomach was empty.

He staggered toward his company. Sinking down onto his knees, h
burst into uncontrollable sobs. Enoch Campbell came to his aid, an
assisted him back behind the breastworks.

As night fell, the men were instructed to entrench themselves b
digging dirt and bringing in logs from a nearby marsh. Bud moved as if i
a trance, unable to come to grips with what he had witnessed. It was a
surreal, sudden, shocking. He knew death was always a possibility, yet
still came unexpectedly. Squeezing his eyes shut momentarily to contr
his nausea, he wondered how something so violent and ugly could befa
such a good man, his good friend. He couldn't fathom any of it, for th
circumstance was beyond his comprehension. Slowly opening his eyes, h
noticed spectacular, strange lights flashing up from the horizon, growin
longer and brighter through the night sky, which caused the men to sto
and stare in awe.

"What do you reckon that is?" he asked, feebly pointing at the sky.

"I've seen it before once," said Enoch Campbell. "When I was in Ne
York."

The sky grew brighter, like it was on fire, aglow with flashing colo
and ever-changing shapes.

"They call it aurora borealis," Chaplain Chaddick informed them, h
head upturned toward the heavens.

"It must be a sign," said Blue Hugh, "that we'll win this here battle."

The men robustly agreed. They went on watching the amorphou
light show, which continued well into the night. Bud hoped the battle wa
indeed over, and that the lights were an indication from God. He hope

the Almighty would accept all those souls lost in the battle, and welcome them into His kingdom. Silently, he prayed for Hiram's salvation, and for his own forgiveness.

The next day, December 15, they waited for renewed fighting, but nothing happened until late afternoon, when they received slight shelling. The Federals spent a good portion of the day burying their many dead, until nightfall hindered their progress.

That evening, Bud lingered beside Blue Hugh and Chaplain Chaddick, staring into the campfire. He withdrew the letter Hiram had given him and considered reading it, but decided it was too personal, so he stuffed it back into his pocket. Rummaging through his haversack, he found Hiram's first letter. Without reading that one either, he tossed it into the fire. The men conversed little but to give each other comfort. Hiram had died for a good and noble cause—of that, they were certain. Unable to sleep, Bud mournfully blamed himself for his friend's demise. He knew he should have prevented Hiram's death, but how, he wasn't sure. Perhaps he should have led the way to the creek. Then he would have taken the bullet instead. It was the ultimate betrayal, and Bud was ashamed of himself for allowing it to happen. Hiram's death would never leave him. The memory would haunt him forever.

The men awoke to find it was raining, as it usually did after a battle. They discovered Burnside's Federals had crossed the river overnight, demoralized into retreating to Washington. A wave of cheers rushed over the Rebel ranks. While the rain dissipated to drizzle, Bud, who was still in a daze, followed some of his comrades out onto the battlefield, which was covered with dead Yankee soldiers. It was obvious from what they saw that the Union army had suffered almost complete annihilation. Some of the Federals died trying to use their comrades' bodies as shields. What it must have been like to lie in wait while bullets thudded into the bodies of their friends, Bud could only speculate. Besides corpses dressed in blue, some wore Zouave uniforms, while others adorned their wrappings with Kelly green. Blue Hugh said they were with the Irish Brigade, because he had heard they wore green boxwood sprigs in their caps to display their heritage. The barefoot Confederates immediately set to work, relieving the rigid bodies of their footwear and clothing, as well as their haversacks' contents. Bud replaced his worn-out brogans, which had developed holes in their soles long ago.

Blue Hugh found a young, handsome Yankee boy, lying dead amongst the others, and motioned Bud over. Inside his knapsack, the discovered chocolate and numerous love letters, which Blue Hugh began to read mockingly over the body.

Bud snatched them from his hand. "These are private," he grumbled thinking of the letter he had stuffed into his own pocket. "We ought t keep them that way, out of respect."

He tore up the letters, letting the pieces flutter away on the cod breeze. They danced across the harvest of dead like little whit ballerinas.

One Alabamian approached, holding three blue-clad soldier prisoner with his rifle. A small white dog tagged behind.

"That li'l' feller looks like Bo," Blue Hugh observed, his usua malevolence gone. "Remember him?"

"Orange Hugh's dog. The one I left with that boy back at Culpepe Court House," Bud recalled out loud. "Course, I do."

"His name's Lucky," said one of the captives. "Because he's alway brung me luck."

"Not this time!" responded his captor with a laugh.

He nudged the Union soldier with the barrel of his gun, and th foursome ambled off.

It had stopped raining, but bitter cold replaced it. Upon returning t camp, Bud and his comrades learned they had lost five, with seventee wounded. Their regiment didn't fire a single shot. The Yankees, it wa estimated, lost over nine thousand after making fourteen assaults tha were all beaten back. The men heard of one brave soul, Sergeant Kirklan of South Carolina, who acquired a reputation as the "Angel of Marye' Heights" for crossing enemy lines and benevolently tending to the Unio wounded by providing them with blankets and water. John Pelham, a Alabama son who was in charge of Jackson's artillery, received prais from General Lee for bravely executing an effective barrage by deceivin the Yankees into thinking his numbers were far greater than they actuall were, and holding their lines in the process.

The Alabamians were told Fredericksburg had been left in terribl condition. The Yankees were allowed to freely loot, ransack, burn, an pillage anything and everything, which infuriated the Rebels. Bud decide the pity he had felt while on the battlefield was wasted.

Those bastards don't deserve my sympathy, he reasoned.

The invaders caused too many innocents to suffer, and although they had been led like obedient lambs to slaughter, they got what they deserved for desecrating the good Southern people of Fredericksburg.

It's God's wrath at work, he decided. *They brought on their own destruction.*

With the battle's end, optimism grew about Europe's possible renewed interest in supporting the Southern cause.

"Since we whipped them infernal Yankees," Enoch Campbell declared, "they might think differently about jinin' us now."

Blue Hugh shook his head in disgruntlement but kept his conflicting opinion to himself by uncharacteristically keeping quiet.

General Lee rode up on Traveller to congratulate his men. Although Bud was heartbroken, he still managed a faint smile as Lee saluted them.

"We've whipped them, General!" one of the Confederates hollered.

Lee nodded in response without displaying an ounce of emotion. He informed the men that those who could go home were granted "furloughs of indulgence," since the winter campaign had come to a close. Bud knew what was required of him, although it was the last thing on earth he wanted to do. Melodic strains from a Federal band wafted across the river, but "Home Sweet Home" only deepened his sorrow.

On Wednesday, December 17, after bidding his comrades farewell, he set off for the train to Richmond. It was one week before Christmas.

As planned, David and his family arrived at the Copeland's for their annual Christmas party. Once they entered, he looked around at the sparkling room, aglow with candles and firelight. The parlor was filled with guests, all of whom he recognized. They were dressed in their finest holiday attire. Someone was playing "Lo, How a Rose E'er Blooming" on the piano. Relieved to see Callie in the corner, standing beside Jake and behaving like her old self, he smiled at the sight of her. She was dressed in a purple velvet gown, her bare shoulders exposed, and her blond hair tied up to accentuate her long, slender neck. Jake was attired in his Sunday suit. Once they saw him, they headed his way.

"Oh, David, darlin'," she cooed. "I am so very happy to see you!"

With a wry grin, he replied, "I'm happy to be here, Miss Callie." He winked at Jake. "Have you received any proposals yet?"

Jake winced at his friend's veiled reference and slightly shook his head, which made David chuckle.

"Why, whatever do you mean?" she asked, the innocence in her voice betraying her demeanor. She slinked up close to David, so close he could feel her warm breath, and it made his face flush. Like a snake coiling around its victim, she wrapped her arm around his. "Were you fixin' to make one?"

It was Jake's turn to chuckle. "Now, honey, leave him be. He's got big news to share." Turning to the room filled with friends, Jake hollered, "May I have y'all's attention, please!" The voices died down, and he announced loudly, "David's pa will be home for Christmas!"

The attendees cheered.

"So will my husband!" added Mrs. Samuels.

The gathering applauded again.

"We must have a feast prepared for our soldiers returnin' from the war!" declared Mrs. Copeland. "In honor of all they have done for us!"

"Here! Here!" responded Mr. Copeland, raising his champagne glass.

Everyone toasted in unison. David glanced over at his mother, who beamed at him.

The following morning, he and his family attended church, where they received a grand reception. The congregation had heard about Hiram's homecoming, and bestowed well-wishes upon them. That afternoon, David busied himself by getting caught up on chores he had let slide over the past few months. He wanted his father to be proud and impressed with his efforts to take care of the place, just like he had promised. Even though it was the Sabbath, a designated day of rest, he worked through it anyway, reasoning that he had only four days to finish his tasks.

The next few days were filled with anticipation and last-minute preparations for Christmas. While the girls decorated, David worked diligently to finish his handmade gifts, and Caroline cooked. The family spent every waking moment getting ready to receive their loved one.

Soon, it was the day before Christmas. David awoke to discover it was drizzling, which wasn't unusual for that time of year. Pulling himself from his warm bed, he dressed, ate a quick bowl of grits, and went outside to tend to the livestock. By the time he had finished, he was cold and damp, so he returned to his room, changed, stoked the fire, and sat down on the bed with his guitar. Although he hadn't played it in quite a while, he decided to learn a few carols, so he practiced "Oh Come All Ye Faithful" and "Silent Night" several times. While he worked out the chords to the "Boar's Head Carol," he heard a knock at his door. Josie entered, wearing a brown coat over her green calico dress.

"Ma says it's time to go fetch the tree!" she announced, barely containing her excitement.

Grinning at her exuberance, he laid the guitar down across his bed. "All right, li'l' sis. If you insist."

Throwing on his coat and hat, he followed her outside to the barn. He saddled Renegade, gave her a foot up, and led the colt out toward the woodlot. Noticing it had stopped drizzling, he clucked to Renegade, who responded by prancing.

"Your horse is the funniest critter!" Josie giggled. "He must know it's holiday!"

"Reckon so. He's mighty high-strung today."

"He's like this every day!" she exclaimed, bouncing atop the colt.

"That's fine if he is. It jist makes him more competitive. He already won those two races I ran him in last month, and I'm fixin' to run him a heap more this spring."

Renegade slowed to a walk as brother and sister approached the woods.

"Reckon tonight ole Santee Claus will be makin' his appearance," David remarked casually.

To their amusement, Renegade blew in response. Caleb and Si came loping up, eager to find out what they were missing, and the two hounds nearly tumbled over each other in their rush.

Josie laughed at them. "Let's find the purtiest tree out here for Pa," she suggested.

"That's a right good idea." He grinned up at his sister, who smiled back down at him.

Bud's arrival in Huntsville went unnoticed. Apparently, the townsfolk were accustomed to seeing raggedy-clothed Confederates milling about. Once he arrived home, his wife greeted him adoringly, but it took only a moment for her to realize something was amiss, so he explained what he had witnessed the week before, but excluded morbid details for her benefit. Shocked by the revelation, she released him to his errand, and he rode out on his buckskin gelding to deliver the sorrowful news.

As he approached the familiar saddlebag house sitting serenely in the glen, he made a decision: his knowledge would remain his alone. He wouldn't tell Caroline exactly how Hiram had died. He couldn't tell anyone. It was far too agonizing for Bud to even think about. His best friend was gone, his comrade, his brother-in-arms, the one man who had gone through the same horrific ordeal, yet regrettably, hadn't survived to tell about it. Bud would go to his grave with that terrible secret. Mustering his nerve, he spurred his horse toward the Summers' farm while tiny, crystalline snowflakes—silent, glistening witnesses to his impending, anguished deliverance—fluttered down from the dark overcast sky.

Absorbed in his dismal thoughts, he rounded a corner, and heard a horse blow. He looked up to see a group of Rebel soldiers ride toward him. One of them accosted his buckskin by grabbing hold of the reins while the other four surrounded him.

"What's the meanin' of this?" Bud gruffly asked, reaching for his pistol. Another soldier produced a rifle, so he reluctantly eased his hand away from the holster on his hip.

"We're scoutin' the area for deserters," the soldier holding the reins responded.

"I ain't no deserter!" After days of sleeplessness, Bud's temper flared easily. "I'm home on furlough."

"Which regiment you with?" inquired another, whose face was hidden behind a thick amber beard.

"The Fourth Alabama Infantry, but that ain't none of y'all's concern." Bud stifled his anger. "Now if you fellers would kindly allow me to pass, I'll be on my way, and we can all go about our business like none of this happened. I have an urgent errand to 'tend to."

"The Fourth you say?" said the first soldier. "Produce your papers."

Bud glared at him. "I don't have 'em with me. I told y'all, I'm home on furlough. I left 'em back at the house." The men exchanged glances and chuckles, making Bud bristle. "Now lookee here!"

The other four soldiers quickly pulled pistols, forcing their quarry to back down. "You're comin' with us," said the heavily-bearded one.

"Hell if I am!" Bud exclaimed.

"You're comin' with us, or you're meetin' your maker right here," said the soldier with the rifle, staring him down with piercing gray eyes.

Bud glanced around at their faces. Forced to relinquish, he drew a heavy sigh. "Damned Home Guard," he muttered under his breath as they led him off. His errand of death would have to wait.

MUSIC IN CAMP

Two armies covered hill and plain,
Where Rappahannock's waters
Ran deeply crimsoned with the stain
Of battle's recent slaughters.

The summer clouds lay pitched like tents
In meads of heavenly azure;
And each dread gun of the elements
Slept in its hid embrasure.

The breeze so softly blew it made
No forest leaf to quiver,
And the smoke of the random cannonade
Rolled slowly from the river.

And now, where circling hills looked down
With cannon grimly planted,
O'er listless camp and silent town
The golden sunset slanted.

When on the fervid air there came
A strain—now rich, now tender;
The music seemed itself aflame
With day's departing splendor.

A Federal band, which, eve and morn,
Played measures brave and nimble,
Had just struck up, with flute and horn
And lively clash of cymbal.

Down flocked the soldiers to the banks,
Till, margined with its pebbles,
One wooded shore was blue with "Yanks,"
And one was gray with "Rebels."

Then all was still, and then the band,
With movement light and tricksy,
Made stream and forest, hill and strand,
Reverberate with "Dixie."

The conscious stream with burnished glow
Went proudly o'er its pebbles,
But thrilled throughout its deepest flow
With yelling of the Rebels.

Again a pause, and then again
The trumpets pealed sonorous,
And "Yankee Doodle" was the strain
To which the shore gave chorus.

The laughing ripple shoreward flew,
To kiss the shining pebbles;
Loud shrieked the swarming Boys in Blue
Defiance to the Rebels.

And yet once more the bugles sang
Above the stormy riot;
No shout upon the evening rang –
There reigned a holy quiet.

The sad, slow stream its noiseless flood
Poured o'er the glistening pebbles;
All silent now the Yankees stood,
And silent stood the Rebels.

No unresponsive soul had heard
That plaintive note's appealing,
So deeply "Home, Sweet Home" had stirred
The hidden founts of feeling.

Or Blue or Gray, the soldier sees,
As by the wand of fairy,
The cottage 'neath the live-oak trees,
The cabin by the prairie.

Or cold or warm, his native skies
Bend in their beauty o'er him;
Seen through the tear-mist in his eyes,
His loved ones stand before him.

As fades the iris after rain
In April's tearful weather,
The vision vanished, as the strain
And daylight died together.

But memory, waked by music's art,
Expressed in simplest numbers,
Subdued the sternest Yankee's heart,
Made light the Rebel's slumbers.

And fair the form of music shines,
That bright, celestial creature,
Who still, 'mid war's embattled lines,
Gave this one touch of Nature.

—John Reuben Thompson
Confederate Poet and Writer

About the Author

J.D.R. Hawkins is an award-winning author who has written for newspapers, magazines, newsletters, e-zines, and blogs. She is one of only a few female Civil War authors, and uniquely describes the front lines from a Confederate perspective. Her *Renegade Series* includes *A Beautiful Glittering Lie*, winner of the 2013 John Esten Cooke Fiction Award and the B.R.A.G. Medallion, *A Beckoning Hellfire*, which is also an award winner, and *A Rebel Among Us*, winner of the 2017 John Esten Cooke Fiction Award. These books tell the story of a family from north Alabama who experience immeasurable pain when their lives are dramatically changed by the war.

Ms. Hawkins is a member of the United Daughters of the Confederacy, the International Women's Writing Guild, Pikes Peak Writers, and Rocky Mountain Fiction Writers. She is also an artist and singer/songwriter. She is currently working on a nonfiction book about the War Between the States, as well as another sequel for the *Renegade Series*. Learn more about her at http://jdrhawkins.com.

Also available from the Author:
A Beckoning Hellfire: *A Novel of the Civil War*
(Book 2 of the Renegade Series)

A Rebel Among Us: *A Novel of the Civil War*
(Book 3 of the Renegade Series)

Horses in Gray: *Famous Confederate Warhorses*

Made in United States
Orlando, FL
02 April 2022

16408315R00125